Child of Light

Child of Light

Diane Bentley Baker

To order additional copies of this book, contact:
Xlibris Corporation
1-888-795-4274
www.Xlibris.com
Orders@Xlibris.com
34318

For Denise, who always knew I could

For color is the child of light, the source of all life on earth.

—*Colors*, Delamare and Guineau

Acknowledgements

A big thank you to my teachers, Linda Clare and John Reed. Thanks to my other eyes, Tim Mack, Sarah Decker, and Carol Lynn, who taught me much and kept me honest. I am grateful to Marcelle Stay for her scholarly editing. And hats off to Gail and Sally.

Thanks to the kind folks at Camp Four Winds, for helping me place the little song, "Laughter," and to Archeologists Elizabeth Wayland Barber and Jeannine Davis-Kimball, Ph.D., who answered emails promptly.

Special thanks to Steve Long, dream guru, who gave me good grades after many years of study. Hugs to my family for their support and especially to my husband, Shane, who patiently went with the flow.

And to all the fiber folk in my life, I am deeply indebted.

Prologue

The burning sand would soon be soaked with blood. He did not want to die; he was far too young. The master dyer had chosen him as apprentice almost two seasons before. Now he was doomed because he was caught wearing the imperial purple. The Emperor had decreed that anyone of non-royal status wearing the purple of the shells would be subject to death. He lived in a fantasy world, a poor soul with the mind of a child.

He wasn't the only one obsessed with the purple. The supply of tiny shells would not last forever. For hundreds of years the wealthy had been provided with color, and the used and broken pieces of shells lined the shores. The recipe for the coveted purple was secret. The master was the only one who knew the entire process. Or was he? When the apprentice had been caught in the purple robe, the dye master thought he himself would be blamed, and ran off into the night. Now the apprentice would lose his life, just as thousands of mollusks had given their small sacrifices. Who would carry on the purple process?

The dye master's wife watched the execution with a great deal of interest. Now no one stood in her way to fame and wealth. She smiled to herself as fresh blood drenched the hot sands and turned purple in the sun.

Part I

The Basket

c. 2500 B.C. East of the garden, on a wide river

"And the earth brought forth grass, and herb yielding seed after his kind, and the tree yielding fruit, whose seed was in itself, after his kind . . ."
—Genesis, 1:12

The River

The tree locusts must have had a leader with a very small baton, who led the others to sing with a wave of authority. All of them started together, sang throughout the day and then stopped together abruptly in the early morning hours, allowing the sparkling voice of a mockingbird to announce the dawn.

The clan traveled on the river in rafts, struggling to find another garden spot. At ten seasons, Poma was the eldest daughter in her adopted family. Because her face was round and her skin creamy, she fit right in. She helped her mother, Ashar, take care of the younger ones. But the very youngest persisted in sleeping sideways in the bed and kicking her in his dreams. The sun rose as she crept out of bed to make her way to the river before the others were awake. The whole world was pink. She gathered up her spindle and some wool. The spindle whorl was a large clay bead, carved with circular lines. She slipped her purple wrist distaff on her left wrist, and strolled down toward the river. She placed her robe and spindle on a fat log and slipped into the water in her shift. It would be washed, too. She dunked her black, curly hair in the water. She had been told that when she was a baby, she was found in this river in a basket, wrapped in a purple blanket, with the purple distaff by her side. She loved to go to the river bank and find a pool to peer in at her round face. She had also been told she had the greenest eyes anyone had ever seen, but she couldn't tell, for the green of the water was the same.

Suddenly she slipped into a large hole and was pulled under the water. She felt the motion of the river pushing her away from the shore and downstream. She fought for her breath, and time seemed to slow as she remembered a few seasons before, when she was also in the water. The fear seizing her now was as sharp as it had been then.

The men had returned from a hunt and warned everyone that a huge elk herd was on the move. Her bath had to wait. The group knew from sad experience if they were in the path of this migration, the only escape was to move themselves downstream on the rafts. They must hurry, for the elk herd was only a short way off. The camp was up in a moment, the night's sleep shed instantly. The women packed the meager belongings, dried food and herbs into baskets and folded up the tents, which were carried to the river's edge. As the children were gathered on board the rafts, they heard a low rumble. The earth shook. The babies cried. The rafts were launched and the people escaped the determined animals. Poma had watched the elk pouring into the river, and had taken a big breath.

Now Poma had almost no breath left, and hit a backwash that forced her down even farther. The pink day was above her, and she clawed at the foam for air, and was pushed down again under the water. This could not be how it ended! She wanted to be alive, to eat and dance and play in the sun. She needed to hunt for the color purple, like the deep purple in her distaff and in her tiny baby blanket. Time slowed again as she remembered Hamora, her red-headed grandmother, who had lived a long life.

Poma's grandmother had always busied herself with the herbs along the river banks, the mushrooms and fragrant lichens from the forest. Her family not only ate well, but wore colorful garments. Hamora always had at least one dye pot on the fire, and the children learned at an early age not to eat out of the one pot that was going to make them a feast for the eyes. From the bounty of the land, that pot gave them all colors of yellow, silver grays and greens like the forest at sunrise.

When the other children played, Poma hung back by her grandmother's side, watched and learned. The flowers made beautiful yellows and golds. Occasionally, if Hamora left yellow daisies in the pot too long, the threads would turn the color of the moss on the forest floor. She had discovered a way to extract purple from certain kinds of lichens. When the boys peed on them in the forest, the ugly lichens eventually turned to beautiful plums and reds, changing their inauspicious beginnings into mysterious beauty. So she had the little ones pee into a special pot in which she soaked the lichens. They made a game out of it, to see who could pee in the pot without dribbling over the side. The urine softened the wool and the smell washed right out. She had even found a mushroom that yielded a beautiful light blue, just like the sky opening now above Poma's head.

Poma gulped at the sweet air momentarily, and saw rapids approaching. Huge rocks caused the water to turn white, and the sound was like thunder. Again, the slowing of time, and Poma remembered her brother, Dunard.

Dunard had been born with a withered leg. He managed to get around, albeit slowly. He was a plump lad, likeable enough, but rather plain-looking, and his adolescence seemed to pile more indecision upon him, more embarrassment and self-doubt. He and Poma had always been close, and Poma felt his pain acutely. She searched her mind for something to do for him, something to help. He seemed especially sad when the others played games he could not. She watched as he sat apart from the other children, staring, dejected, at the water. He was wearing his brown shirt and his mood seemed to match it. Finally, Poma knew what to do. With Hamora's help, she started some pink socks for him. They dyed the yarn with some special mushrooms, and then Poma began one-needle knitting with a bone needle. Her thumb was just the right size for the small loops required for a fine pair of socks. She and Hamora had learned about one-needle knitting by examining the small purple blanket.

Poma had been sent down to the water's edge to mind the younger children. As she watched them, her gaze settled on the greens and blues of the water. How could a substance so sparkling and full of sky-filled colors blend and flash to dark in an instant? Streaks of green, cold as the forests of winter, suddenly erupted into midnight blue, or the color of the sky at dawn. Small eddies sparkled. Great pools muddied a bit where animals had come to drink, and where the children now played. The river she had loved as friend and respected when it became powerful in springtime took on an ever-beautiful palette of colors in the summer. Every year she reveled in its beauty because she knew it would roar into black when the grey rains came.

Suddenly, Ashar ran down the bank screaming. Poma dropped her yarn and quickly searched through the children with worried eyes. None of the little ones was missing. She glanced back at her mother to see why she was so upset. Ashar ran into the river, screaming Dunard's name.

Poma had seen the older boys swim out to the middle of the river and then head back again. It was a game they used to test each other. She couldn't see Dunard. The boys were swimming back toward Ashar, who waded out into the water, yelling and searching for her son. Poma thought she was at fault, and ran and hid under a big bush. They never found Dunard's body. After he drowned, Ashar was inconsolable. Hamora took over the family's needs. As the weeks wore on, it was apparent to Poma that her parents, indeed, loved her and she understood that the death of Dunard was not her fault. She still felt a small spiral of guilt, however, that was to never really leave her for the rest of her life. She took the half-finished pink sock she had been making for him and tearfully tucked it away in her basket.

Poma tried to grab another breath of air. It was laced with water. Was this how Dunard had felt? Her legs were cramping. Why was she to die this way too? Was her mother to lose two children to this beautiful river?

After the drowning, Poma had become a somber child. She always felt a little lost, different somehow. She and Hamora had spent long hours over the pots by the fire. She stared in wonder at the greeney-yellow pot of indigo when the threads were lifted out and turned expertly to blue in the air. Because Poma was the only one of the little girls to lag behind to watch and listen, Hamora taught her as much of the lore of herbs as she could handle. She also taught Poma that she was a special child. "The Goddess told us there may be one of us chosen to disappear into time, to take the hand of the Goddess and make a different journey. She told us these special time travelers live however long they are needed in one place, and then move forward in time to live somewhere else. I pray if you are that one, that what I have taught you will be of value for a long, long time." Poma didn't quite know what Hamora meant by all this, but she was intrigued by the old woman.

Poma's fingertips found a rock. She struggled to reach and grab whatever hold she could get. But the rock was smooth and slippery and it slid away, and with it, her hopes. Her tears mixed with the water as she remembered her tears of last night.

Mordach, one of the elders, had come home wounded from a hunt, and Hamora cared for him, as she did everyone in the clan, with herbs and strong tea. Mordach fell asleep in the big family tent. Poma's father was across the tent, snoring. Ashar finally erupted in an old hatred she held for Mordach. Poma lay on her back, shivering. She was upset and could only listen. Ashar was sobbing. Poma listened in disbelief as Ashar related to Hamora how she had to allow his advances when Poma was a baby. Mordach wanted to drown the infant when she first appeared in her little basket. Ashar had saved the little one's life by giving in to the horror of his demands.

Poma shed tears right along with her mother, and knew it might be a sleepless night. She pulled the fur up over her head, so the women would not know she was awake. The two women cried together into the night. And the third, now a woman too, cried herself to sleep in the big fur bed.

Now she would never be able to console her mother, to thank her for saving her as a baby. In the midst of her panic, she felt a hand take hers. Had she been chosen? A warm energy captured her and slowly rose toward her face. A voice that sounded like the river spoke to her.

"Poma!" She looked up to see a white light through the water. Was this the face of the Goddess? "Poma!" The rich scent of flowers almost overpowered her. A deep, purple light replaced the bright face in front of her. It flickered at the edges, and filled her whole being. Suddenly, in a loud snap, time stopped. As the water receded, her hand was dropped.

Ashar went on to have many more children. Mordach died mysteriously from poisonous mushrooms. Hamora died peacefully, taking many secrets with her. She was the only one in the clan who felt sure that the Goddess had chosen Poma and rescued her from the river. No one else knew what happened to Poma or her basket, its tiny blanket, or the purple distaff.

Part II

The Nile

c.1540 B.C.—The delta of the Nile

"Have your distaff ready and God will send the flax."
—old proverb

The Distaff

Poma found a baby rabbit in her grandmother's indigo pot. The rabbit wriggled away from her, turning blue in the process. It jumped down and skittered off through the trees. She followed it, but it kept just ahead of her. Every time she would grab for it, it would get away. She couldn't even lay a hand on it. The rabbit had turned into a blue man who hid behind the trees. Then her grandmother was there, much smaller, stirring the indigo pot with great care. The pot was big enough to hold the blue man, who jumped into it and peered at Poma over the edge. The whites of his eyes glared against the blue background of his face. She was frightened of him, yet drawn to him at the same time.

Poma's throat was parched. Her mouth was dry and her skin was hot. Her dream came rushing back to her. She kept her eyes closed, so as to remember it. She felt like that baby rabbit, learning from Hamora's dye pots. Her instinctual gift derived from the passion for color. Who was the blue man? She must explore this later, after she found out why she was so hot. As she opened her eyes the dream was forgotten. This was a very strange world. She was bathed in brilliant, glaring light. As her eyes focused she saw two colors: green overtaken by brown. The sand she lay on was the same color as the strange tree trunks. She looked up. In the brightness of the sun, she saw trees, tall and skinny with a sudden burst of green at their tops. Stark, brown treeless mountains stood in the distance, indistinct in the oppressive heat. She sat up. The river behind her was wide, calm, and green. It was not the river she had started to bathe in that morning. This river played hostess to a narrow band of green on both sides and then as far as could be seen, right up to the barren mountains, it was a wasteland: brown, ugly, and hot.

Poma was struck with fear. Everything had changed. Where was this place? Where was her family? Now she remembered the bright face of the Goddess, the purple light, her hand being dropped. This is what Hamora meant by being chosen. Had Hamora and the Goddess forsaken her? Was she still dreaming? How could she get home again?

As the tears streamed down her small face, she looked all around for some clue. Her eyes rested at last on her basket. Her robe sat folded on top of it and the little spindle was there, leaning against one of the strange trees. Had the Goddess put them there? She opened the basket. There was the purple blanket. It was comforting somehow.

A noise from the distance brought Poma back to the problem at hand. A drum was beating and there were strange sounds accompanying it, almost like cicadas in the heat of the summer—a summer she had known before, she corrected herself.

The wide leaves beside the river shook and moved, and out of the center of a large plant emerged the head of a small camel. Poma watched in astonishment as it moved toward her, its lips rippling. She backed up, but before she could turn and run, she tripped on a root and fell backward. The little beast walked over, sniffed and gurgled at her, and then waited patiently as she got to her feet again. Poma's surprise turned to appreciation when she came eye to eye with the little camel. Its eyes were large and soft-looking, and were rimmed with beautiful lashes. Poma had never known an animal to be friends; all the animals she had seen had been killed for food. This little animal almost seemed to know her.

The drum grew louder and the accompanying cicadas proved to be stringed instruments borne by a long line of people marching to the drum. Most of them were dressed in white. Poma tucked her robe and spindle into her basket with the blanket and hid behind one of the strange trees to watch. The little camel tried to nibble on her hair.

"Get away, beast," she said. Poma pulled her hair away and crouched down to watch the procession. A large gold statue, carried by a group of struggling men, swayed in time with the marching throng toward a tall building with round pillars holding up a fancy roof. It was covered with colorful paintings. Poma's eyes grew big. She had never seen such wonderful, ornate decorations.

The procession turned down a long pathway toward the building. The people followed, clapping and chanting. The camel dashed out of the bushes and started chasing the last of the people and joined the procession. She whispered at the camel to stop, but on he went, trotting behind a small group of children. The children stopped to catch the camel, saw Poma's hiding place, and came running toward her. She searched desperately for another place to hide. There was none. She clutched her basket to her and waited. Her heart was pounding.

"Who are you?" asked a little boy.

Poma barely understood him. "What is this place?" She heard herself speak in a voice that did not seem like hers.

The boy only stared at her. The children lined up in a row, staring at Poma. An old woman walked toward them and called to the children. They still just stood and stared. Poma tried to smile at the old woman. She didn't know where to begin or what to say. The woman smiled back at Poma, and motioned her to join them. Poma felt hungry, and the old woman and children seemed harmless enough, so she fell in behind them. The camel smiled too, and seemed pleased with himself. He wanted to chew on her hair again, so she hurried after the others.

They came to a large portico. The chanting and drumming reached a crescendo, and then stopped. Poma sat with the children and watched as a group of men dressed in white robes and elaborate headdresses emerged from the large building, a signal for everyone to bow to the statue, which was ensconced on a low platform. They carried torches which they used to light something in large pots. Poma could smell a sweet aroma rising with the smoke. One of the men repeated more chants for the audience to enunciate in a reverent way toward the statue. Young women then emerged from the building all in dazzling white pleated gowns, and scattered flowers from baskets all around the statue and into the gathered crowd.

Poma had never seen such ceremonies. Her family had been taught to make offerings to God, but this seemed much more civilized and beautiful somehow. The worship of a gold statue seemed wrong; however, she was impressed with the seriousness of the young women in their beautiful gowns. When all the flowers had been lavished on the crowd, the girls crept behind the statue and sat with solemn faces in a corner of the big porch. After some more music, the people marched off down the road.

Then Poma was all alone. Even the lovely young girls had disappeared. Poma was frightened and hungry. How would she find anything to eat? Where would she live? What was to become of her? She put her head down on her arms and cried.

An impatient voice broke through her bewilderment. "Who are you? What is your name?"

She looked up to see an angry old man on the steps of the building. He had blazing blue eyes which bore right through her. She could only sniffle.

"I said, who are you?" he repeated, frowning.

Poma tried to top crying. She couldn't catch her breath. "Poma," she said. It didn't come out right.

The man grabbed her by the arm and pulled her toward the large doorway. "We'll just see about this," he said, and he snatched the distaff from around her wrist. "Get in here right now."

One of the shaven priests met them at the door. He looked at Poma and the old man in surprise. "Ambassador Norek!" he said. "What seems to be the problem?"

"I found this waif right outside, with this," and he waved the purple distaff at the priest.

The young man's eyes widened. "Come in and sit here, and tell me what this is all about."

The old man's face relaxed just a bit. They entered the big building and he dragged Poma over to a stone bench. "This purple—" he explained—"This purple is the imperial purple, as you know. In our land, this color of purple is worn only by people of great wealth. It is rumored our ruler may impose the death penalty on anyone wearing this purple, who is not of royal lineage."

"I see," said the priest. He frowned at Poma.

Poma wanted to be anywhere but in this big, frightening building, being accused of wearing a "forbidden" color. These people must be crazed from too much sun.

"I'm sure, Ambassador, that there is a good explanation for this. She is just a child, and as you know, we have no law in our country concerning the wearing of this color."

The old man's eyes softened. "If this is true, then I am mistaken. But you should find out from this child where she acquired such a treasure." He handed the offending purple distaff to the priest. "If she is not a temple maiden here, she's obviously a thief."

The priest seemed to want to calm the old man down and claim some authority. "We will question her, and if need be, take her to the Pharaoh."

With that, the old man stood up. "Speaking of the Pharaoh, I must leave. I have an important meeting with him. I will leave this matter in your hands." And he bowed to the priest, scowled at Poma, and turned and hurried out.

Poma looked closely at the priest's puzzled face. *I am not a thief!* She wanted to wail, but her parched throat wouldn't let her. She swallowed. "I've had that distaff all my life."

She almost said she arrived on earth in a basket with a distaff of purple, but thought better of it. She would not be believed. Then she wanted to say that the Goddess had given her the distaff, but that would be believed even less. Oh, how she wished she were home! "I am not a thief!" This time she wailed, and the tears came afresh.

The priest called out, his voice echoing through the building. "Heptle!" One of the young girls came running. "Heptle, make her ready to meet Enash. If he agrees, then she can join us here." He seemed to have almost forgotten about the distaff. He handed it back to her and left her with Heptle.

Poma took a big breath and studied the older girl. She was a great beauty, with blonde hair and dark blue eyes. But her beauty was diminished by the disdainful look on her long face.

"What is this place?" Poma asked, wiping away her tears.

"Come with me," said Heptle, immediately taking charge. "You are in Avaris, home of the great Pharaoh."

"Great who?"

Heptle frowned at her. "Our scribe will talk with you," she said, leading Poma into the sudden coolness of the interior of the building. The other girls in white followed, whispering among themselves. Poma watched Heptle with curiosity. She made up her mind this situation would have to do. If the Goddess had protected her from two great rivers, she would protect her from this tall, thin young girl.

Poma noticed that these girls were different from the other people outside earlier in the dusty crowd. Not only could she understand these young women, but instead of the black hair and very dark skin of the people outside, these girls looked more like her own family, some with brown hair, one with light brown hair, and one with auburn hair like her grandmother. The scent of flowers seemed to emanate from them. She wondered once again about her family. Would they think she had drowned?

They guided her to a small area in the rear of the building attached to an open courtyard and began preparing a noontime meal. She felt famished and a little weak. She sat down on a large floor covering and tried to control the tears which streamed down her cheeks. Heptle sat down next to her and took her hand.

Heptle looked Poma over from head to feet. "What is your name?" she inquired.

"Poma." Her name echoed through the large hall.

"Come, Poma, and you may bathe." Heptle guided Poma down a long hallway. The ceiling was so high and dark it could not be seen. There was a small anteroom where she told her to undress. Poma was struck with another stab of fear until she saw a small private courtyard. Here the roof made way to an open space with a patch of blue sky and sun, which warmed a small pool. Relieved, she allowed Heptle to help her bathe, and put Poma in a white dress.

"Heptle, you have been so kind to me. Thank you."

"I'm glad to help you," Heptle's face did not reflect her words.

"What is this place?" She looked up at the ceiling.

"This is the temple of the great Goddess Isis," Heptle said. Her blue eyes gleamed with pride.

Poma's eyes widened. *The Goddess had a name.* Poma wanted very much to fit in here. She pretended to know about Isis. "Oh, yes, Isis. She taught my great grandmother how to spin."

Heptle stared at her in astonishment. Then, after a moment, "Just wait here, Poma, and the girls will bring your meal." Poma waited, wondering if she had said something wrong. Two of the other girls came in bearing fruit, bread, and milk. They stared at her. Poma thanked them and began eating. The two were at first aloof and then giggled together as they returned down the hallway. Poma was almost too busy eating to notice. As she finished drinking the cool milk, Heptle returned with a very tall young man. He had a shaved head, as did the other priests, but his manner of dress indicated he was of great importance, contradicting his youthful appearance. Like his fellows, he was dressed in white, but he sported an elaborate gold headdress. A long scar ran through his brow and curled up on the side of his face. But he was kind looking, with twinkling brown eyes.

"I am Enash, the chief scribe of the temple," he said. "And what is your name?"

"Poma," she said.

"I hear you have a famous great-grandmother." He sat down across from Poma and gazed intently at her.

Poma took a big breath. "Yes, the Goddess was all dressed in a white light, and made a spindle from a tree branch and taught Eve to spin." Her story became animated. "And when Eve came back from finding her own spindle, the Goddess was weaving—"

The scribe stopped her in mid-gesture. "Who did you say?"

"The Goddess—"

"No, your great-grandmother."

"Well, she may have been a great, great-grandmother, but my own grandmother, Hamora, told me how the Goddess taught Eve to spin."

By the look on the scribe's face, Poma wasn't sure he believed her. After a moment he said, "Poma, tell me about what your grandmother Hamora taught you about yourself. What did she think about you? What did she teach you?"

Poma frowned. "Well," she said, "Grandmother taught us all to tell the truth and be kind to one another." She smiled.

"What else?" he said, smiling back.

She thought for a moment. "She taught me about herbs for medicine and for color." She thought some more. "Oh, and she taught me about one-needle knitting."

"Really?"

"Yes," she went on. "From this." She reached into her basket and drew out the purple blanket.

"That's very nice," he said, his eyebrows raised. "And where did you learn how to make this?"

"I didn't. I came wrapped in it when I was a baby," she said with pride.

"In the basket?" he said.

"Why, yes." She was surprised.

"Tell me how you got here, to this place, today."

Poma was unsure if she should trust this young man. "I woke up this morning by the river," she said carefully. "And there was a little beast . . ."

"I mean before that."

She examined his face, and decided to plunge right in. "You may not believe me," she started, "but the river this morning, the one right there, is not the one I went bathing in earlier."

"You are right to be cautious," he replied. "If you are who I think you are, you should never reveal these secrets to anyone."

She felt the fear again. "Who do you think I am?" she asked.

"Well, little one, every once in awhile there is a special traveler who is chosen by the Goddess . . ." he began.

"That's what my grandmother said." She was amazed.

"Poma, you are, indeed, a special little girl, sent to us by the Goddess, and I would advise you to stay here, join the girls here in the temple, and we'll send you to school." He got up and beckoned Heptle from the hallway. He seemed excited to have Poma visiting his temple. "Heptle will show you where you will stay."

"Can't I go home?" she said.

He looked down at her. His eyes grew dark. "That's not possible, Poma. You must look forward." He studied her face. Poma felt her chin quivering. She blinked back the tears. The Goddess had directed her to this kind young man who seemed to know much more than he revealed. She thanked Enash and accepted Heptle's outstretched hand. Poma did not notice that Heptle's hand had grown cold and her smile frozen.

The Dapple Grey

The next day as Poma awoke, she didn't know where she was. Piece by piece it all came back to her; the new land, the temple, Enash, Heptle and the other girls, and school. School! She wasn't quite sure what this meant, but the girls explained it. Taki, the youngest one, took her by the hand after their morning meal and soon had her smiling with her banter. She never stopped for a breath as she told Poma about the school.

". . . and we learn about the Gods and Goddesses, and the moon and stars, and the Pharaoh's sons are there, and Enash talks about writing, and . . ."

Taki only filled Poma's head with questions. She finally reached a saturation point and her mind turned from listening to noticing the girl's fair skin and blue eyes. She looked much different than the people outside the temple.

They moved down the hall and into the large sleeping room to make their beds.

"Where are you from?" she said.

Taki stopped for a moment. "I'm from here. Right here in Avaris. Many generations back, my family is not from here. We are all related to the Pharaoh Apophis. The Egyptians call him a shepherd king. I'm not sure why. Enash told us all about how the God Seth helped us to be the best soldiers in the world. Our Pharaoh had horses, and the other Pharaoh didn't, and my father loves horses, but my mother didn't care so much for them. You should see my horse. He's black and has a curling mane, and . . ."

Poma helped her fold her blanket and watched in awe as she rattled on and on about her father and the horses. She finally broke in. "May I see the horses soon?" she asked.

"Oh, yes, of course. Come, I'll show you."

Taki grabbed Poma by the arm and pulled her through the courtyard and into a large open space next to the temple. A three-sided mud building stood next to a circular walled-in space. Poma had never seen horses, and immediately fell in love with the beautiful animals. But they were frightening.

"Taki, they are wonderful!" she exclaimed. "But they are so big."

"Come on, Poma," said Taki. "I'll show you Ach-La."

The two found the big black horse, who seemed gentle despite his commanding presence. He nuzzled Taki, who fed him some treats she had brought from their small courtyard kitchen. It was then that Poma laid eyes on a big dapple grey with a silver mane and tail. Before she could ask Taki about him, he walked over to her, lowered his head and stood waiting. Poma was astounded. He had one blue eye and one brown eye.

She was enchanted with this stately beast. "Taki, look!" she whispered.

Taki started in all about how dapple greys can start out any color and sometimes end up white. Poma couldn't even hear her for the noise her heart was making. As Taki went on and on, Poma sidled over to the big animal and shyly touched his nose. He nodded at her and nudged her arm.

". . . and she turned white as a cloud." Taki finished up.

Poma patted the horse on his neck. "What's his name?" she asked Taki.

"He's just new. He doesn't have a name, really. He came in last week with a big group of horses from the north, from a place far away." Taki looked wistful.

A slight little man appeared at the door of the enclosure. "Good morning, Taki," he said. Taki ran over and put her arms around him in a big hug. "Hello, Papa," she said. "This is Poma. She's new, and wanted to see Ach-La, and it looks as if the grey has a new friend. Poma, this is my Papa. He's in charge of all the horses here."

Papa smiled at her, his blue eyes bright. "Would you like to ride him?" he asked.

Poma backed away. "Oh, I don't think so," she began. "I just—I think he's so big," she said.

"Here," he urged, "Step here, and up you go."

Poma felt frightened, but wanted ever so much to be up on that broad back. She took a big breath and stepped into the small man's cupped hands, and he lifted her onto the big horse. The grey stood patiently until Poma was settled. She looked over to see Taki already up on Ach-La.

"Hang on to the mane, like so," Papa said, and gave the horse a pat. The horse followed behind Ach-La, and around the enclosure they went.

She felt the power as the animal changed pace beneath her. Intoxicating! Before long the horses were trotting and Poma felt her dark hair flying behind her, whipping against her back. She laughed with Taki as they rode around and around.

Soon the little Papa announced it was time for school, and helped the girls down. "Taki, can we come again tomorrow?"

"Of course," Taki said. "I ride every day."

"Can I ride him every day?" Poma asked.

"Well, for awhile, but he's going to be sent south soon to be with the soldiers." Taki said. Poma was crestfallen. She had heard long ago that soldiers often did not return from their battles, and she was fearful for the big grey. Whenever she found something to love, it was taken away from her, or she from it. She swallowed some tears and kissed the big animal on the neck, fed him a treat, and whispered that she would be back the next day.

The two girls then ran into the temple courtyard and through the big building to the other side where the chattering of children announced the school day. They knelt on some cushions with Heptle and the other girls in the back of the schoolroom. The school was held in one of the temple courtyards where there was shade from the suffocating sun. The Pharaoh's two sons were in front and the children of other dignitaries took their place behind the pair. The oldest son lay on a large cushion and appeared to be somewhat fragile. The other was very young and sat huddled at his brother's side. Taki whispered to Poma, explaining who everyone was while they waited for the teacher.

The courtyard also had a pool with a small waterfall and a profusion of great white flowers floating in the water.

"What are those?" whispered Poma.

"What are what?" Taki said.

"Those." She pointed to the white flowers.

Taki frowned at Poma. "Those are Lotus flowers. Have you never seen a lotus flower before?" She was incredulous.

"Are they used for dye?" Poma asked. She suspected one could achieve at least a good yellow from the stems.

"We don't use those for color," Taki said. "The temple priests use them for the fruit."

"And what are those?" Poma said, pointing at some red flowers.

"Hibiscus," Taki replied.

"Surely you could get a good color from those," Poma said.

"I suppose. I haven't seen anyone try it."

Poma found this hard to believe. But with everyone wearing white, she guessed the folks here had gotten lazy. All their efforts in the way of color had to do with decorating buildings, not clothing. She would have to look into this Hibiscus thing later.

Enash was the teacher for the day, and they were to practice writing. Poma and two of the other young ones were given glyphs to copy. Poma marveled at the thick paper and colorful ink pigments and spent the morning carefully copying the pictures and painting them. School was fun. Wouldn't Hamora have been proud of her!

Then it was time for a story. Enash sat cross-legged on a large mat in front of the children. He was tall and regal and looked very much like one of the handsome statues that decorated the temple. His soft voice almost put Poma to sleep.

"The Tocharians far, far to the east tell a wonderful story about their neighbors, the Celts, who had a princess named Morrek. Now, Morrek had great beauty."

The little girls were immediately interested. Their chins rested in their hands.

"Her flaxen hair framed her elfin face, and her eyes were like lapis."

The little boys fidgeted.

"Morrek traveled about the land on the back of a flying crocodile named Estwynd."

Poma was astonished. She had seen the pictures of the crocodiles. "Crocodiles can fly?"

"Well, not really, but this was a magic land," said Enash.

They all quieted down to listen. Enash told a long tale about how Estwynd wounded his wing, and Morrek was sent on a quest for ingredients for a healing potion. She gained courage, patience, and determination by finding the three things needed for the potion: a snake's smile, a baby's sigh, and a golden toe.

Enash still had everyone's attention at the end of the story.

"The new King asked Morrek to marry him, and they all lived happily from that day to this."

The children applauded.

After school, Taki and Poma sat in the small kitchen, eating lunch.

"Have you ever seen anyone who looked like Queen Morrek?" Poma asked.

Taki dipped her bread into her milk. "Yes, we had a visitor one day, a man and his family—he was an important person from some government in the north. When Enash described Morrek, I thought immediately of the daughter in the family. I'll never forget her face. She was wearing this blue gown, and . . ."

As the girls walked back to their beds, Taki went into one of her meandering descriptions, but Poma was too sleepy.

Poma rode on the big grey. She felt him lift her into the sky. She reached out to touch a cloud, but it faded away. She looked down and saw rivers and forests. The big horse whinnied at her.

When she woke up, Taki was not there. She had an idea. She washed her face and ran out to the horse enclosure.

"Taki, I'm going to name the grey Estwynd, just like the flying crocodile!"

Taki looked up from some horse trappings. "That sounds great! Let's see if he likes it." The girls rode together, round and round, and it was decided that Estwynd did, indeed, like his name.

School Lessons

Every morning Poma and Taki went to the horse enclosure and Papa taught them the finer points of riding. Then they would return to the temple in time for school. Their meals were prepared by a group of Egyptian women in the service of the Pharaoh. They lived in mud huts just beyond the temple gates.

In the middle of the day everyone slept under filmy gauzes which kept the insects away. In the late afternoons the girls bathed and made ready for their duties in the temple by cleaning, cooking sweets, and learning the fine arts of dancing and playing on small stringed instruments similar to the ones being played when Poma first arrived. They were taught to be guardians of all that was sacred within the temple. These things, in addition to school, were expected of all the temple maidens.

But she missed spinning. She was anxious to learn to spin the beautiful light linens she now wore. The Pharaoh's spinning was done in a special building by a team of Egyptian women who were farmers' wives. Taki took her to see the weaving and spinning. Long strips of the finished linen cloth were laid out to bleach white in the hot sun. She watched in awe as they spun extremely fine threads and wound them onto long spindle shafts. She assumed she would be learning more about dyeing when it was time for the harvest and all the plants would be ripe for gathering, as her family had done when she lived in the forest. She now lived a rich life, but school was becoming more difficult.

As the days went by, Poma learned to love glyphs and hate mathematics. Enash gave Poma special lessons and tried very hard to get across the importance of mathematics, but Poma wanted none of it.

In school one morning he said, "What if you wanted to walk to the sea and you needed to know how long it would take you?" He wiped the sweat from his brow.

"I would go on the river, in a boat." Poma said stubbornly. *What was so difficult about that?*

Enash took a big breath. He moved closer and stood in front of her. "You're missing the whole point of the lesson, Poma. If you *were* to walk, and you knew how far it was, and how far you could walk in a day, how would you figure out how many days it would take?"

Poma and Enash stared silently at one another. The elusive answer dissolved in the air between them.

"Couldn't I at least ride a horse?" Poma said.

Enash threw up his hands. "We'll do this another day. It's time now to read the star charts." He returned to his place at the front of the class.

"This man is crazy," she whispered to Taki. Taki rolled her eyes. Poma saw Heptle watching them. She was uncomfortable with the disapproving look on Heptle's face. She turned her attention to Enash and the large chart he was lecturing about. It was something about the movement of the stars and how one of the Gods ate the sun every day. This only confirmed Poma's theory that Enash needed a good talking to.

After class that day, Poma saw Heptle earnestly whispering to Enash. His eyes followed Taki and Poma as they left the courtyard.

"Taki," she said, "why does Heptle watch us like that?"

"Like what?" Taki said. Her eyes grew big.

"Like she hates us."

"Do you think she hates us?" Taki said.

"She seems terribly unhappy about something," Poma replied. "Did you see how she was whispering to Enash?"

"She acts all the time like she knows everything," Taki said, disgusted. The two reached the small kitchen where a large bowl of fruit was waiting for them. Poma bit into an apple as they headed for their beds.

"She seems jealous, or something," Poma said.

"Well, I remember one time when all of us were going to a festival across the river and when Enash got sick and she stayed behind to take care of him, she became one of his favorites. No one ever stays home from the festival of the Queens. Why, the last time we went . . ." Taki went on and on as usual, but Poma could only concentrate on Heptle's jealousy. Finally, despite Taki's ramblings and the heat, she fell asleep. Her dream on this hot afternoon was vivid.

A long, skinny snake was carving its way through the sand. It had big red eyes and a long green stripe down its back. Poma ran after the snake to catch it, but it was too fast. It disappeared into a garden and when Poma looked for it, she

found it coiled around a hibiscus flower. The older of the Pharaoh's sons grinned
at her from the branches of a tree. His aura was white and thin. He said to her,
"Poma, you must ride to the sea, but ride on a camel instead." When she looked
back down for the snake, it was gone.

Poma woke up and didn't move, so she would remember her dream,
as Hamora had taught her. The snake's escape meant she didn't
understand Heptle's jealousy. She remembered Hamora telling her about
thin, white auras. This was almost always a sign of death. She shivered. She
wasn't sure about riding a camel. She giggled to herself to think how
much Heptle looked like that snake. As she lay thinking about the snake
and the Pharaoh's son, some of the older girls were bathing in the nearby
pool. She could hear Heptle's voice ringing in the small courtyard.

"I told him they need to learn respect." Heptle said. Someone else
said something she could not hear. Then Heptle replied, "They're not
too young to learn to respect their elders."

The older girls walked back down the hall to dress at the other end
of the large room where the girls slept. Poma opened her eyes. So
that's what was bothering Heptle. Poma felt angry and humiliated. Her
parents had taught her respect and she didn't think Heptle was justified
by her remarks. She decided to keep them to herself and not tell the
sleeping Taki.

She got up quietly and went to bathe. She dressed and went down
the hallway toward the front of the temple. She was exploring the great
statue when she found a small room in back of it. Curious, she wandered
to the doorway and peeked inside. Her mouth fell open in amazement.
She beheld a room full of the greatest treasures she had ever seen. There
were painted statues, much gold jewelry, and stacks of rugs, cushions,
and fabrics that were startling in their colors. Precious gems and beads
decorated many beautiful wooden boxes. Wooden papyrus scrolls lined
the walls on tall shelves. Poma was awestruck. Her eye caught a familiar
color in a dark purple tapestry with a pharaoh's head appliquéd on it.
Poma was immediately drawn to the purple. Was it exactly like her distaff?
She turned to run back for her distaff to compare, and fell directly into
the arms of Enash.

"Enash, look at the purple!" She dragged him over to the tapestry.
"Where did you get this? Who made this color?" she begged.

Enash looked surprised. "Well, Poma, such excitement. These are
gifts to the Pharaoh. We keep them here for the Gods to protect them.
I don't remember where this came from, but I can look it up."

"Oh, Enash, thank you."

Enash searched through the scrolls and finally came to one with a
long list of gifts ". . . from a land not too far away, but across the great sea.

It is called Canaan," he told her. He named some other things on the list, some boxes and fabrics from beyond Canaan far to the east.

As he read the list, Poma examined the fine fabrics. Her hand ran over the soft, fine silks. She was almost breathless. "Enash," she exclaimed, "How could anyone spin anything so fine?"

"Our linens are just as fine, Poma," he said.

"Yes, but not so soft." Her eyes shone.

"And what would you do with silk like this?" Enash said.

Poma didn't hesitate. "A dress for dancing." She could imagine herself twirling around and around, the beautiful silk billowing and flitting around her. She could dance through the clouds.

Enash smiled. "And what else?"

It brought Poma back down to earth. "I would want to learn to spin this silk. Where does it grow?"

"It grows far away in the east."

"Tell me, Enash, why don't people here wear color?"

Enash spoke like the teacher he was. "It's just simply cooler to wear white. Colors are much hotter. And the Sun God loves white."

"But people certainly can't be happy wearing white all the time," Poma persisted. She remembered Hamora dipping more and more wool into her dye pots in order to get every last drop of color. Some of the light colors produced this way couldn't be all that hot to wear.

Her mind came back to the purple tapestry. "Let me go and get my distaff, to compare," she said, and off she ran. A few minutes later she returned, breathless, with her distaff. She held it up to the tapestry, and it matched almost perfectly. Poma couldn't contain her excitement. "Enash, where is this Canaan? What makes this purple? Can we make it here?"

"Whoa, Poma," Enash said, "One question at a time. The purple comes from a tiny seashell, which we don't have here, and Canaan can be most easily reached by the sea, because no one really wants to go over the desert."

"I want to go to this Canaan. When can we go?"

"It's many weeks away, and we have responsibilities here. But I'm sure some day we could . . ."

Poma's face fell. "Oh, I want to go soon," she said.

Enash frowned. "There is one problem, little one. This dye is very valuable and they say the dyers keep the process very secret. Many important people who wear this color are in a position to make laws against anyone else wearing it."

Poma was confused. She almost whispered, "Then how come I got this purple distaff when I was little?"

Enash smiled. "You certainly are a mystery, aren't you?"

"Why?" Poma's whole being wanted to know who her real mother was, why she had been chosen, and where she would go next. Would she never get back home?

"Sit down over here," Enash said. "Those of us who are chosen are chosen because we are teachers. Our lives will be used . . ."

Poma was amazed. "You are chosen too?"

"I feel it is so. When I came here, I found some old manuscripts concerning the needs this world has for people who can learn quickly and then can be sent to specific places and times to be influences for the good of culture and art."

"What does this have to do with me?" Poma was almost ready to cry.

"Don't cry, Poma." Enash took her hand. "Sometimes when the world cries out for help, someone comes along who is a helper."

Enash hugged Poma as she cried, and stroked her hair. Soon she was comforted enough to wipe her eyes and thank him.

Enash and Poma did not see Heptle standing in the shadows of the statue, listening. She turned and slipped silently away.

Born to the Purple

The next morning in school, Poma noticed the Pharaoh's sons' seats were empty. In the middle of the lesson on the rhythms of the Nile, one of the other priests burst in, approached Enash and whispered something to him. Enash turned to the children.

"We have been invited to visit the Pharaoh and his family. Everyone, put your work to one side and follow me."

Poma looked at Taki. Taki's face had turned white.

"What's wrong?" Poma asked.

"Sh," Taki said. They held hands and followed the others through the temple and outside toward some large buildings beyond the horse enclosure. The heat hit them like a hammer.

"Where are we going?" Poma asked.

"The Pharaoh lives over there, in that palace." Although the palace was imposing, it was rather low and sprawling in comparison to the temple. Poma clung tightly to Taki's hand. It was hard for the children to keep up with Enash's long stride, and they all scampered after him like baby ducks. The pathway in front of the palace was lined with statues of lions. It made the palace all the more splendid. The palace was guarded by fierce-looking men carrying spears. Enash's way was parted by the guards and the small entourage made its way up the grand stairway and into the cool, dark palace. The scent of flowers drifted through the air. The floor was polished stone and pillars led to the back of a large room which housed the thrones.

The Pharaoh was a stocky, grey-haired man with a worried face. His wife, who looked almost exactly like him, square and puffy, sat next to him. His family and attendants gathered around him, the sickly son and his brother at their father's feet. As usual, everyone was dressed in white.

Enash got on his knees and bowed down with his head to the floor in front of the Pharaoh. Everyone followed suit. Everyone, that is, except Poma. Taki pulled at her gown. She could only stand and stare. The Pharaoh spoke.

"Arise." He saw Poma. "Wait!"

The children all waited, on their hands and knees. "You—come here." He pointed with his scepter at Poma. She stepped forward a pace. Everyone else sat down.

"Closer." The Pharaoh scowled. Poma walked toward the frowning man with growing apprehension. She stopped just at Enash's side. Her knees shook. "Who are you?" the Pharaoh asked.

Poma's voice faltered. "I . . . I am Poma."

"Oh, yes. The little one who came to us out of the river with a camel."

"The camel wasn't mine—" she began.

"Silence!" The Pharaoh's wife hid a smile behind her hand. "Arise, Enash, and tell me again, who is this child, and where does she come from?"

Enash got quickly to his feet, bowing slightly. "She is Poma, from the river. She is from an honorable family who taught her much about the herbs." Poma smiled.

The Pharaoh's eyes narrowed. "A magician, then?"

Poma's smile faded.

"No, your eminence. She's wise beyond her years in the ways of medicines and color." Enash said. Poma tried to smile again. The Pharaoh's face sagged into a worried expression.

"Look at my son," he said, rising. Poma noticed the faint white aura around the sad little boy on the pallet, just as in her dream. Her heart beat faster. The little boy was not far from death. His tired little face drooped in unhappiness. Suddenly Poma remembered about Dunard and the pink socks. She had an idea.

"Sir," she said to the Pharaoh. "I'm sorry your son is not well. But I think I can help him."

The Pharaoh's brows rose slowly. "Oh? And what can you, just a little girl, do for the dying son of the great Pharaoh?" The question rang through the quiet hall.

Even Enash seemed surprised. "Perhaps . . ." he began.

"Silence," the Pharaoh said. He turned to Poma. "Well?"

Poma took a big breath. "He needs to be wearing purple," she said. She surprised herself with an even voice.

"What?" Everyone stared at Poma.

"Purple, sir," she said. She managed another step forward. "If the Gods decree that he should die, then he will at least be happy until then." She held her breath.

The big man looked in surprise at his son and then at Poma. The only sound was water, echoing from a far-off fountain somewhere within the palace.

The Pharaoh's wife broke the silence. "There is nothing else to be done," she said quietly. "Certainly it could do no harm."

Poma watched the man's face. Finally, resigned, he agreed.

"Go, Poma, and bring us back some of your magical purple."

She breathed again.

The little boy looked at Poma and managed to pull his small face into a lopsided smile. She became determined at that moment to find the most wonderful purple she could find, and they would have a festival, and everyone would dance and there would be music and feasting. She also decided it a good idea to bow in thanks to this Pharaoh. She turned and made her way over to Taki. She had a hunch. "Come, Taki, we're going to find some more hibiscus flowers." The other children followed as they ran back toward the temple. All except Heptle. She waited and walked back with Enash.

Poma and Taki negotiated for the horses for a ride along the river in search of hibiscus flowers. Enash and Heptle walked by the horse enclosure, deep in conversation. Poma glanced at them and felt a chill, even in the heat of that fateful morning.

The Quest

"Be careful," Papa warned.

"We will," shouted Taki, and she and Poma rode off down the path toward the river. The dusty path gave way to muddy spots left by the receding water. Poma searched carefully along the water's edge for the hibiscus plants. They finally found a few scattered clumps of the red flowers and stopped to fill their linen bags with beautiful blooms.

Taki stopped in her tracks. "I remember someone who might help us," she said.

"Who?"

"I'll show you." She maneuvered her horse, Ach-La, nearer to a large rock so she could climb on his back. Poma did the same with the grey, and they rode off away from the river and far out into the desert.

Poma felt the change of the rhythm of the horse between her knees. What power! The twosome galloped off across the sand as if in pursuit of the wind. Estwynd did, indeed, seem to love his name. Poma was thrilled with the ride; the breeze cooled her down in the heat she hated so much.

Through the ripples in the air above the ground there gradually appeared a small cluster of mud houses close to a muddy creek and a cliff that hid a series of short waterfalls. Poma and Taki rode up and slowed the horses down to a walk. The water made its lazy way toward the river. A very old woman sat in the shade of her house spinning linen with a long spindle. The woman looked a little like Hamora, but she was much darker and had large, sad brown eyes. Her greying hair was tucked under a white head covering, and much to Poma's delight, a blue apron covered her white gown. The woman smiled at Taki, a big, happy grin.

"Greetings, Lila!" Taki shouted. The girls slid off the big horses. "This is Poma." Poma smiled shyly at the older lady. They led the horses to the creek.

"Hello, Poma. You two come riding in here like the wind," Lila said. "What would your father say?" The girls looked at each other and giggled. "Come over here and sit in the shade." Lila motioned to a long stone bench by her house with a large tree shading it.

Poma stared at Lila's spindle. The shaft had a small slit running vertically to the top. The linen yarn was then centered and made the spinning balanced. The carnelian whorl fairly flew. Lila's wrinkled hands made quick work of the flax and a slender thread emerged almost like magic. Poma was entranced at this technology—only a small slit—and the economy it introduced to the craft.

Lila smiled at the girls. "Tell me now, how is your father?" she said. The girls joined her on the bench with their bags of flowers.

"He is well. We have come to ask you about something we need help with. Poma needs very much to find some purple dye."

Lila looked at Poma. "Purple dye? For your hair?"

Poma was surprised. "Oh, no, it's for the Pharaoh's son. He's kind of sick, and we need to . . ."

"Pharaoh's son?" Lila said. Her brows wrinkled together in a frown. Her eyes looked frightened. "Is he still alive?"

"Do you know about him?" Poma said.

"Oh, too well, little one. My husband was his physician, and couldn't help him. The Pharaoh banished us out of sight. My husband died in disgrace." Her eyes filled with tears.

"Oh, Lila, I'm so sorry." Taki said. She put her arm around the old woman's shoulder and kissed the wrinkled cheek. "I didn't know. Papa didn't tell me."

"I guess word has not spread that far yet." Lila wiped away a tear.

Poma felt sorry for the old woman. "What's a physician?" she asked.

The old woman looked at her in surprise. "It's someone who heals people. Physicians know about the herbs and all the incantations that go with each one."

"Incantations?"

"Yes," Lila said. "The herbs do not work unless one knows the correct words to say along with them—the right prayers."

"Oh, I see." Poma said politely. Hamora had taught her to pray, and taught her about the herbs, but never connected the two. She thought it was a good idea that physicians pray. It could do no harm. Except—she grew uneasy. What would become of her if the purple robe she envisioned for the Pharaoh's son did not make him happy? She just had to succeed.

"Your apron is so lovely." Poma said.

"Thanks, dear. I get weary of white all the time."

"Oh, Lila, you are wonderful!" She felt a sudden kinship with this old lady.

"Now, what's this about the purple?" Lila asked.

"I told the Pharaoh that if his son wore something purple, at least he would die happy."

Lila's face eased into a smile. "And what will you use for a dyestuff?" she asked.

Taki pointed at the linen bags. "We are gathering hibiscus flowers."

Lila examined the blossoms. "That's a good choice for this time of year," she said.

"Do you know where we can get more?" Poma said.

"I have some right on the other side of the house," Lila said. "But let me show you the color they make." She got up and disappeared into her little house, and reappeared with another apron in a bluish purple.

"It's beautiful," Poma said, petting the linen fabric.

"Put as many flowers as you can into your pot." She thought for a moment. "Do you have a copper pot?"

"No," Poma said. She had no idea what the temple kitchen held in the way of pots.

"You girls go back and get the linen yarn together and bring it back here, and we'll make it as close to purple as we can," Lila said. "The weaving can be done by the palace weavers."

The girls were excited. They gave the flowers to Lila, climbed on their horses and raced back to the city and the temple enclosure. Poma was glad the dye pot was out in the desert and away from prying eyes, just in case the pot gave them an unexpected color.

The Celebration

Estwynd loved to run, and Poma raced him over the desert at a full gallop. Exhilarated by the wind in her hair and the freedom to explore the desert and the secrets of the cliffs, she felt good about the new land she found herself in. She and Taki raced to Lila's mud house every day, bringing linen yarn from the Pharaoh's storehouse to the dye pot. They searched for purple and red hibiscus and filled the hungry pot every day. Lila showed them how to take the red linen and dip it into the Indigo pot where it turned beautiful shades of violet and purple.

They kept the palace weavers busy. The weavers employed the latest invention for their craft—upright looms with weighted warp threads. It made their work more comfortable and went faster than the old horizontal looms, located flat on the ground. So the work went at a fast pace, and soon enough fabric emerged to dress the whole royal family in various shades of purple, violet and red.

Poma prayed to see the Pharaoh's son smile once more. If the purple didn't work, she might be in trouble. The children dressed themselves in blue and learned to dance from the older girls. The excitement was palpable as they made plans for a festival. The Pharaoh's attendants prepared a large feast, and flowers from the river decorated the large room and the thrones.

When the festival day arrived, Poma led the way with the purple garments and the children followed. Such colors in clothing had not been seen for a very long time. The Pharaoh watched as the preparations were completed.

Poma reached the great throne with her colorful following. "Sir, I have the purple robes for you and your sons."

44

The Pharaoh glared at her. "And you think that by wearing purple, my son will somehow be happier?"

Poma remembered her mother's hug when she wanted to make the pink socks for her brother. She never got a chance to give them to Dunard. Her grandmother and mother had faith in her. She took a deep breath. Even though her heart was pounding, she knew the answer. "Yes, sir," she said. She managed to make it sound brave.

"We will see if your idea works," he said. The Pharaoh's wife pulled her frowning husband into an ante-room to change his clothes. When they returned, their little son was wrapped in his purple robe, his face beaming. Then the celebrations began. There was a great feast and dancing. Poma and her classmates danced in their blue aprons as dignitaries in hibiscus red and purple watched, and then they all sang songs of praise to the gods. All in all, it was quite a day.

Poma was happy and proud, but she kept a careful eye on the sickly son of the Pharaoh. He seemed relieved as those around him gave him hugs and food.

The wife of the Pharaoh came over to Poma. "Thank you, my dear," she said. "Your idea was a good one. Festivals are always good ways of celebrating the important events in our lives."

"My grandmother taught me that when we wear color, it makes us happy," Poma replied.

"You have a very wise grandmother," the older woman said.

Poma almost saw her grandmother smiling at her. She wished she could feel Hamora's hug. She took comfort, however, in the knowledge that Hamora's wisdom had been passed on.

When the celebration was over, Enash rounded up the children, who were still excited. He allowed them to dance their way back to the temple. He and Poma stood in the doorway talking.

"Today was a success, Poma," he said, "but we'll have to wait and see if the effect is lasting. Do you understand that?"

Poma was all too aware of the danger she was in. But her enthusiasm kept bubbling to the surface. "Yes, I understand very well," she said. "I think about poor Lila all the time. She was banned to such poverty, but she still had the courage to help me. She's a real heroine."

"Indeed she is." Enash said.

Heptle approached the pair. "Aren't you quite the queen of the day?" she said to Poma. "I saw the Pharaoh's son just before I left the palace. He was coughing so much they had to take him back to his bed." She sneered at Poma and glided past her.

A small cloud of fear touched Poma.

"We must wait and see how the purple will help him," Enash said, trying to be encouraging.

Poma sighed. "Thanks, Enash," she said, and turned to enter the temple and hunt for Taki.

Three weeks later, the Pharaoh's son died. He had worn his purple robe until the end. It was reported he died with a smile on his face. After an appropriate time, his body, prepared for his journey into the underworld, was ensconced in a small tomb next to that being built for the Pharaoh. The Pharaoh's second son came back to school, still wearing his purple robe in tribute to his big brother. Poma stayed in the back of the room, a little frightened for her future.

Soon the Pharaoh sent a messenger, asking that Poma come to see him. Poma was very uneasy. She didn't know whether to trust the temple gossip or not. If she were also banished, where would she go? She bit her lip as Enash escorted her to the palace.

"Don't be afraid, Poma," Enash said. "I'll be right there with you."

When they reached the palace, guards ushered them into a small courtyard where the Pharaoh and his wife sat, eating their lunch. The tired-looking Pharaoh gestured at a large cushion across from them and told the two to sit and eat. Enash smiled at Poma, indicating that her worst fears should perhaps be put to rest.

"Well, little one," the Pharaoh began, "it looks like your idea worked. My son seemed to be the happiest after your purple was employed to cheer him up."

Poma was speechless. At last she managed to say, "Thank you, sir."

The Pharaoh's wife touched her husband's arm and frowned at him. "Oh, yes, Poma," he said. "I—that is, we—" He smiled at his wife. "We would like to reward you for all your hard work. Tell us, what would you like?"

Poma felt her mouth open, but nothing would come out. Finally she collected her wits. "Oh, sir, I don't need anything for myself. But there is someone who needs a new home."

The Pharaoh's brows rose in surprise. "Who is that?" he said.

"You used to have a physician. He is dead now, but his widow, Lila, needs a new home."

The Pharaoh's face was red. "How do you know Lila?" his voice was low and threatening.

Poma thought for a moment. Did she make friends with the wrong person? Regardless of the consequences, truth was the best path. "Lila is a true friend," she replied. "She helped us make the purple for your son, even though she was out of favor. I think she's a hero." Even though Poma's stubborn chin was firm, her heart was racing.

The Pharaoh squinted at Poma. He looked at his wife. She nodded to him.

"I suppose we could arrange for a new home for Lila," he mumbled. "And you want nothing for yourself?"

Poma didn't have to think for very long. "There is one thing," she said.

"What is it?" the Pharaoh studied her carefully.

Poma glanced at Enash. Enash nodded to her. She gulped. "I'd like to have Estwynd," she said. It was almost a question.

"Estwynd?" The Pharaoh's goblet stopped in mid-air.

"The big dapple grey with the one blue eye," Enash said.

The Pharaoh looked at Poma; his eyes narrowed. His wife poked him with a long pointed fingernail.

"Done," he said, resigned.

Poma was too excited to eat the lavish lunch laid out before them.

"Go," said the Pharaoh, gesturing again with his goblet.

Poma rushed out of the palace and ran toward the horse enclosure. Taki was there with Papa.

Poma ran up, breathless. "Taki, he's mine!"

"Who?" Taki said. "Estwynd?"

"Yes."

"Oh, Poma, that's wonderful!"

Poma spotted the big grey at the far end of the enclosure. She called to him, "Estwynd," and over he trotted. She threw her arms around the dapple grey neck and buried her face in the silver mane. Poma had never been happier. Laughing and shouting, she and Taki raced the horses out into the desert past the low hills and out to Lila's once more, bearing the good news.

The Soul Mate

Poma and Estwynd grew together to be tall and handsome. Riding in the Egyptian sun added gold to Poma's dark face. She learned much during this time, and at sixteen seasons, she had become a beautiful and well-educated member of the Pharaoh's court. It soon became time for a slightly different education. The temple maidens learned the ways of spiritual love-making, and were well-versed in the ceremonies connected with this age-old practice. Some of the older girls would come back to their large sleeping room with wonderful stories about the temple priests. Others became unhappy and eventually left to become wives of minor dignitaries. Those who eventually became too old for temple duties moved on to make important alliances with foreign potentates. The Pharaoh gave them as wives to ameliorate political grievances.

Poma was seen as a favorite of the Pharaoh, but she tended to draw back from the court as she realized her destiny was not bound with these people. Soon the Goddess would pull her through time once more, to be instrumental in the arts of other people. The Goddess knew best where to send her. She and Enash had long discussions about religion and politics and their own uncertain futures. They also talked of the sexual duties of the maidens.

One warm day in the fall it became time for Poma to begin with the spiritual love-making and her first time would be with Enash. The day was clear and sparkling after a very rare rainstorm that swept through the land in the night. The humid air had dissipated. Poma came to Enash bearing fruit and anointing oils. She smiled at her old friend as he greeted her, nude, and turned to walk toward his bed. She was amused at his small behind. She had mixed feelings of excitement and fear, so she focused on her duties. She slipped out of her linen shift and they bathed in his small courtyard pool. He sat, relaxed, as she danced her last dance as a true maiden. She uncovered a small basket and produced some fresh fruit and small sweets she had made early that morning.

Barely 20 seasons, Enash was nevertheless learned beyond his years in the ways of spiritual love-making. He acknowledged her beauty and her role as a mother in the short prayer. "A man has seed for a woman," he said. "But as a priest, I will not expend that seed. A woman's energy will help a priest to reverse his energy. When the God and Goddess are present, it goes to a whole different level."

Poma wasn't quite sure what he meant. "I will do my best . . ." she began. They fell silent to gaze into each other's eyes. His gentle touch made her body blaze. He kissed her with a sudden passion. Her wonder was fed as his knowledge of her unfolded. Their union was urgent and focused. Her body exploded and she saw a shower of stars. The energy hit her feet and hands as her toes and fingers tingled. For one sacred moment, she was the only force in the universe. He kissed her softly. She lay only for a few moments and then got up and stepped into the pool once more. He joined her there and took her hands in his. She smiled at him.

"Poma, my wish for you is that you have a long and happy life, the Gods willing."

She shifted away from him and buried her nose in a water lily. "Why do you always speak of the many gods? I know you believe in the one God," she said.

"Before you can approach the one God, you must come to know and experience the many Gods. They manifest themselves in our behaviors. Man's true nature is many-sided, and we play out their stories." His slender fingers arched in cadence with the words, framing them with meaning.

Poma just listened, waiting for something she could really understand.

He continued. "Our task in life is to incarnate the Gods and Goddesses and become aware of their presences, acknowledge and celebrate their forms."

She came closer and kissed the curling scar on his face. "What is incarnate?" she asked.

"Hmm—to bring alive." Enash ran the back of his finger down her cheek.

"Like us?" she said.

"That's still a mystery. I don't know exactly how it works with us," he said, frowning. "But I have learned the more you elevate your energy, the closer you get to God."

She placed her hands on his shoulders. "What about prayer?" she asked.

"Prayer should be used always," he said. He returned her serious gaze.

Poma knew now she loved this man. But she remembered her duties. She kissed his forehead, and stood up to leave.

The Visitor

It was just before dawn that Poma, smiling to herself, tiptoed across the room in front of the great statue and down the hallway to her bed. The God neither approved nor disapproved. She didn't know for certain who to thank for this night, but she suspected the God to thank was not encased in stone.

Poma crept into her bed. She and Taki, who was snoring in apparent bliss, were side by side. Poma's foot brushed against a lump in the bottom of her bed, and thought it might be her shawl. She kept it to cover her feet in the cool desert nights. Just as she drifted toward sleep, the shawl moved against her foot. In the longest instant of her life sleep flashed away and instinct obeyed an ancient reality. She should lie very still. The calm she felt was wrenched away by an almost unreasoning fear.

"Taki," she whispered. She hoped her feet were not sweating as her face was.

"Taki," this a little louder. Taki snored on. Poma did not want to disturb the visitor at her feet. Among the creatures which were likely to take refuge in a warm place were scorpions and snakes. Poma admired scorpions from a distance, and snakes were all right if she knew which way they were going.

"Taki," she whispered again. Light snoring. What to do? Could her unwelcome bed partner feel her tremble, smell the fear? Poma reasoned that she had not been bitten when she slid her feet next to whatever it was, and if she were to ever so slowly slide her foot away, perhaps she would be lucky again. But the motion might also mean her death. The next prayer included salutations to every God and Goddess she could think of.

Once more she pleaded in a whisper, "Taki!" Nothing. Closing her eyes and clenching her teeth, Poma eased her foot away from the offensive lump. She eased a little farther and was crouched, shaking, when Taki woke up at last.

"Poma . . . are you back?" She said.

"Don't move, not even a tiny bit," said Poma.

"What's wrong?" Taki sat up.

"I said, don't move. Sh, quiet. There's something in my bed."

Taki froze. "What should we do?" she whispered. The room had grown pink in the coming light.

"I think we should wake the others, one at a time," said Poma. Heptle and the older girls were still attending to duties in other parts of the temple. Poma and Taki woke the four younger girls who were left and told them to wait in the kitchen until they could dispose of their small visitor.

"Let's get Papa," said Taki.

"I'll stay and watch, to see if it goes anywhere," said Poma. Taki raced out the door. Poma sat and stared at the lump in the bottom of her bed, wondering how it had gotten there. She prayed it wouldn't move, so Papa could kill it. She could hear the younger girls whispering together in the kitchen. After waiting what seemed an eternity, Taki appeared with her father.

Poma pointed at the lump under the blanket. "Right there. It moved—I felt it when I was almost asleep," she said.

Papa had brought a large hammer from the shed by the horse enclosure. "Stand back, girls," he said. His pounding was muffled by the bedding. After two strokes he stopped to look under the blanket. A small asp gave a last gyration before he finished it off with one last smash.

"Ugh!" said the girls in unison.

"Ugh is right," said Papa.

"Where did he come from?" said Poma. "How did he get in here?"

"They usually stay away," said Papa. "But the cool nights must have brought him in to get warm."

Poma and Taki grimaced as Papa wrapped up the dead snake in the blanket.

"You're a lucky young lady, Poma," he said. He took the snake out in the blanket and Taki followed him. Poma went to the kitchen to tell the others it was safe. Just as she rounded the hallway corner, she almost ran into Heptle. When she saw Poma, the tray of dishes she was carrying clattered to the floor. Her eyes were wide and she turned very pale.

"Poma!" she exclaimed.

Poma bent to pick up a bowl which had rolled to her feet. Heptle stood staring at Poma for a moment, and then tried to collect herself. "I thought you—I mean, haven't you—I mean—"

Poma was startled by a Heptle who was usually calm and aloof. Heptle now looked like a frightened child. "You look as if you'd seen a . . ." Poma stopped, stunned. In a flash she understood. "It was you! You put that snake in my bed!" The pink morning turned red. "Why you little . . ." She heaved the bowl at the startled Heptle and lunged at her, pinning her against the wall. She could only see that twisted face in front of her. She grabbed for Heptle's hair and started clawing. Everyone screamed, but Poma barely heard it.

"Hippopotamus!" screamed Heptle. Her long fingers pushed Poma's face into the kitchen table. Poma tore at Heptle's clothing. They rolled on the floor. Pots flew everywhere. Poma felt something warm on her face. Two of the priests ran into the room and pried them apart. Her arms were pinned to her sides as she was pulled to her feet, her breath coming in gasps. Enash came running in. Heptle immediately collected what composure she had left.

"What's going on here?" Enash said, his brown eyes flashing.

Poma managed to speak. "She put a snake—in my bed!"

"I did not, you little frog!" They both wriggled to get away from the big arms holding them back.

"Here, now—that's enough!" Enash spoke with authority.

Poma became limp enough for the priest to let her go. She felt the warm spot on her face and stared, astonished, at her hand. It was bloody. Some of the anger dissolved to fear. As she collected herself, Heptle spat at her, and stormed, shaking, out of the room.

Everyone followed her into the large sleeping room, which was filled with disarray. All the bedding had been searched for more intruders. The younger girls were crying. Taki and Papa came through the outer door.

"What's happening?" Papa's face was anxious. Taki saw Poma and her mouth fell open.

"Poma, you're bleeding!"

Poma tried to take in a deep breath, but was suddenly wracked with sobs. Taki took her in her arms.

"She—put that—snake in my—bed!" Poma said between gasps and tears.

Suddenly one of the little girls, her face white, stepped forward.

"I saw her do it," she said, then bit her lip.

"Well, then," said Enash. "We must all go to the Pharaoh to settle this. Heptle must be punished for what she has done."

Poma felt a strange mix of relief and sadness. She had been harassed by Heptle from the very moment she had arrived here, and now it might all be over with. But at the same time, she felt sorry for the hapless Heptle. The Pharaoh's judgments were usually swift and harsh.

They moved to the palace, where they had to wait while the Pharaoh finished his morning bath.

"Now, to what do I owe this intrusion?" the Pharaoh snarled.

Enash came forward to explain. "Heptle tried to kill Poma by putting an asp in her bed. She just barely escaped with her life."

"And did anyone see this happen?" the Pharaoh asked tiredly. "I am too busy to be interrupted with school girl pranks."

The little girl stepped forward. "I saw her do it," she said again.

The Pharaoh's lip curled. "Heptle!" Heptle was pushed forward by one of the priests. "Heptle, you are to be sold as a slave. Now, the rest of you, out of here. Let a man at least take a bath!"

Poma was shocked at the swift justice. She took one last look at Heptle, who was being led away by two guards. Her face was white despite her defiance. Poma took a deep breath. Then she remembered the time with Enash. She had a good lesson about jealousy, and promised herself to keep her love of the priest in a secret place close to her heart. The love was right and good, and she was filled with happiness, despite the evil Heptle and the snake.

The Amulet

Winds of change reached every part of the land in the weeks that followed. The Pharaoh gathered soldiers and sent them south to protect his part of the country from attack by the new Pharaoh. Poma felt more and more unease about her situation at the temple. The girls sometimes talked of what would happen to them if war should come. Some could go home, others might marry, but Poma felt that the girls were the only family she had. She and Enash talked often of their futures.

"Where were you before you were here?" she asked one day. They were by the river, in the shade of some acacia trees. Farther along the shore, smoke from cook fires arose straight up into the blue sky, accompanied by the soft tones of a flute.

"I lived on a great river, as wide as this one," he said, nodding at the water. "I was very shy, and I was reared by my grandmother."

Poma thought it amazing that both of their past lives were much the same. "Have you ever made any goals for yourself?" she said.

"Well, I never thought much about it until recently. I guess I'll go on teaching. I think I have a spiritual message that most people will take a lifetime learning by themselves." He frowned.

"That's a noble cause," said Poma. "Why the frowning face?"

His eyes penetrated hers. "I just don't feel my path is that of a teacher," he said.

"But that's all I've ever known you to be, is teacher," said Poma.

"For now it is a matter of survival. When I got here, I could understand these Hyksos people and I was able to teach some of them to read and write. This Pharaoh tries to be a good man, and it has been a joy to teach his children and their young friends. But I'm not sure I'm that good of a teacher."

"Oh, that's not true," said Poma. "You're a wonderful teacher. You have taught me much." She kissed his chin.

"Well, thank you." He kissed her cheek, and let her hug him. He was so tall she could only reach around his middle. They planned to meet again in three days' time, when his temple duties allowed him to be free for a day.

Poma was flushed with excitement as she dreamed of the time to come when she didn't have to share him with anyone else. She realized the spirituality he sought as a temple priest with the other girls was not an earthly relationship such as marriage, but she couldn't help the small pangs of jealousy she felt, however tempered they were by the episode with the asp. She took particular care with her skin and hair in the beauty rituals she learned from the Pharaoh's wife and her hand maidens. The women spent long hours mixing cosmetics and elixirs to enhance their skin. They mixed these potions in small batches so they could be used up before the oil got rancid.

On the appointed day, Poma arose early and bathed with the flowers she loved, the hyacinth and floating lilies, and rubbed fragrant oil into her skin. She met Enash at the horse enclosure, helped to saddle Estwynd and a big black and they galloped off across the desert toward Lila's new house. The old mud house had been demolished, and she now lived in a comfortable villa with her family.

Enash and Poma rested the horses here and enjoyed a small breakfast with Lila. Her family had gone to work in a nearby orchard. She was to join them later, to pick apples. "Where are you two going today?" Lila said.

"We're going to follow the creek up into the mountain," Poma said.

"Be careful of the cliffs," Lila said. "Some of the rocks are not as steady as they look."

"Don't worry, Lila, I'll take good care of her," Enash said. He and Poma each hugged Lila and bid her goodbye. She insisted they take a picnic lunch with them. She packed some bread and fruit into a linen sack, which Enash slung over his shoulder, and the pair started up the small creek toward the cliff above Lila's home, leaving the horses to rest below.

They reached a series of waterfalls which parted the canyon and left steep walls reaching up on two sides, except for a small space where a cliff reached down deep into a rocky abyss. A small tree offered shade, and it was here they stopped to have their picnic. As they ate, Enash asked Poma what she would do with the rest of her life.

"I'm not sure," she said. "I do know that I have a deep love of color and I know the important part it plays in people's lives. If only people understood, if they only just knew—people pick colors to wear depending on what's missing in their auras. Some colors are healing, some have deeper meanings. The Goddess has need of teachers, and before my life is done, I want to sit at the feet of all the great teachers of the world and perhaps pass along what they have to say." It sounded lofty when she put words to it, but it felt right and made sense.

"That's a wonderful goal. I'm so proud of you," Enash said.

Confidence comes from knowing where you are going, she decided.

As they rested in the shade, Enash became increasingly uneasy. He got up and paced for a bit.

"What's bothering you?" asked Poma. She made her voice just loud enough to be heard above the rush of the waters.

"I don't know, little one." Then he gave her a look she had never seen from him. He reached down for her and drew her to him with a passion that was almost frightening. She sensed his fear of something. His silver amulet caught the sun and the lapis scarab danced as he kissed her again and again. The sound of the waters disappeared as she absorbed his very energy. In an explosion of passion he turned from priest and teacher to boy and man. She could hear bells from deep within. A sudden rush of aroma of the incense of dying Gardenias overcame her. They slept in each other's arms. When she awoke the sun was high. His face was peaceful and bathed in a lavender light. She crept away from his sleeping form to bathe in the pool at the bottom of the waterfalls.

"Enash, come and bathe. It's so cool," she said. No answer. She turned to look at the spot where he was sleeping. It was empty. "Enash? Enash!" She stood up and looked all around. He had vanished. Something lay on the edge of the cliff, gleaming in the sun. It was the blue scarab in its silver necklace. She ran to the spot and looked over. She knew before she looked what she would see: nothing. Just the barren rocks staring silently in the heat. No Enash lying broken at the bottom of the cliff. Nothing. Her naked body became cold and then hot, then cold again as the tears passed down it. The Goddess had taken him; he was still alive somewhere, some time, but where, and when?

She dressed slowly and the first thing she put on was the lapis scarab. He had left it for her, and she would wear it always as a symbol of his love. She gathered Lila's bag and made her way down the mountain. When she approached the house, only Estwynd was there to greet her. The desert was empty. Lila was curled up on a mat, sleeping in the shade, a basket of apples by her side. She awoke as Poma approached.

"Did you two have a nice walk?" Lila said. Then she saw Poma's face. She sat up and looked around. "My dear, where is Enash? Come here, sit down and tell me what happened."

Poma was still too stunned to speak. She sat down obediently and cried on Lila's small shoulder. She felt as if her world was dead and gone, only here it was, going on in spite of how she felt. Lila's reassuring pats brought back the reality. She would have to continue without him. But how?

Poma looked up at Lila. "I love him so much—don't understand why he had to go." She started to sniffle once more.

"Hush dear," Lila said "I remember once when I was about your age— I loved a young man who did the same thing—just rode off and left me. I felt as if the world had stopped." She patted Poma's hand.

Poma remembered that at least she might have another chance to see Enash again in another time and place. She took a big breath and attempted to smile at Lila. "Thank you, Lila. You've been such a dear person and sweet friend." She promised Lila some more hibiscus for her dye pot and some basket reeds from the river, and said goodbye. She moved Estwynd to a gentle walk and rode home in sorrow. When she reached her bed, on it lay the two scrolls from the storeroom. She could read some of the glyphs, but had to content herself for now that this was Enash's way of saying goodbye and leaving her with information she may need later. She knew he was not dead, but had moved on to his next destiny. She cried herself to sleep. The dream that came to her she would treasure all her life.

Poma stood on a cloud. The heavy aroma of gardenias came to her. The amulet floated in the air just out of reach. Enash's voice came to her as if it were echoing down the temple hallway. "I will be your friend as long as I am in this world," he said. His face appeared in front of her. Instead of his priestly headdress, he was crowned with a small lavender cloud. He smiled and gave her the same look he had earlier in the day. As his face faded, the amulet drew closer.

Poma awoke. Her mouth was parched and rivulets of sweat ran down her arms. She lay contemplating her dream, fingering the sacred scarab. Her own destiny came clearly into focus: Enash was gone. She would follow the dream she had shared with him. She would teach little girls to spin and dye. She would give comfort to others through her knowledge of the herbs. She would search for those who taught about the making of the royal purple. And she would search for Enash until she found him, even if it took all the days of her life.

Winds of War

Poma grew up quickly in those years and before she was twenty she had taken on duties as advisor to the Pharaoh's wife. They experimented together with various leaves and flowers, and established quite a repertoire of dye colors. The linen took the dye differently than wool did; the colors were slightly muted, but lovely nonetheless. She taught the women of the court about using oak galls or alum for mordants to fix the color and make it lasting.

Poma couldn't help but think that the alum represented the structure needed in life to make one feel safe. Just as the colors would not fade, her life felt secure because the power of good was fixed into her being. There was joy in constancy.

Poma learned the great secret of the Egyptian economy, which was teamwork. When a new building arose out of the desert, and it was time to paint the outside of it, she watched as teams of workers would move across the walls and paint them expertly, with the work divided between the team members. She thought when she watched this that it may have been good for getting buildings done, but did nothing for the art. The workers were not encouraged to expand on what they knew, and she was sad to see how their lives were affected by the sameness of each day. However, perhaps they felt good about contributing to their community, which seemed to be the only saving grace.

She felt very fortunate to be in the company of the Pharaoh's family and part of his staff. She had the freedom to experiment with her dye pots and then teach what she knew. She longed for Enash and thought about him every day. He had helped her to know about herself and celebrate the goodness she found deep inside. As she taught the children, she thought to emulate his teachings.

The temple school now included sessions with the palace spinners. Poma helped the children learn to spin and weave. They watched in awe as the accomplished craftsmen separated the flax from its woody stalks, spliced the long strands end to end, rolled these into balls and then used spindles to ply them together and make linen ready for weaving. Soon the class had spinning projects and Poma was happy to see the children learning these skills. She became much admired and respected as advisor in the Pharaoh's court.

Every once in a while she would go into the storeroom and study the purple in the little tapestry. She still dreamed of going to Canaan to find the secrets of that rich, deep violet. Knowing the process of that dye was almost an obsession with her, but she was beginning to understand that this obsession needed to be kept in check. It was a dream for some day, and for now, it was just good to dream.

She pored over her scrolls and began piecing together what they said. There was a long story about the beginning of the earth and detailed descriptions of animals she had never seen or heard of. She wasn't quite sure these scrolls were true. She felt a small tingle of excitement at the prospect of finding out.

One of the scrolls had a section entitled, "Oracle Poems: The Mysteries Unfolded." Among them, two were of special interest to her. The first was as follows:

Incense arises
Awakens the Goddess.
She sleeps within the deep white bosom.
The bosom heaves a sigh,
And the white turns brown.
Herein is the death and life.

Incense . . . the white turns to brown. Did this mean the aroma of the dying gardenias?

Another was equally mysterious. It went:

Your way through life
Lives two seasons
To ten of yours.
Two seasons of love and service.

Two seasons of patience and
Depending on unknown truth.
Two seasons to ten of yours.

Perhaps her "way through life" had something to do with Estwynd. She would have to sleep on these things. She committed them to memory, for she felt they might be important to her, but she wasn't sure just why. She wisely kept the scrolls in her basket, knowing they would go with her when it was time for the Goddess to make a change in her life.

The Flight

The fire happened in the middle of the night. As Poma awoke, the girls were scattering like frightened butterflies. The wooden supports in the roof of the temple were orange with flames. Smoke filled the great hall. The smell was frightening. Taki was pulling at her. Poma screamed at Taki to run for the horses. Then she threw her shawl over her head and ran toward the storeroom. Two of the priests were there, filling their arms with scrolls. She did the same, and then, on her way out through the smoke, remembered the tapestry. She dumped the scrolls into a large basket on the portico and then ran back for it. Smoke burned her throat and eyes. She gathered up the tapestry and some more scrolls, and made her way out of the great room. Her basket! She dropped the scrolls into the arms of the waiting priest and ran down the long corridor. Flames licked at her from the kitchen door. She ran to the large sleeping room and grabbed her basket, shoving the tapestry inside it. She fought her way back through the flames and out the side entrance. Papa and Taki were leading horses out of their enclosure. Where was Estwynd? She ran over and saw the frightened grey in a corner. She was cautious in her approach, and tried to calm the large animal. The fire had not reached the enclosure yet, but the orange sky and shouts of the Pharaoh's men had filled the animals with terror. She threw her shawl over his eyes, and guided him out of the enclosure and through the yard toward the other horses.

Taki and Papa led the other horses to safety. When they reached the river, they heard from the gathered crowd what had happened. The Egyptian army, led by the southern Pharaoh, Kamose, had come through in the night, killing the palace guards and destroying everyone in its path. No one knew if the Shepherd King was still alive. The entire town was on fire. Papa was herding horses with the other men, and Poma saw that Taki was shivering in the dark, her face white and drawn. For once she was speechless.

"Taki!" shouted Poma. "Over here!" The girls huddled together by the river. The sky was filled with orange flames and black smoke. People screamed at one another in the confusion. The acrid smoke took its toll. Soon Papa found the girls, and they decided to take refuge at Lila's house. They could not go back through the temple compound because of the chance of running into the enemy soldiers, so they made their way along the river, through pockets of people who had escaped the fires.

Men attempted to protect their families. Ashen-faced women consoled crying children. The wounded and dead were everywhere. It was a sight that Poma would never forget. Finally they came to a spot where it was time to ride across the desert toward Lila's house. There was no moon that night, and riding in the dark was difficult. At one point, Papa pulled up his horse and cautioned the girls to silence. Horses were galloping in the distance. They waited, silent. Poma was trembling in fear. Stories of war before in her life had been told around the nightly cook fires. Now she was living one of these stories. Life had changed in one night of fire, smoke, and horror. The coming dawn would reveal their way to safety, but would also make them more vulnerable.

As they rested the horses to wait for the dawn, Papa warned them about what might come. "We must be ready to ride hard. If I give a yell, we will split up and meet out at Lila's. Poma, you may have to ride by yourself. You know the terrain out here, and the enemy does not. We have the advantage. You can reach Lila's by skirting the valley of sheep on the south, but first travel through the hills. Taki can head back toward the river and hide with the reed people, if necessary. I will lead the enemy away to the north. We can meet at Lila's at nightfall. Agreed?"

"Agreed," said Poma. It was good to have a plan. It calmed her mind. They would do what they had to do to survive. Papa was not only good with horses, but he was a student of past wars. Both the girls loved and trusted him.

As the sun rose, they mounted up and started out toward Lila's, trying to keep in the low hills to have the advantage of high ground until it was time to make a dash across the open desert. They came to the last oasis before the open desert ride. The girls jumped down to drink at a small pool. Their faces were blackened by the smoke from the night before. Their hair was in tangles. Their images in the water caused them to collapse in laughter. They splashed each other in relief from the stressful night.

It was time to make the run for Lila's house. The horses sensed the urgency and were anxious to be off and running. The three hugged, got on their horses, and off they went. The dry, hot wind seared Poma's face as they galloped across the desert.

A small dust cloud appeared far off in the distance. As it grew, Papa yelled, "Aieee!" the signal to split up. Poma's heart skipped a beat. She smiled bravely and, waving at her friends, urged Estwynd toward the low hills. Estwynd seemed to know her safety was up to him. He stretched out his strides and raced with the wind toward a large outcropping of rocks. Poma glanced over her shoulder. The tiny puff of dust had grown large. But it seemed to be headed now in another direction. Poma drew Estwynd up behind the rocks and peered out at the dust cloud. It looked like it was headed in the direction Papa had taken. Poma felt angry and helpless. The plan was working, but she worried about Papa.

She rested the big grey for only a moment and then they headed off toward the mountains. They skirted the valley of the sheep and at long last arrived at Lila's villa. It was strangely quiet. Poma hid her horse behind the villa and then watched the house for a moment. Nothing moved. She slipped into the back courtyard. It was here she found the first of the carnage. Two of the servants were lying in a great pool of blood.

"Oh, my God," whispered Poma. Her heart beat like a drum as she entered the house. The entire family was slain. Grief engulfed her as she kneeled by Lila's lifeless form. She could only shake in anger as the tears streamed down her face.

She didn't know how long she had huddled in the yard with Estwynd. Her body throbbed with anger at the beasts who had done this atrocious thing. Taki found her there.

"Poma! You made it! Poma! What's wrong?" Taki was at her side.

"Oh, Taki. They're all dead—all dead." She started to cry again.

Taki's eyes grew big. "What? Oh, no, oh no, not Lila. How could they?" She rose to her feet. Poma pulled her down again.

"You don't want to look."

"Oh, Poma!" The two cried in each other's arms.

Sunset came and Taki grew anxious. The girls had taken the horses up the creek to a spot where they could hide the animals and see anyone approaching. A small dust cloud announced an approaching horse. Taki was ready to run back down the path, but Poma held her back.

"Wait, Taki. It might be someone else," she cautioned.

"It just has to be him," Taki whispered.

The horseman drew his mount to a cautious walk. Poma remembered the awful silence when she had arrived earlier. Before they could make it back down the path, Papa had discovered the awful silent secret the villa held. His voice arose and echoed up the canyon.

"Taki—aieeee!"

"I'm here, Papa," she yelled. She hurried down the creek and into his waiting arms.

"Thank the Gods," he said. "You're alright. I thought—I thought you were—" They wept in each other's arms. Poma joined them.

"Come, girls, there is still enough light. We must get as far to the north as we possibly can. I know a man with some camels. We'll have to leave the country. These Egyptians have built up a century of hatred."

Poma was relieved that she would have these dear friends to travel with. She went back, tears streaming, and collected Lila's spindle. The long, slotted spindle with its carnelian whorl seemed like a torch. *A torch being passed on,* thought Poma. They gathered up a stash of food, and Poma placed the spindle and the food together tearfully into her basket. The three mounted up and started out toward the northern coast.

Their journey was a short one; however, they had to find fellow countrymen along the way to make their way safely. They arrived in a town not yet ravaged by the enemy army. A few camels were left. Poma grew apprehensive. They may be her only chance to get to the purple and the secrets it held. She needed to stay close to the seashore. Camels meant crossing the desert. Should she try to convince Papa and Taki to go by boat, or should she go by camel? She remembered her long-ago dream about the Pharaoh's son who told her to go by camel. How could she give up Estwynd? Her heart was torn. She must give him up sooner or later, because she certainly couldn't take him with her by sea. It seemed as if whatever scraps she had left of her life were slipping away. Yet she needed to follow the plan she had set up for her life only a few years before. The Goddess would protect her.

That night as they sat around the camel driver's fire, she decided to tell Papa and Taki her plan. The mournful sound of flute music made it harder to speak of what she must do.

"Papa," she began. "I need to tell you . . ."

"You hate to part with Estwynd, I know, but this fellow will give us a fair price."

"Papa, Taki—" She took Taki's hand. "I must go a different direction . . ." She started to cry.

"What's this?" Papa said.

"I have a dream I must follow, Papa."

"But why?" Taki whispered. She was crying now, too.

"The passage by water is not safe, Poma," Papa said.

Poma set her mouth in determination, wiped away her tears, and spoke with confidence. "I feel I must do this, Papa. I have a dream—a duty, if you will, to take a different path. Please understand."

Papa's face was sad. "If you must, Poma. I remember when you came here; no one knew where you were from. I had the feeling then you would not be here long." He attempted to smile.

"Poma!" Taki was almost wailing.

"It's all right, Taki. We have to let her go." He reached into his saddle bags and drew out a small sack, and pressed it into Poma's hands. "Take this; you will need it for the journey."

Poma looked into the pouch. It held a goodly amount of gold. She was relieved. "Thank you, Papa. It's good to know I'll be safe." She gave him a big hug.

The girls hugged silently. Poma smiled at her dear friend and brushed her hair from her face. "Remember the fun we had, Taki. As soon as I have found what I need, I will come and find you." Poma didn't think this was possible, but it gave Taki hope.

The next morning, Poma left before anyone was awake. After she took one last look at her friends, she and Estwynd headed north to the sea.

The shore was covered with people. Poma was awed by the vast blue waters and the throngs of refugees. For only a moment she wanted to turn Estwynd around and head back to the camel herder's camp. Most of the people on the beach were not of Egyptian descent, and were trying to get out of Egypt before the Egyptian army approached. She and Estwynd set up camp near a large family of dark-haired children. The little ones came to pat Estwynd's nose. "Where are you going?" asked one.

"I want to go to Canaan," Poma said. The children laughed. Poma didn't see the humor.

"Is it hard to find a boat?" she asked.

The children laughed again. Poma frowned. This was not a good sign. The oldest girl approached her.

"Please excuse my brothers and sisters," she said. "We have been waiting many days. The people are many and the boats too few." Poma thanked her and squinted at the horizon. There was nothing to do but wait. She unsaddled Estwynd and settled down on the sand to wait. She fell into a restless sleep. When she awoke later, it had gotten dark. Estwynd had vanished. The saddle was gone. She got up and called. She surveyed the gathered horses in a small enclosure. No Estwynd. She searched the entire beach. Nothing. Poma sat down in despair. She was crying and thinking about Enash. She felt so alone. Then she remembered the day Enash had disappeared. His horse had also vanished that day. Temple gossip had it that he had simply ridden away and never returned. Poma knew better, but this was the first time she even thought that horses might go with them, to be their way through life. Then she remembered the little poem on the scroll. . . . *Two seasons to ten of yours* . . . It was now that Poma knew that it was time for her to move on. She had successfully brought color to the clothes of the Egyptians. She had introduced many wonderful colors to the Egyptian court. She had learned much from this place, much that she could teach somewhere else. It was time to go. She could only pray that Estwynd would be there, whenever it was, wherever it was, to help her.

As she waited for a boat she repacked her basket. Among her belongings it now contained the small purple blanket, the purple distaff, the half-made pink sock, two Egyptian scrolls, the small purple tapestry, and two spindles, one hers, and one Lila's. The gold was hidden safely with some flax seeds. Before the fire she had also tucked in some alum and a few skeins of fine linen. What wonderful memories!

Far into the afternoon there came two boats, one headed east to Canaan, the other headed west, to Crete. Both of these places were sources of the precious purple. She would try for the boat to Canaan, and if it filled up, the one to the west would have to suffice. When it came her turn to board, the boat to the Isle of Crete was where she ended up. Would she ever see Taki and Papa again? Bravely, her plans changed as she dreamed of the lands to the west. Perhaps she could find the purple in another land, and go to Canaan later.

They set sail that day under a cloudy sky. The ancient boat was filled with people and animals, boxes and bedding, food and water. The old vessel creaked under the weight. The captain was a large Phoenician with a dark, worried face. There were many people in his boat and he must be wealthy from the politics of the time. Poma thought he had probably collected as much Hyksos gold as he could while he had the opportunity.

The heavy-laden craft was far from any shore when the storm hit. The boat tossed up and down. The rain poured down and the waves got higher and higher. People were sick and children were crying. The sounds and smells were frightening the animals. Poma clung to her basket and prayed. Each wave seemed bigger than the last.

The old craft could stand no more. In a great shudder and crack, the entire boat capsized. People flew screaming into the cold dark water. In a second heave of water, Poma was thrown overboard. Her basket was torn from her grasp. In desperation she swam toward a large piece of wreckage. Just before she could grab hold, a huge wave engulfed her, pushing her under the water.

Suddenly someone grabbed her hand. *"Poma!"* She clung to the hand. She looked up and saw the face of the Goddess in the white light. Again the face disappeared. A deep purple light almost consumed her. Where would she go now? Time snapped again. Just as her hand was dropped came the faint scent of old Gardenias.

Papa and Taki went to Canaan over the desert. Taki married an innkeeper and made Papa a proud grand-papa. She became a famous story-teller. Heptle had a rude encounter with an asp and died a day short of her 25th birthday. The Pharaoh and his wife had been killed in the night-time raid on the palace. Their remaining son was spirited away to live in the south with the Nubians. He became a trader in spices. And no one ever knew what became of Poma and her basket of treasures.

Part III

Saka!

c. 490 B.C.—The northwestern slopes of the Tien Shan

"Laughter runs by in silver sandals shining,
Stops in at every wide-flung, friendly door.
Warm be the gypsy fires that we keep burning,
That laughter may stay ever more!"

—Ruth A. Brown

The Nomads

Poma was drenched. Water lapped at her feet. Something nuzzled her neck and breathed warm air in her face. She opened her eyes to a familiar nose. Estwynd! Sure enough, one blue eye and one brown eye blinked at her. And his saddle was in place. The sun was warm, but the air had a clear, icy tinge. She smelled the sweet familiar smell of grass and lichens. She sat up and stared in disbelief at the mountains. Almost surrounding her were great, jagged, snow-capped peaks. The hills nearby were green and nearly barren of trees. The lake at her feet was the bluest she had ever seen. The only sound interrupting the licks of clear water on this strange shore was the cry of an eagle. It was a cry she had not heard since she was a child. She leaped to her feet and hugged the big horse.

Where was her basket? She looked all around her, and finally saw its familiar shape farther down the shore. She fetched her basket, checked to see that all its contents were there, and then drew in a long breath. The clear mountain air was a tonic to her tired spirit. She felt almost as if she had come home. A large rock made a good place to sit and dry out in the sun. She took off her cloak and laid it out to dry. As she sat in the sun, she once again thanked the God and Goddess for her life and good health.

She got on Estwynd and together they made their way along the creek through the tall summer grass toward a broad valley. The meadow sage provided a dark purple carpet along portions of their pathway. There were large groups of trees; Poma recognized the pine and fir, but could only admire the other trees she had not known before. Partridges flew up in the horse's wake and eagles soared above. Feather grass swept across the steppe in silver, sea-like waves. Red thistles poked their heads above the waves like bristling sailors. Poma was enraptured with the scene, and entertained thoughts of exploring this new wonderland, dye pot in tow.

A sudden thud punctuated her reverie. Estwynd reared up, almost dumping her off. He broke into a full run. She glanced behind her and saw two horsemen on small pony-like horses. They were shooting arrows at her! She couldn't imagine why anyone would want to kill her; she had only just arrived. She clung to Estwynd as he opened his stride and ran for his life. She suddenly realized it was her horse they were after. Then her shoulder was hit with a searing pain. An arrow went completely through. She cried out as the big grey raced on. But where were they going? She could see no sign of habitation, no smoke, and no village, nothing except the wide expanse of silver grass bordered with the huge mountain crags.

The horsemen were far behind her now; Estwynd had again matched his name. All Poma could do was cling to the silver mane and pray they would find help. Her shoulder burned with pain and she began to feel faint. Could it be the blur in front of her was a herd of animals? Try as she might, she could not stop the grey fuzz from enveloping her.

The next thing she knew, a beautiful face framed in red appeared over her. Was this the Goddess, again so soon? She reached her hand up, and the face started speaking to her.

"There, there, my dear—just be still. We'll take care of you."

Poma tried to sit up, but the pain in her shoulder kicked her back onto her side on the soft fur bed beneath her. "Estwynd . . ." she said through clenched teeth.

"Lie back now, and drink some of this. We need to get rid of that arrow. Hold still."

"My horse . . ." choked Poma, tears streaming down her face.

"Your horse is just fine. He's been hidden in the herd with the other horses." Poma peered at the kindly face above her. She could only believe the Goddess was watching over her once more. The tea that was offered her had a bright, snappy taste. She pushed her mind to remember. It was a small green mint her grandmother had shown her. How long ago had that been? She thanked the lady. She knew the arrow would be broken off in the back and drawn through the front, and she braced for the pain. There were two women attending her, the plump red-head and a thinner version of her who appeared at the tent opening carrying hot water. The plump one held Poma down while the other one broke the arrow. The snap quivered all though her body and the pain reverberated into her neck and down her arm. She almost passed out again.

They let her rest for awhile before they pulled the evil arrow out and again the pain was almost unbearable. As they patched her up, they spoke in low tones together.

"She doesn't look like any of the western tribes, except for those green eyes. She reminds me of Aristagoras' new wife, the one from the islands of the big sea. And did you see the linen she's wearing?—it's the finest I've ever seen," said one. And then a whisper: "And the purple distaff. What do you think?"

"She's a puzzle, all right," was the reply.

"And that necklace . . . it's not any workmanship from the tribes," continued the first. "I wonder if she's of royal blood."

"Those Mongols must have been after the horse," said the other.

The first hummed in disapproval. "Bunch of greedy toads," she said.

Finally Poma had the courage to speak. "What is your name?" she asked the plump, blue-eyed woman.

"I'm Boot-Ru, and this is my sister, Madga."

"I am Poma. Thank you, Boot-Ru, for helping me."

Boot-Ru glanced at Madga, and smiled back at Poma. Poma looked around. Her basket was tucked neatly in a corner. The tent she was lying in was covered with felt. Many strange herbs were hung drying on the walls. There were also horse trappings the likes of which she had never seen. Bright silvery animals bedecked the saddles and knife hilts. Their craft and imagination far outstripped Egyptian jewelry.

Boot-Ru was digging through a basket of herbs, frowning.

"Do you have any comfrey?" Poma said.

Boot-Ru raised her eyes to met Poma's. "Why yes, that's exactly what you need." She picked some leaves from a bundle hanging on the wall and dropped them into the warm water. She formed them into a poultice which she placed on Poma's wound, which comforted her. Her wound was no longer bleeding, and she rested in the warmth of the fur bed.

Another head appeared at the tent opening. A very old woman climbed in and sat down on a stack of furs, her arms around her knees. Her eyes were very bright and grey hair surrounded her small head like an enormous halo. She was smoking a curious pipe with carved animals on it, and around her neck was a gold amulet with a leopard ridden by an owl. The gold animals appeared to be in a fog from the pipe smoke as a sweet aroma rose and filled the tent. She looked at Poma with what appeared to be only a modicum of curiosity. However, her gaze was hypnotic. So was her voice.

"Do not fear, Poma. My name is Tigrax. These are my granddaughters. I saw you by the lake."

Poma was confused.

"Tigrax is our shaman," said Boot-Ru. "No one does anything without her knowing all about it. You rest now."

Later she awoke to the shouts of men and galloping horses. The front of the tent had been opened, and Poma saw that the tent was perched on a wagon. Other wagons, some with six wheels, carried the rounded tents. Huge herds of animals grazed lazily in the distance. One of the men rode up to Boot-Ru's wagon leading a horse with a dead warrior draped unceremoniously across its back. The soldier was lifted off and laid by the wagon.

"Not again!" exclaimed Boot-Ru. She opened a large bin and frowned at the contents. "Let's see, here's the frankincense and anise. What did we do with the parsley seed?"

Madga searched in another of the baskets.

"And hand me the sedge," finished Boot-Ru.

Poma had never seen such an array of herbs and spices. She knew clearly from her experience with the Egyptians that Boot-Ru was gathering everything needed to stuff the warrior's body with, in preparation for his burial.

"Juniper works well, if you have some," Poma said.

Boot-Ru looked up at her. "We're too high here for Juniper," replied Boot-Ru, eyeing her with curiosity.

The air was filled with sudden shrieks as a woman apparently lamented the dead soldier. Then there was silence. Two men appeared, carrying the limp body of a woman. Her body was being prepared for burial as well. Poma frowned to herself. She tried to get up to see what was happening, but found it almost too painful to move. *Better to rest,* she told herself. Boot-Ru, Madga and Tigrax were joined by more women. Poma could hear them talking softly as they went about the work of preparing for the burial.

"So young, this wife—too bad when they go so young; but at least he will have her by his side."

"Did you see the new girl who rode in on the big grey?"

"That's one huge horse!"

"They say her linens are the finest anyone's seen."

"And she's wearing a necklace that's not from here."

"I heard she was of royalty."

More whispering. The only thing Poma heard was—"The imperial purple?"

Different curious female faces appeared at the tent opening.

"She looks like the king's new wife."

"No one has come after her; she must not have a husband."

"Did they catch the bandits?"

"Oh, yes. They are hanging deep in the forest." The warrior and his wife were stuffed, smeared with honey, and sewn up in furs for burial later.

Narmet and Solok

Poma fell into a fitful sleep. That night, she awoke to several bright cook fires. People were gathered for the evening meal. Long shadows played on the happy scene. Flute music floated over the camp from far away. Fires crackled under cook pots while children played. The aroma of beef and spices cooking filled the air. She eased up and sat on the wagon seat to watch.

Boot-Ru noticed her and brought her a silver bowl filled with stew. "Eat this, it will give you strength," she said.

The stew filled her with warmth and comfort. The other women eyed her from their fires. Soon two men of large girth approached the wagon. They looked for all the world like two shaggy mushrooms. The older one of the two stepped forward. His great presence filled an orange-red robe trimmed in elaborate appliqués. Some of the festive flowers in the design were a deep, dark purple. Poma put her bowl down, trying to concentrate on the man's hairy face and not his colorful robe.

He pointed at the horses with a pudgy thumb. "Is that big grey yours?"

"Yes. He saved my life," Poma said

He squinted at her out of his beard and moved a step closer, cocking his head. "Where are you from?" he said.

Poma thought quickly. "My family lived by the sea," she said.

"Mmmm," he said, raising his brows. "It is rumored you may be kin to the king's wife. Is this true?"

"Which wife?" she shot back. She felt beads of sweat breaking out on her forehead.

"The new one. What's her father's name?" This over his shoulder. No one knew. To Poma he said, "Well?"

"Sir, I will leave soon if you can tell me the way to the big sea." Poma said.

"Well, now, don't be so hasty. I heard of your misfortune with the bandits. You will need to rest. The sisters here have room for you, don't you, Boot-Ru?"

"Of course. She has a way with the herbs. There is plenty of room." Boot-Ru refilled Poma's bowl with stew and passed it up to her, smiling. For a brief moment Poma felt as if everyone was being a bit too nice to her.

"Besides, we are headed toward market in the fall. You can find the road to the sea from there." Most of the crowd nodded in agreement.

"And what is your name, sir?" Poma said.

"I am Narmet, Chieftain of this clan. This is my nephew, Solok. We follow Aristagoras, King of all the Sakas. You and your horse will be safe with us." Narmet turned his ample form and bounced away. Solok squared his fat shoulders and followed. Boot-Ru sidled over to Poma as soon as they were out of earshot.

"I would do as he says, Poma. He is a powerful warlord. He didn't kill you for your horse because he was afraid you might be of royalty. He is as interested in your horse as the bandits were. He wants to breed him into our herd, and will offer you protection as long as your horse performs well."

"A most interesting man," Poma said, smiling.

Boot-Ru pulled her shawl around her. "Interesting, yes," she whispered. "but he can be treacherous as well. A powerful man must at least sprinkle truth with trust if he is to keep his power."

Poma continued to smile to herself. If she kept her own council, Estwynd would provide her with survival.

That night there was music and dancing. There were several stringed instruments and the people seemed to be a naturally happy bunch. Tigrax's pipe smoke contributed to the general ambiance. As the stars spread in a purple canopy, Poma rested on her fur bed and slept soundly.

Purple appliquéd flowers floated through her dreams. Boot-Ru gave her a silver bowl filled with purple flowers. Estwynd danced up to her wearing a crown of purple flowers. Boot-Ru rode Estwynd and laughed at her. Narmet had turned into a strange animal. He had the head of a lion and the body that looked like it might be a fat crocodile.

It was just getting light when she awoke. She smiled at herself and all the purple flowers. This was indeed a mystery. She would ask Boot-Ru about the flowers. She felt confused about Boot-Ru riding on Estwynd. On one hand, Boot-Ru had confided in her, but she still didn't know if she should trust her or not. And Narmet was indeed of royal presence, but perhaps not to be entirely trusted, either. Here she was, thrown into this beautiful land and in just two days the people in it had completely complicated her life. *Patience,* she told herself.

The Purple Owlet

The pain in her shoulder kept her close to her bed for a few days. It gave her a chance to get to know her temporary family. Tigrax came visiting almost every day. The old woman was now bedecked in a red shawl. And the smoke from her pipe circled around her head, enlarging her sunburst of grey hair into a hazy nest. Poma was intrigued by this apparition.

"How did you know I came from a lake?" she asked the old woman.

Tigrax's black eyes pierced through the halo of smoke. "I should be asking you what you were doing there," came the reply.

No one had questioned Poma quite so closely. Her mind raced to answer the little woman. "I thought I was going to drown," she said. "I don't remember much about that day, until I woke up by the lake's edge."

Tigrax's eyes narrowed. She puffed another puff on her pipe. "You smelled of the sea," she whispered. "No one else noticed, but it was clearly there. I knew you'd be coming." Her teeth re-clenched around the stem of the pipe.

"I just don't remember, Tigrax. All I can tell you is I was glad to be here until the bandits started shooting at me."

"I don't need answers, Poma. When you dream next, come and we'll talk some more." She winked at Poma and crawled off her perch of furs and climbed down from the wagon.

Poma was at once amused and curious about the wily old seer. She wondered if the shaman knew about her and her true destiny.

Boot-Ru crawled through the opening of the tent with a bowl of soup for Poma. "Is that old lady giving you problems?" She asked.

"Oh, no, she's quite amusing," said Poma. "But she certainly seems to know a lot about me."

"She even dreams your same dreams right along with you. She's a very powerful shaman. Narmet consults her about everything. She's had the sight all her life," said Boot-Ru.

"She's an amazing lady," Poma said. Poma tried to sleep, but she was afraid she'd dream. She decided to consult Tigrax about Narmet having the head of a lion and the body of a crocodile in her dream.

Later, the sisters rummaged through a large basket and drew out a beautiful red wool tunic and baggy pants for Poma. They also had deerskin boots. "I'll never wear these again," Boot-Ru said. Poma was amazed. The tunic had sleeves, and was decorated with appliqués. The clothing just fit her. Her golden skin was set off beautifully by the deep orange-red.

"Oh, Ru, thank you!" she exclaimed.

"You look beautiful, dear."

"I need to consult with Tigrax. Is a gift expected?" Poma asked.

"Yes, she will accept a small gift," Boot-Ru said.

Tigrax's wagon was just next door. Poma dug deep into her basket and found her small stash of flax seed, and decided this would be a fitting gift for the elderly shaman. As her eyes became accustomed to the darkened tent, she beheld an altar which held small carved statues, precious stones, cowry shells, and a small mirror. The aroma of incense burning was overcome by the shaman's pipe smoke. Poma squinted into the darkness.

"Welcome, little bird," Tigrax said.

"Little bird?"

"Purple owlet," Tigrax replied.

Poma was entranced. "Do you have purple owlets here?"

"Have you not been here before?" countered Tigrax.

She has more than one way to know things, thought Poma. "I brought you a gift of flax seed," she said.

"Thank you. Seeds are more than just seeds. They hold promise for the future. Perhaps your dream has seeds, too. Tell me about it."

"I do have a question about Narmet. In my dream he had the head of a lion and the body of a . . . well, something like a big lizard," Poma said carefully.

"And what does that mean to you? Have you done any work on this?"

"I feel like Narmet does have a royal, lion-like appearance, for he is a great warrior," Poma said carefully. "But it's the rest of it I don't understand."

"And you won't unless you tell me the truth," Tigrax said, squinting through her halo of smoke.

Poma hesitated for a moment. She wasn't going to keep much from this lady. Finally she said, "Do you know what a crocodile is?"

"A crocodile means Narmet has a very primitive side—some might say treacherous. The combination of lion and crocodile makes him comfortable in many different atmospheres. This may also be a symbol to our tribe to remind us that our leader is one to be reckoned with. You have also conjured up a means of thinking like the Saka. Our art is born out of dreams such as this. You are a very special young lady." She smiled at Poma.

Poma grinned back at her.

"May I ask if anyone taught you about your dreams?" Tigrax said.

"My grandmother," Poma said. Hamora seemed so far away now.

"Just as a bonus, I'll read the shells for you. Here, hold them for a moment and think of a question dear to your heart."

Poma took the small, even shells and held them near. They felt cool. She threw them down on the small woolen square of cloth Tigrax had spread out between them. The shells were all the same size, and one stuck to her hand.

"That bodes well. You will always have wealth—enough for your needs. The shells are used in some lands as money. We like to think of them as seeds of the Goddess." Tigrax squinted at the shells, her pipe providing its usual complement of smoke. "Mmmm," she said. Her eyebrows rose slowly. "The one you love is very far away. And the one who loves you is as close as a crow's hop."

It was Poma's turn for raised eyebrows. "Close as a crow's hop?" she said. "Who would that be?"

Tigrax settled back, her arms around her knees, smoke going everywhere. "You will know very soon," she said.

Arle

Poma thanked the old seer and hopped down from her wagon. The fresh air felt good on her face. As she sat spinning with her new aunties she thought about what Tigrax had said. She thought it best to keep these things to herself.

Boot-Ru and Madga went searching for herbs every day.

Poma joined them one morning. "What are the wooden spades for?" she asked.

"We found a patch of madder," said Madga. Poma remembered the Pharaoh's stock of madder roots. Now she would see the plants. Some of it had never been picked before, and the roots were almost as big around as a child's wrist.

Boot-Ru explained how she extracted the dye. "I let it soak for a moon or more, and then add the yarn. Then it soaks some more. I never cook it, otherwise it turns brown. I'm going to turn the world red, the color of life!" she exclaimed. There was no need to explain to these folks the value of color.

"I noticed some purple flowers on Narmet's robe," Poma said. "Which plant makes that purple?"

"We have a cousin who lives on a farm," said Boot-Ru. "She does the madder purple for us."

"Madder purple? Madder makes purple?"

"She keeps the recipe a secret," Boot-Ru said.

Poma thought about the royal purple from Canaan and the great sea. "Why a secret?" she said carefully.

"Well, she sells purples at market and does quite well."

Would purple never cease to be a secret? thought Poma.

"When do we go to market?" she asked.

"You mean you've decided to stay with us?" Madga said.

"As long as I can," Poma promised. The nomadic life of these people would get her safely where she wanted to go. She would find the sea again, and the secrets of the purple, and perhaps this cousin could help. And a city with many people—people who might know of Enash. This time the Goddess had put her in a place where the dreams of her life could be realized. She was secretly very excited about all these prospects.

The renewal of her mission was reinforced late in the spring when she rode Estwynd out to a small hill in the midst of the rolling grassland. The sun was up, making pink and gold outlines on the jagged grey clouds. Estwynd walked dutifully up a much-used path which spiraled around the small hill. On the third spiral, she stopped the big grey and surveyed the expanse of green. She jumped down, her heart pounding. She drew her breath in as the sun rammed slender rays into the valley below and rested for a moment on a tree, as if sent by God. Proud and alone, the young tree gloried in that moment as a symbol to Poma that, even if alone, she would nonetheless be favored by heaven as a messenger of the Goddess. As the sun evaporated behind the clouds, Poma etched the image of that tree deep in her heart. She eased back on the stallion and glanced back at the scene she would never forget. That day was near summer, a time of warmth and growth.

It became time to spin the winter wool. Some of the women spun with rocks instead of spindles. Madga showed Poma how to wrap a thin cord around the rock and secure it with a flat twig. When the day's spinning was over and they were ready to move on, the rock was thrown away and a new one found at the new camp. As the summer days wore on, Poma taught the other women the one-needle knitting. Soon all the weaving came to a halt and the women were knitting instead. Many of the women made small needles of wood or bone and then did the needle binding stitches to decorate their winter clothing.

Boot-Ru tried to contain her excitement over this new craft, but she was transparent. "I'll wager we can knit even on horseback," she said. Poma thought it best not to tell her she had tried it already, and found it completely compatible with a leisurely walking horse if there were no particular destination in mind. Boot-Ru even came up with a new stitch which was quickly incorporated into her next blanket.

Occasionally all the women would gather around as the red yarns were dipped into the indigo pot and wonderful violets and purples emerged. But none was quite like the purple in her distaff. And the fact that the recipe for the royal purple was secret made it all the more enticing. Poma thought some of the deeper purples were like the enormous panoramas of sunsets when thunderheads came and went across the vast expanse of the grasslands, and one or two of the tall clouds lingered into the night to capture the last vestiges of the light of the sun.

On one occasion, near sunset, a rainbow appeared, arching across the sky opposite the sunset. Poma was thrilled. She was alone by the trees where she went to gather wood. She sat down to watch the colors. Her breath was taken away, just like the time when she first saw the great mountains. *God must love us all very much,* she thought. Never had the colors been so heavenly, even and clear. It was as if the purple from the sky had been used to create her little blanket and her distaff.

That night Poma felt like dancing. Madga showed her the steps. Soon the children gathered to watch. She caught on quickly and combined this new dance with one she learned from long ago. As she danced, she smiled, knowing she was teaching the folks here much more history than they realized. She writhed to the drums and the fire cracked back at her sharp movements. She thought she heard a flute playing, but she couldn't tell where the music was coming from.

She noticed a tall, auburn-haired man watching her from the shadows. She stopped dancing. The history lesson held more than just history. The assembled crowd of little girls cried, "More, More!" so she bowed, and danced some more restrained steps for the children. Soon they were dancing with her. One of the men played a stringed instrument and plucked out a tune she could sing. She danced until she was breathless. The little girls gathered around, giggling. She laughed with them. They all ended up in an adolescent heap, arms and legs flying.

Later, she and the sisters were preparing for sleep. As they rested on the fur beds, they talked of the men.

"Did you see how Arle looked at you?" said Madga.

"Which one is Arle?" Poma said.

"He's the tall one with the dark red hair. He just lost his wife to a strange illness. He is a good soldier and huntsman. He's almost ready to take another wife."

Poma thought about the burial and the shrieking wife; the men here had better be good soldiers, or the entire clan would disappear.

"I'm not exactly in the market for a husband just now," she said.

"Do you have a man where you are from?" Madga asked.

"Well, you might say that." Poma said.

The sisters looked at one another.

"I mean, I'll keep an open mind." Better to keep them guessing. "Have you ever been married?"

The sisters snickered together. "Well, we were both married when we were younger, and our husbands both disappeared. It happens occasionally; a man just gets tired of the responsibility and off they go," said Boot-Ru. "The clan takes care of us because I know the herbs and Madga is a midwife. And, we are kin to one of the greatest Shamans of the land. But I guess you'd say we haven't stopped looking at men." The three of them laughed softly together.

"When will we be going to market?" asked Poma.

"When the leaves start turning." Madga said. "Ru and I are making felted caps and woven tunics to trade for spices and dyes from the east. We have to make a lot of clothing to trade, because the indigo is so dear."

Poma could well imagine that indigo would have to be purchased; these folks were not in one place long enough to grow any crops. "What about wheat?" she said.

"We get some at market, but we also have cousins in the valleys that have farms. They grow enormous amounts of wheat and also oats for our horses," said Boot-Ru.

So all the people here also have to depend on one another, thought Poma. That night the purple canopy over the steppes turned a dark indigo blue.

The next day, Poma needed to get away and think. She needed to make some more decisions about which way to turn, and if she should stay with these folks. The best way to do this was to take Estwynd for a walk. The big dapple grey was as anxious as she was for some exercise. As she passed by the big cattle herd, Arle saw her go by and started after her. She stopped as he caught up with her.

"You shouldn't go too far alone," he said.

"I'll be alright."

"May I join you?" Arle asked.

Poma wanted to be kind, and said, smiling, "I'd rather be alone." She turned Estwynd's head and started down a little draw. A moment later he followed behind. She turned and waited again for him. "Do you think I need a nursemaid?" she demanded, annoyed.

His face turned red. "Of course not," he said. "Couldn't you call me guard?"

She grinned at him. "What are you guarding, me or my horse?"

"Both," he said

At least he is honest, she thought. Then she had an idea. "If you need to be my guardian, you'll have to catch me first," she said. She guided Estwynd away and down the green steppe, skirting a forest of walnut trees. He took out after her. She glanced back. He seemed to be enjoying the chase. Poma felt free as the wind again as Estwynd stretched out and raced along. She felt a little sorry for Arle, whose little mare could not keep up. She pulled up near a little creek and waited for him.

"Whoa—ho! They told me your horse was fast, but I didn't know he knew how to fly!"

Poma grinned at him. "Alright, you may join me, but remember, I can beat you home every time," she said, laughing. She saw the admiring look on his face. This time he was not admiring Estwynd.

"How does anyone so beautiful know how to ride so well?"

Poma felt herself blushing. "Estwynd makes me look good," she said. They rode slowly down the stream.

"I saw you herding sheep yesterday," she said.

His face lit up. "We have to keep them away from the feather grass when it sheds, or it gets deep into the wool and is dangerous for the animals. I'll be glad when we get back to our winter pastures."

"How far away are they?"

"Not far. We go to market first, and then head north, but we keep to the valleys. The sheep do better without so much heat. The wool is better."

"Why are you concerned with the wool?"

"Right now we have plenty here—plenty of everything—fox, ermine, even snow leopard. But some day we may not be so lucky. We will have to depend on better and better wool. The day will come."

He seemed so serious. Poma had not thought of running out of fur. But she assumed it was possible, maybe some day. And it would be nice if wool were softer.

"It's an honorable thing—thinking of the future. Have you ever thought of being a farmer?"

"Yes, but not right away. I love the mountains too much." He looked embarrassed about his plans and dreams. Poma liked this man. At least he thought about things other than making war on his neighbors.

As they rode back toward the camp, their talk turned again to the horses. "Do you always ride the black mare?" she asked.

"Old crow and I are on good terms," he replied.

Old crow? Poma smiled to herself. So far, Tigrax was operating at one hundred percent.

Out of the clear sky came the sound of thunder. "The herds!" he exclaimed. Poma wasn't sure what he meant, but his face was white with fear. They raced back toward the camp. The scent of smoke drifted up to them. It was not campfire smoke. They could hear the women shrieking. Poma realized the terror at last. As they rounded a small hill, the scene was devastation. Fully half their herd of horses was missing. The cattle were gone. Small dark horsemen dressed in black were riding through the camp with torches. Two of the wagons were on fire. Arle drew his bow around and tried to shoot as he rode. Poma raced to the wagons to find Boot-Ru and Madga. Their wagon was intact, and the women were shooting from the open tent door. She raced up and leapt through the back opening to help. Boot-Ru was shooting steadily. Madga's face was ashen. Hope returned when about ten of their clansmen came back from a hunting trip. The eerie war cry rang over the hills: "Saakaaaaaa!" as they rode in at top speed. Narmet led the charge on his small bay with Solok close behind. Arrows rained down on the marauders, killing three or four. The rest took off over a rise, the hunting party in close pursuit.

The women looked around for only a moment, and then jumped down from the wagon. Madga went hunting for Tigrax. "Go and help the others put out the fires," she called. Poma and Boot-Ru ran toward the burning wagons. Old Crow appeared and made a slow descent into the camp. Arle clutched his arm.

Poma ran over and helped him off his horse. "Where are you hurt?" she asked. His face was still white, this time from pain.

"I got stabbed, here in my side," he said.

She helped him into the wagon where she found some wool to bind his wound. "I'll be right back," she said.

He grabbed her hand. "Thanks, Poma."

"You rest." When Poma looked out the front of the wagon, the fires were gone. Thick, black smoke still rose from the felt portions of the collapsed wagon-tents. She stepped down out of the wagon to get water to wash his wounds with. Some of the women were standing, helpless and in shock. Others were gathering families together and rounding up the children. The animals left near the camp were milling anxiously about. When the men rode back, there were extra horses with horse trappings just a little different than theirs. They had killed or scattered all the invaders.

Sudden cheering pierced the air. Madga and Tigrax emerged from the grandmother's wagon. Tigrax was almost screeching in triumph. She had survived another skirmish.

"Aieeee!" she cried. "That will teach them!" Only her age kept her from jumping up and down.

Narmet strode toward her, Solok a shadow behind him. "How many dead?" he snarled.

The women looked around. "I think we're all here," Madga said. Everyone looked around. No one seemed to be missing.

Solok was excited and anxious. His beady eyes darted around. "Let's go find the rest of them. They all need to hang!" he whined.

Narmet wheeled around, almost stepping on his erstwhile nephew. "Not now. We must stay here to guard the clan in case they come back."

Solok managed to pout behind his beard.

"I hope the hunt was good. We must have a feast to celebrate," Tigrax said. When the herds were reestablished, it was, indeed, time for healing and celebration. Only a few minor injuries were certainly reason for feasting and dancing. This they did for the next few days as new wagons were erected. Most of the cattle and horses were rounded up. Arle was closely watched by Poma, supervised by Boot-Ru. Arle and Poma became almost constant companions. They rode together to help the others round up stray cows and oxen. Poma was not a little awed by this gentle man who was both warrior and herdsman, a man of honor and one who loved the land as she did.

Market

As the weeks went by, the clan prepared to head south toward the city of Marakanda, on the banks of a narrow River. Poma helped the aunties pack for the trip. Boot-Ru was packing herbs into a basket. "Here, Poma, put this under the wagon seat," said Boot-Ru. "And leave room for the goatskins." Madga was folding blankets. The fires were extinguished and cooking pots hung in their accustomed places on the sides of the wagon. Poma watched the scene for a moment. The smaller children ran and played while the older ones herded the sheep together for the trip. Men on horses whooped at the cattle. The big move was underway. Soon the wagons were lined up and all the children were gathered in. Narmet's wives and family were in the lead wagons, which were richly adorned with the most colorful felt tents. The women of his family were proud of their status, as it was announced to any who saw the handiwork to be a token of the wealth of their chieftain. Tigrax followed next, with a compliment of men on horseback to guard her rumored stash of gold. Boot-Ru urged the big oxen into line with the others.

The herds moved southward at a slow pace. The oxen had one speed, hauling the large wagons. The clan stopped after weeks of traversing the huge steppes. Some of the days were spent preparing hides for trade with the Greeks.

The sunny mornings were now spiced with cool breezes that flicked their way through the vivid fall leaves. The sight of yellow aspen brought out busy spindles, and the summer wool became the work of the new season in a flourish of twirling movement which mirrored the dance of the small yellow leaves. Poma was excited as the women talked of the city and its people, and the things they would see and do. They camped near a large lake where many other tribes had already gathered. The night before they were to ride into the city, Poma could hardly sleep. Her basket was filled with felted children's caps, and she was proud of the beautiful array of colors she had captured in the wool: reds, blues, soft yellows and moss greens. Boot-Ru said they would do well at the bazaar. When Poma finally slept, she had an extremely vivid dream about Estwynd.

She was riding him down a narrow road, south toward the city. Enash was standing at a crossroad. He was pointing eastward. Estwynd suddenly reared up, and Poma found herself flying off the horse and far up into the sky. Estwynd galloped away toward the east. Out of a fog emerged a ghost horse, his mirror image, running in a westerly direction.

She woke up slowly, the sensation of flying still clinging to her. To fly like a bird must be wonderful, she thought to herself. Why was Enash pointing to the east? Had he gone that way? What was the meaning of the other, west-bound Estwynd? She would ponder these questions later. It was time for market.

The sun hit the felt tents and the dew turned to steam as the clan roused itself for the day. Soon the wagons that would go down the river valley to the city were piled high with cow hides and furs, and such bright metal treasures as they would hold.

Boot-Ru, Madga and Poma rode horseback behind one of the other wagons, their trade goods entrenched with another family. The procession made its way single file over the road which had emerged out of the grass the day before. Suddenly, over a rise, they could see the city's mud walls rising up out of the hillside next to the river. Another road, east-west, as in her dream, lay just before them. As Estwynd approached the road, his ears flickered for an instant, and he hesitated momentarily. Poma gingerly urged him on through the crossroads, and as they reached the center, an unexpected wind rippled Estwynd's mane and blew Poma's robe into an instant billow. She managed to guide the skittish horse back into line, and then glanced back over her shoulder. The wind scurried through the tall grass up a small rise and there, for an instant, was the other horse from her dream. He had a silver mane and tail, just like Estwynd. He reared up and then disappeared in a westward direction over the small hill, leaving Poma shivering and stunned.

Boot-Ru rode up behind her. "What's the matter, Poma? What's wrong with Estwynd? Was there a snake?"

Poma's mouth came closed with a spiral of determination. She smiled at Boot-Ru. "No, no snake," she replied. "Just a bird or something." Their attention turned toward the road ahead where the wagons were pulling up into a large space with other wagons and tents by the side of the road.

They followed the wagon of their clansmen to a spot beside a small stream. Here they rested the horses.

"What frightened your horse, Poma?" inquired Madga.

Regardless of Tigrax's words, Poma wanted desperately to find Enash. She believed in order to do this it was best to fit in and not cause her new aunts any trouble.

"Oh, it was nothing, Madi," she said casually. "Just a bird, frightened up out of the grass." This seemed to satisfy them. Poma knew she must not give them any reason to leave her behind, especially now, when she could look for her priest.

Men from other tribes gathered around Estwynd, gazing at him with admiration. Narmet had guards posted in the encampment, and Estwynd garnered three of the best guards all by himself. Poma knew he would be safe.

Marakanda was bustling with people, animals and the trade which brought them all to this crossroads. Poma stared, wide-eyed, at the scene. Outside the gates of the city the animals were pastured by the river along with tents and wagons that had come from far away. Row upon row of booths had sprung up along the city wall, where all manner of goods were being sold and bartered. The air of excitement included aromas of strange spices and foods. Arle was busy with fleeces, so Poma joined Boot-Ru and Madga, and they wandered through the maze of stalls and saw soft fabrics made from cotton, wool carpets, and copper lamps, with strange oils such as castoreum. There were tents, stirrups, bridle-heads and straps. These trappings were highly decorated with silver and gold. Poma thought Estwynd would look very handsome wearing them. Asafetida, linseed, and huge bins of spices and dyes completed the scene. The variety of goods was almost overwhelming. When Poma saw the silk, she stopped in her tracks. She walked over to the silk merchant's stall to feel of the precious stuff. Her face screwed up into a fierce desire. She vowed to sell all of her felt caps and come back for some silk.

Toward the end of the rows of stalls was a large gathering of people. The women stopped momentarily to see what was of interest. A squat little man spoke. They pressed closer. He was speaking to a man who sat at his feet. Some small white stones were laid out before them. Everyone was listening intently to the oracle.

"Change and liberation indicate a great and pressing need within your being to be free from the strangulation of identifying with the reality of things . . . material possessions. You should be free to understand your symbols."

Madi and Ru exchanged glances. Poma stared, her brow furrowed. The little man's voice resonated through the crowd.

"If you have plans for your life," he continued, "they will be ripped away from you, as a tear in your tent. Your beliefs will be bare for you to examine anew. Do not look to blame others. This will come from within."

Madi's head moved slowly toward Ru. "What did he say?" she whispered. The question hung in the air as he spoke again.

"Everything in your life will be challenged, and you cannot fall back on your previous inner guides."

Ru shrugged. "Let's go," she whispered. The aunts moved toward the back of the crowd. Poma stood rooted as the little oracle smiled at the man at his feet. She joined the other women. She didn't want to get lost in all this crowd of people.

"He's interesting," she said.

"Really?" replied Ru. "He may sound important, but I can't use what he says. Now, if someone were to talk of the things I do every day, I might listen."

"You think *he's* interesting," said Madga. "You should have seen the oracle that was here last year. Remember him, Ru?"

"Oh, yes, I remember. He was so tall and handsome. He kept talking about the Gods being part of us—some such nonsense."

Poma's heart stopped. She trembled uncontrollably. Did they notice? She steadied her voice. "What was his name?" she asked.

Boot-Ru fingered some rugs. "I don't remember. Do you remember, Madi?" Madga shook her head, eyebrows raised.

"Why?" said Ru.

Poma collected herself somewhat. "It's not important. I just thought I may have heard him speak somewhere else a long time ago." She tried to sound nonchalant.

"Well, he was very tall, wavy brown hair, brown eyes, and a curious curling scar over his eye."

Poma felt the blood draining out of her face. She turned away, pretending interest in a nearby stack of copper pots. "Oh? Well, that fits," she said. "Did you see him here?"

"Oh, yes, every year there are several. It seems like it's a growing thing—so many different religions and ideas—this is the place to hear it all."

"Do you know where he went?"

"Well, he said he was headed to the north."

Poma's heart sank. To the north? She had her heart set on going west, to the sea and her beloved purple. Now what? The confusion brought tears to her eyes. She found herself standing again in front of the silk merchant's stall. Madga and Boot-Ru tasted honey in a nearby food stall.

Poma remembered Enash's silken voice. Only she was standing here feeling the silk instead of hearing it. She took a deep breath. *Alright, north it is,* she thought. *I'll stay with Madi and Ru.* But why would Enash go north? Perhaps he was with another clan of the Sakas. This thought filled her with hope. Her mind calmed a bit by the feel of the silk. As she rubbed the tears away she spied a beautiful scarf the color of willow branches in early spring. She remembered as a child seeing the willows by the river looming like grey and green ghosts in the fog. The scarf would look so pretty on her. It would go with her green eyes.

That night she couldn't sleep for all the want in her soul. She kept seeing herself dancing in green. And she thought about Enash and she could almost hear his voice: *"I will be your friend . . ."* She finally fell into a deep sleep.

The next morning she sat with Madga and Boot-Ru in a small stall to sell the clothing they had made. The Sakas had much to trade. There were many beautiful furs, sables and ermines, and the fur of the steppe foxes. They had amber and gold from the far mountains, swords, armor, horse trappings, and beautifully worked gold, silver and bronze pieces. They cautiously eyed the things they needed: indigo and spices from the east, silks and wheat. The soft white "wool" from the cotton plant was said by the Scythians to be made from small lambs which the plant produced. From the west came glass, colorful and expensive.

Poma loved to watch their customers examine her little felt caps. But they weren't selling. She watched the other booths next to them and saw how the bartering went. Later in the afternoon she began to put together a plan. She snatched up her basket of caps and headed straight for the silk merchant, her mouth set with determination.

"I will trade four of these caps for this scarf," she said, pushing the basket closer to the dark little silk merchant.

"Well, now, let's see what you have there." He fingered through the caps. She watched his dark eyes darting from color to color. "Mmm . . . How about six caps?" he said. She pretended to ponder this offer for a moment. "Four," she said. "The blue ones cost a little more to make."

The merchant's face remained immobile. "The silk comes from very far away," he grumbled finally.

Poma held up the green scarf, scrutinizing both sides very closely. "Alright—five caps, but that's as far as I can go."

"Sold!" he said. As they exchanged caps for scarf, Poma thought perhaps it had been too easy. But she had her silk. She smiled at the man who folded up the small green scarf for her and put it carefully in her basket. She immediately went to find Tigrax in search of a mirror. The old shaman was nowhere to be seen. So she climbed up into her wagon and found the mirror on the altar. As she put the green scarf over her dark curls she thought of the other valuable thing she had from this trip. "Everything in your life will be challenged," she whispered to herself, smiling at the reflection. So far, she had prevailed, and now she had a silk scarf at her command.

"What else do you see in there?" Tigrax appeared at the tent opening.

"Oh, I hope you don't mind . . . I had to see what my new scarf really looked like," said Poma. "What do you mean, 'what else?'"

"The mirror is a sacred tool, little bird."

Poma stared into the mirror at a questioning face. "How is it used?" she asked.

"The person who knows how to use the mirror must get beyond its earthly form," Tigrax replied. The questioning face in the mirror turned to a frown. "But not now, little owlet. One day soon I will show you. We need a quiet winter's day. Go ahead and admire your beautiful silk."

Poma's happiness was only marred by the fact that Enash was not at her side. It was so sad to know that she had come so close to finding him. She decided to get some paper from the silk merchant and write Enash a poem. She could express her love and then save it in her basket until she found him. He would be proud of her for practicing all the things he had taught her so long ago. How long had it been? That night, with a piece of charcoal, she scratched her poem:

A Poem for Enash

I say goodbye, yet love me.
You have me not, yet hold me,
Keep me always near.
The summer winds will not blow
Tall green grasses for us, I fear.
The ripe green leaves that swell
Are cold without you here.
Our memories are scattered
As leaves upon the wind.
Has the tree now borne us all?
I am full to over-flow.
Can your heart, as mine, be tall
With wine-tears never to be tasted
As are the golden wines of fall?
'Til again green grasses blow
And small green leaves echo back
Our love to us again,
My heart is an ache of fall.

Hope for me will keep the pain
When grasses stir,
Having winter long in silence lain.
I say goodbye, yet love me,
You have me not, yet hold me,
Keep me always near.
As summer to autumn passes
And brings another year,
Will part of me be there,
As part of you is here?

Poma rolled the little poem around a small tree branch like the temple scrolls and tucked it in her basket. She cried a little then, and slept.

Market was not only a feast for the eyes and the soul, but for the stomach as well. Bins of spices conjured up childhood memories for everyone, although the remembered meals were different. Marakanda was one of the most famous cities along the road running east and west. Many strange spices and dyestuffs passed through the ancient town. The smell of Rakhabin cheese filled the air and stirred hunger in the fresh mornings. Boot-Ru and Poma found honey, hazelnuts, and sesame. Boot-Ru started stocking up.

"What will you make with all this?" Poma said.

Boot-Ru's eyes widened. "Ooooo, cakes and sweets for the children," she replied.

"Oh, yes—the children!" And they giggled together.

Poma was amazed at the price of indigo. In Egypt the peasants grew woad for the treasured color, but the silk merchants told her about a different plant that also produced the beautiful midnight blues, and took far less of the plant in the process.

"Where does the silk come from?" she asked one.

"From a land many months away," he replied.

"No, I mean, is it a plant?"

"They keep it a secret," he said. "I have heard they kill those who tell," he whispered.

Poma was astounded. Then she was sad. "Knowledge like this should be shared," she mourned.

"Well, little lady, the great China makes a lot of money. If everyone knew the secret of silk, then the price would come down. Their government would fall apart. Everyone there would go hungry. Some say there would be war." His eyes were squinting, and he sat back and folded his hands.

Poma thought the dark little man was almost proud of this fact. From his rich clothing, she figured maybe he was part of the problem. She vowed to go and see this China place with her own eyes one day. Such beautiful fabric and wonderful art—even their paper was very fine and precious—and now a better way to make blue. She heard among the food stalls there was even a religion spreading here from this China.

Poma and Boot-Ru were standing at a stall full of jewelry. The Saka's pieces were at least as good if not better, and they were skeptical of the prices. Next to the jewelry was a large collection of knives and swords. Poma noticed two very tall blonde women just as interested in the hunting and killing paraphernalia as she and Boot-Ru were in the jewelry.

"Ru, where are those women from?" Poma whispered.

Boot-Ru glanced over. "From the west. I'll tell you about them later." The two blonde women wandered to where there was a large group of men in a heated discussion over some goats. Poma watched as they slowed and stared at the men in a very un-lady-like way.

Poma and Boot-Ru rested on a pile of Saka skins. "Those are part of the women who came from the sea in the north to steal our husbands. They are mostly blonde and very war-like. I can tell you, if I had a husband, they wouldn't be messing around with my man."

"That's outlandish. Didn't the men do something about it?" asked Poma.

"Why would they? More wives mean more wealth, more children. They welcomed them. But the Scythian women weren't happy at all. And these women are warriors. What could our women do? They'd better not set their caps for any of our men. They'd have a fight on their hands, alright." Boot-Ru's mouth was fixed in a determined grimace. Poma suspected this fiery red-head could be a handful when she wanted to.

Boot-Ru and Poma came across a wonderful collection of new cooking pots made of iron. They were very heavy.

Ru scoffed at them. "Way too much weight," she said. "My oxen would give up and sit down right in the traces," she went on. "Who would have such a thing, anyhow? The copper and brass ones work just as well, and aren't nearly as heavy," she sneered.

The pot-seller looked down his long nose at her. "But the iron ones will last a lifetime," he said.

As they wandered through the market, a new scent accosted them. Poma made a face. "Ugh! What's that?"

Boot-Ru mirrored her expression. "Camels," she replied with disgust.

A long line of camels had arrived out of the desert, bearing large loads of goods for the market, and weary travelers. The sharp smell of camel dung arrived with them. Then the horse trading began. Done with the desert, some of the camels were traded for horses for the journey west. The camels would go back into the desert with new owners.

And so the days went, trading, haggling and wondrous sights. There were crowds of people. Other Sakas came in from their summer pastures. There was much laughter around the huge campfires as old friends and relatives met. Mongols came in from the northeast bringing bins of wheat, hides and gold. They were dressed in bright reds and deep blue-black robes. Poma thought back to the day she had first come to this place, and shivered just slightly. There were Greeks and Persians, folks from India dressed in indigo almost as dark as their skin, and light-haired Celts from the northwest. Their yellow and white plaids caught the eye. There were Sudanese bringing perfumes and spices. Poma wondered to herself how many years had passed since she last saw a Sudanese, when they came through the Pharaoh's court at least twice a year. They were selling the same kinds of spices here, and she mused about the fact that some things never change.

Children from all over the known world played together between the stalls and underfoot. Mystics from east and west debated in the town square. The air was filled with strange aromas—spices and perfumes held together with the constant smell of too many animals in small spaces. The autumn nights grew cool and as the colors deepened in the trees from green to yellow, gold, orange and deep red, people gathered around fires that matched those colors at night to feast and dance, drink and boast, gossip and tell stories.

One night the stories turned to the great battles of the south. Ban, a grizzled old warrior with few teeth and one eye, was telling once again the story of how the Sakas had led their enemy into the great desert and left them there to die.

"We had better horses." His one eye reflected the firelight. "They had many men and all of them were armed with mighty swords." The children scooted closer together to listen.

"We never slept or ate for two days. We only rode. We had enough extra horses, and this was the first secret to our victory. The Persians had come a long way from home, and we knew where to ride and where the water was."

The old man paused for effect, and hunkered down to reveal the final secret of their great victory. His audience was totally charmed. It waited in anticipation. The story was an old one, but it got better every time it was told.

His one eye never blinked. "They chased us clear over to the great— Taklimakan!" The sentence ended in a reverent whisper. The children waited.

"The foolish army rode right after us. Then we disappeared into the Tien Shan and left them to die in the sands." A tremble went through his audience.

"A few weeks later we went back for the prize—all the armor, spears and swords became ours. Now we knew our enemy better than they had known themselves. None of them lived to tell the tale. Even their skeletons were soon covered with sand. Ahh, but the word spread. Everyone feared the great Saka!" The audience gave the battle cry, "Saakaaaa!" and cheered.

Arle was across the fire from Poma. She could see the wry smile on his face. Perhaps it was just a campfire story, perhaps not. Who could ever know?

Confederation

When the tribes were done with trading, bartering, gossip and drink, it became time to go back to the herds and set out for winter pastures.

One of the families whose wagon had been destroyed by the fire in the last attack decided to stay and try a season or two at farming. Poma and Arle visited with them shortly before the clan moved north. Arle was in an animated discussion with the husband about the price of wheat. Poma watched while the wife stirred their supper.

"I guess we'll be alright," the wife said. Her face looked tired. "We lost everything in the fire, except for the livestock. He managed to trade one of the oxen for a plow and some seeds. We're going to help his brother with his wheat until we know the land will support us."

"I'm glad you have family to help you. It would be very hard doing it alone," Poma said.

The wife gave her a wan smile. "It will seem strange, not seeing the big valley again. But we're not young any more. And the boys will maybe get a chance to go to school." Her eyes brightened.

Poma knew well the importance of school. "They'll have good opportunities," she said. Later, Arle and Poma sat and talked about the couple.

"He's tired of always being on the move," he said. "But I can't understand being so poor, let alone giving up the mountains."

"Their boys can go to school," Poma said.

"School can't teach you how to tame a horse or breed sheep for the best wool. It can't teach you about the weather or how to protect your family. School's just a waste of time." Arle's face was serious, his blue eyes darkening with the argument.

Poma had to disagree. "School helps you do all of those things better," she countered.

"Those boys will be needed on the farm." Arle spoke the truth on this point. "At any rate, we must remember when we come back next year, to buy our wheat from these folks, to help them along."

Practical and compassionate, thought Poma.

Tired and happy, the clan headed back toward the herd. When they were all back together, Narmet called a meeting.

"I have news of great importance. It is rumored that these marauders from the east are banding together to make more raids on our herds. For this reason, I have made a new pact with some of the western tribes, and in the spring we may be at war. We need to unify ourselves and stay strong. As we grow, we will prosper, for the caravans cross our lands. We will be charging a tax on travelers through the southern east-west road, and this will soon make us wealthy." His eyes sparkled through his bushy brows.

Solok and his young friends seemed happy with this news. He folded his arms in approval.

Tigrax stepped closer to the bushy little chief. "Why was I not consulted about this tax business?" she demanded.

Narmet fidgeted. "Because they've been doing it for years, and now that we are part of this new confederation, we will profit not only from their protection, but from the outsider's gold as well."

"Nothing good will come from a road tax," she muttered.

Narmet flinched slightly. "My first responsibility is to protect my people, Tigrax. And that's the way I choose to do so." He pulled himself up to his greatest height, which was only a little more than his width, and with finality, bounced off toward his wagons. Solok sneered at Tigrax and as usual, followed close behind his uncle.

Tigrax mumbled to herself, then settled down, face immobile, to glare at the fire, her button eyes shining.

Poma and Boot-Ru went to sit beside her. Arle was in quiet conversation with the other men. They all seemed to agree with their chieftain.

"People should be free to move about," Tigrax said finally. "We shouldn't be taxing something that's free to begin with."

Poma could see both sides of the argument, but tended to favor what Tigrax was saying. Travel cost money, and this might force people to find a different road. But she felt she shouldn't interfere. "The merchants from the east will simply charge more for their silks and spices," she said.

Tigrax wagged her head. "Still, it doesn't seem right," she maintained.

Poma thought about her travels and she now felt lucky to be with a people who had as much freedom as they did. Their life was restricted by the herds, but their love of the land and the animals in it prevailed in their lives. They simply were fighting fire with fire.

The Women

The approaching winter now took precedence in the thinking of the nomads because survival depended on finding just the right pastures for their herds. Luckily with the fall rains came plenty of green grass low enough so they could stay warm for the duration of the long winter on the steppe. Most would stay in their wagons, but a few made temporary yurts to house the large families.

Everyone had something to do to pass the time. Madga used leftover wool to make small felt bandages. Boot-Ru and Poma gathered a large harvest of wild herbs to dry for medicine and the dyeing of yarns and felts. Every once in a while the women got up early to braid each other's hair.

"Ru, it's too bad you have no little girls to share this beautiful red hair," Poma said.

Boot-Ru just hummed to herself, her face in the sun. She smiled. "I'll just remain one of a kind," she said.

Poma remembered when Hamora had taught her to braid. "I'll make you into the queen you are." She proceeded to form the braids into a crown.

Tigrax was poking at breakfast in a pot. "She's always been a queen," she said. "But not like the Queen Tomyris."

Boot-Ru rolled her eyes. Poma took this to mean that the story which was surely to ensue had been heard many, many times. As Boot-Ru braided Poma's hair, they all settled in to listen.

"Tomyris was Queen when her husband died, and the Persians wanted our land. She kindly gave them enough room for trading in peace, but the Persian king was greedy."

Poma remembered listening to stories in school. Where was this one going?

"He took Tomyris's son into captivity, and then let him go. The young man was so embarrassed at having been caught, that he killed himself."

Poma frowned. That wasn't enough reason to kill oneself. Perhaps he had problems with his mother.

Tigrax waved her spoon in the air. "The Queen was so angry at the Persian King, there was a huge battle. She had the King's head brought to her and she dunked it in a big skin filled with blood, and proclaimed that if he was so bloodthirsty, now he could drink all the blood he wanted. And no one ever bothered her again," finished Tigrax, folding her arms.

It was all Poma could do to keep from speaking her mind. "Well, that was a long time ago," she managed.

"My grandmother was there," Tigrax said with a triumphant grin. "She was just a child, but she told me all about it."

How can we have peace, if the women set such examples? Poma thought. And what was she to do to make some kind of difference here, in this place? She got to wondering anew about Queens and Goddesses and her path as a woman through all this maze of religion and politics.

The Proposal

That day they made felt patches to repair the tents. They laid out layers of wool on the ground. This was wetted down and whey was added to facilitate the binding of the fibers. When it came time for stomping the large sheets of wool, the women all took off their deerskin boots and started trampling it with bare feet. To Poma's delight, it soon became a dance. It was a lively thing with a song to go with it. The children gathered to take turns "helping." Before long the large felt pieces were done, and everyone was laughing and out of breath. It didn't seem like work at all.

Some of the men lounged around the fire, smoking and laughing at the comical scene the women made. Arle sat with them, grinning and whittling.

Poma saw him tuck something in his saddlebag as he ambled over to her.

"Let's go for a ride," he said. "Some of the sheep strayed last night, and we need to bring them home." His blue eyes sparkled.

"I'd love to help," she said.

The day was a shining one. One more rain and fall would be done. Tigrax had said only the day before that she smelled snow in the air. Poma laughed at her, but the old woman had been serious.

"I'll get the horses," said Arle. The herds were situated now at a point far to the north and east of Marakanda. The steppe meadows displayed forests of plum and apple trees, honeysuckle vines and sweetbriar rose thickets. Many of the trees were almost bare now, and the day welcomed a late fall sun. They rode through the meadows and up the steppe and into a stand of maple trees, almost devoid of their red leaves.

"Let's stop here. I can gather some lichens from that rock," Poma said.

They dismounted, and Poma started collecting the lichens. Soon they sat on the rock to enjoy the warmth of the golden day.

"What color will you get from the lichen?" he said.

"Well, there are several different kinds. I'll probably get some yellows or golds and maybe even orange, and if my guess is right, this one will give me purple." She gazed at the ugly green lichen with admiration and a certain amount of excitement.

"I love the green of your eyes," he said. "It almost matches some of the lichens."

She looked at him with surprise. "Arle . . ."

He put his finger over her lips. "Sh," he said. "I have something for you." He got up, reached in his saddlebag, and pulled out a beautifully carved comb, and held it out to her. The handle of the comb was a series of owls. "Poma, you will marry me, won't you?"

Her green eyes filled with tears. "Oh, Arle . . ."

He bent down and kissed her. She felt herself melting into his arms. She couldn't help herself. There was a twinge of guilt as she succumbed to the warmth. *Why is this happening to me? And with this gentle, caring person . . .* "Arle . . . I want you to know . . ." He kissed her again, and this time displayed the passion that was inherent in the art of these people: raw, animalistic, yet sensitive. And for her there was the longing for a place to be, the constant search for a home and just simply someone to share with.

They made love that day in the shadow of the rock on the edge of a high mountain meadow. She would always remember the smell of the campfire smoke in his hair. As the afternoon grew chill, they rode slowly back down the mountain toward the camp. Arle did not press for an answer to his proposal. He seemed to understand she needed time to get used to the idea. He spoke softly to her of the weather and the dye plants they found on the way home.

"Ru will love the gold we'll get from the Ephedra," she said,

He smiled at her. "Your love of the dyes gives you an art to live by, and it's one of the reasons I love you so," he said. "And the steppe is rich with color. I can help you explore it all."

Her secret smile was bittersweet. How could she ever explain to him who she really was and how short a time they would have together? Where could she turn for help? They rode into camp in time for dinner. Boot-Ru eyed them with curiosity. Tigrax only puffed and grinned a big grin at Poma. That night an owl kept her awake until almost dawn.

The next evening Poma sat and stared into a pot full of Ephedra. A little Ephedra made a medicinal tea. A lot of it made a nice golden yellow. The yarn had turned a tawny gold and was cooling beside the fire. She felt as if she were willing the pot to cool. Why did her life have to be so complicated? Is it possible to love two men at the same time? Would she ever see Enash again? Why couldn't she just let herself love Arle without wondering about Enash? She sighed and stirred the yarn expectantly. The pot was still hot. Arle said he loved her. He was ready to make her a home in his wagon. Enash had only said he would be her friend, and was God knew where. But he had left her with his amulet. Arle had carved her the beautiful comb. What if she had children, and then had to go off and leave them? What to do? She stared at the pot as if it had answers hidden deep within.

Boot-Ru sat down beside her. "Won't that pot cool off without you?" she asked.

Poma felt tears well up. "Oh, Ru . . . hoo hoo hoo!"

"Oh, honey, what's the matter?" Boot-Ru hugged Poma and patted her shoulder.

"Oh, Ru, I'm in . . . . in . . . . in love, hoo hoo hoo!" Poma couldn't stop crying.

"Gracious, is that all?"

This only brought more tears. Poma couldn't explain about any of this. This was something she'd have to solve by herself. But it was nice to have a comfortable bosom to cry into. She took a big breath. "I guess I just don't know if Arle is the right one for me," she said.

"Who else is there?" Boot-Ru stirred the coals, launching a small yellow flame. Poma stopped crying. "I guess you're right, Ru." She was tired, and a little relieved that someone in her life was being practical.

"Arle is a wonderful man. Don't pass up the opportunity," Boot-Ru said. Something shifted in Poma's mind. Boot-Ru was right again. She was a true offspring of Tigrax when it came to earthly matters. Poma decided firmly that things spiritual in her life were best left to the God and Goddess for the time being. She felt a certain peace with this decision, but decided at the same time to sleep before talking with Arle. But this was not to be. Arle appeared out of the shadows and sat down with the women.

"Good evening, Arle," Boot-Ru said.

"Good evening, Ru," he replied.

Their mock civility was not lost on Poma. She could only smile at him, for the tears were welling up once more. This time they were tears of relief and joy. Now, instead of a bosom to cry into, there were big arms to hold her and gentle hands to stroke her hair.

The Wedding Trip

The wedding day was grey. One or two red leaves clung to otherwise empty branches. The morning harbored warm air which turned later on a cool wind. The fires were built high for the celebration. Boot-Ru and Madga made sure that Poma experienced the excitement of brides through time. They spent days making her a beautiful dress which announced with appliqués and beads the festive importance of the day. Wool, dyed red and then purple, was woven into fabric. The ermine trim was dyed in indigo. Many of the other women took up needles to help decorate the outfit. Her headdress was a tall, pointed hat of felt which erupted in a silk cascade of bridal veil. Tigrax insisted that owl feathers should complete the look.

The couple endured words of wisdom from Tigrax, who, accompanied by the red wool shawl and usual haze of smoke, spoke of life's journeys and destinies.

"And wherever life takes you, if you rely on one another and teach your children the same, your marriage will be a happy one." Her final words: "Be kind to one another."

Then it was Narmet's turn to bless the couple. He spoke of his ancestry and the noble folks who had gone before, and urged the celebration of marriage to be one of happiness and laughter, so as to pay homage to the ancestors of the clan.

"It is strong families that make the clan strong. So live long, be happy, and I bless you with many strong sons!" He raised his gold scepter, which was the signal for the feasting and dancing to begin.

Poma was indeed grateful for this family who had taken her in as a stranger. The warmth of her new husband completed her wedding day and the celebration wore on into the night. She came with a basket, a girl from none knew where, possessing only a few trinkets, and a great grey horse. She had a good knowledge of the herbs and household arts, but her greatest possession was two pronged: an artistic passion and love of life, and an almost epoch wisdom for someone seemingly so young.

She danced with Arle far into the night, and when it seemed appropriate, they made their way to his wagon. Their wedding gifts included the prize furs of the clan and their tent was cozy and warm. They laughed together and fell asleep in each other's arms.

Arle woke her up the next morning. "It has gotten colder. If we are to make it over the mountain, we should leave soon," he said.

Poma looked forward to their wedding trip. Arle wanted to visit his cousin in the Pazyryk Valley and barter hides for a prize ram which was the talk of the local shepherds. It would strengthen their flock and improve the wool. She was always anxious to travel. Her soul was fed by changing scenery and new places to explore.

"Are you awake?" he asked.

"I am now," she grumbled. The best reason for an early rising was travel, so she couldn't grumble much.

He seemed wise enough to let her greet the day in some semblance of silence. "I'll get the horses," he said. He kissed her brow.

The morning was cold and breezy. No one else stirred, nor would they, for all the fermented mare's milk consumed the day before. The pack horse was ready with hides and gifts for relatives, and so they started out, Old Crow, the pack animal, and Estwynd bringing up the rear. Poma enjoyed the warmth of a new fur-lined cape and breakfasted on cold bread and dried meat. The changing landscape soothed away the shock of the early morning awakening. Forests of walnut and plum gave way to the maple trees, now barren of leaves, their grey fingers reaching out to match a grey dawn tinged with pink. Leaves crackled under the horses' hooves.

It was a steady pace up the great steppe toward the mountain pass which would aim them to a valley of farmers who lived in a high mountain meadow near the edge of the great Taklimakan.

They stopped in the middle of the day to eat and rest the horses. Arle took her in his arms and kissed her. His blue eyes sparkled in spite of the grey day. Poma thought of Enash, and discovered to her dismay she could not see his face clearly in her mind. In the warmth of Arle's embrace, her thoughts of Enash faded a little. As she looked deep into Arle's eyes, she saw the promise there, and thought it well that Enash had faded a bit. She smiled her secret smile. Arle would protect and love her.

The wind picked up, and it became time to continue their journey. "We'd better hurry if we are to beat this storm," he warned. Huge black clouds formed over the valley far below. Tiny streaks of lightening threatened rains there and snow above. Scurries of cold wind announced snow and freezing rain. Poma urged Estwynd up the rocky path. Rain pelted them with sheets of cold and wet. Estwynd plodded upward as best he could. The sleet turned to snow and it quickly built up around them. Soon the air hurt Poma's lungs. The darkened day turned to an envelope of white. She could no longer see the trail. Arle had disappeared ahead. Ice hung from Estwynd's bridle. The aloneness challenged Poma's very being with cold and fear. At long last she was relieved to see Arle ahead of her.

He stopped his mare and the pack horse to wait for her. "We'll be safer if we stay together," he said.

Poma tried to be assured. The low roar of an icy waterfall competed with the howling wind. They poked along through the deepening snow. As they rounded a huge rock the waterfall came into view. Water fell from high above, and on either side the cliff housed long, pointed icicles. The new-fallen snow sparkled from tree branches, giving the whole scene the look of a home for ice fairies Poma heard about from a story told when she was very young.

Before she could absorb the beauty of this spot, an enormous snow leopard leapt down from the rock and attacked Arle and Old Crow, knocking Arle off the horse and over the cliff side, sending the frightened mare and the pack animal down the snowy trail. Poma had a flashback to a warm autumn day on an Egyptian cliff. She shrieked, "Arle, Arle!" and tried to calm the startled Estwynd. Her voice could not be heard over the roar of the falls.

Arle had disappeared into the storm below her. The other horses had disappeared ahead. The leopard now stood in the trail ahead of Poma, his long tail twitching through the wayward snowflakes. As Estwynd reared and turned, the great cat leapt at them. For one searing moment she and the leopard were face to face. For the rest of Poma's life, she would never see such a look of anger and fear on man or beast. Before she managed to turn the big grey back down the trail, she saw those fierce eyes framed by the enormous paws, whose claws sparkled like ice bracelets against the white snow. Estwynd barely escaped the slashing cat.

After a brief lunge down the mountain, the big horse launched himself into a large patch of snow, and was struggling to get out. Poma jumped off and into the snow, thinking to help the big animal by lessening his load. She brushed the snow from her quiver, and fumbled with her bow when the leopard, snarling, appeared again, this time below them.

It seemed to take a lifetime to line up the arrow in her bow. Her fingers were freezing. Her whole body was shaking. Before she could take aim, the leopard simply watched her for a moment or two, and then in another instant, the anger and fear dissolved into a piercing, intelligent release. Inexplicably, he turned and, ears back, evaporated into the storm.

Poma sat down, exhausted, relieved, and awestruck. Estwynd managed to break free from the snow drift and stood beside her, warily eyeing the trail. She was still shaking as she climbed back up and headed the horse back up the trail to the waterfall.

Arle was just crawling his way back up the embankment and his worried face eased into a relieved grin as he looked around. "What was that?" he asked. Icicles hung from his beard.

She laughed in relief. "Only the biggest snow leopard in the world," she replied, her face turning from smiles to tears in a wave of relief from the terror.

"Oh, Poma, thank the Gods you are alright!" As he hugged her, he looked around again. "Where is he now?"

"He decided I was not worth his trouble," she said. "He disappeared like a ghost."

Arle peered around them into the storm. "Where are the horses?" His face turned back to its worried expression.

"Both the horses disappeared up ahead on the trail," she said.

"I'll ride behind you and we'll hunt for them," he said, climbing up behind her on Estwynd.

The storm had changed to a docile and echoless snowfall. The flakes were large and wet. Poma took a big breath as the horse made his way across the short summit and they started down the other side of the mountain.

Within a short space, the mountain changed from forest to high desert with the rocky trail leading down out of the snow. The enemy now was a cold, biting wind. At a vantage point they spotted the pack horse, grazing in the sparse grass close to the trail. Old Crow was nowhere to be seen. The pack horse came obediently and they continued down the trail.

In a small forest of tall fir trees, they set up their tent and tucked their bed just inside, where they could watch the fire. As they cuddled that night in their furs, Poma told Arle about the snow leopard.

"He didn't act like he was afraid of me. He just gave me a very intelligent look and turned and walked away. It was amazing."

"The old ones tell about some whom the animals seem to recognize as being special souls and do not harm them," Arle said.

Poma thought back to the asp in her bed. *Do you think . . . ?*

"You know," he continued, "one of these furs is a leopard fur."

Poma was glad she hadn't seen this leopard face to face. "Did you kill this leopard?"

"Actually, I traded a prize foal for this skin. The leopards are hard to catch."

The next morning they re-packed the horses and moved on down the mountain. The day was bright and clear. The great Taklimakan spread out far below, a vast, empty space. They stopped for a moment to adjust their senses from the damp forests and the changing, challenging mountain peaks to the deadly beauty of the far horizons of emptiness. The scene was sobering and took Poma's breath away. She had seen some of the Egyptian desert, but the great Taklimakan, even from far off, seemed to reaffirm its reputation when its wind whispered, *"Enter if you dare!"*

Poma broke the silence. "I'm glad we don't have to tackle that today."

"Thank the Gods," returned Arle.

The trail turned into a broad canyon and a high meadow protected from the wind. Green crops lined the big space. At the far end of the fields a small mud house sprouted like a mushroom under a grove of aspen. Arle's cousin, a red-haired woman of about 35 seasons, stood on her porch, smiling as they rode up. Her boys stood behind her, wide-eyed at the strangers and their wondrous grey horse. They were thin, dark young men with snapping black eyes. They disappeared behind the house to care for their guest's horses. Arle and Poma were greeted with warm hugs. The smell of freshly baked bread spilled out of a nearby outdoor oven and civilized the sharp fall air.

"Welcome, Arle! And who is this?"

"This is my wife, Poma. Poma, this is cousin Anad."

"Poma! How lovely you are!" she said. "Come in out of the cold."

Poma entered the small house to find warmth and comfort. A low fire crackled behind a stone hearth. Colorful rugs lined the floor. In an adjacent anteroom was a large upright loom made sturdy with huge logs. A beautifully patterned rug waited, half-way done. Some of the border patterns were etched with a deep, dark purple.

Poma stopped to admire Anad's handiwork. "What a beautiful rug!" She was almost reverent.

"Thanks. Come and sit by the fire. Batu will be home soon. He is up at the barn feeding the sheep. Arle, I'm so glad to see you. How many seasons has it been?"

Before he could answer, she turned to Poma. "We used to play together as children. I remember going to Marakanda to the market. Have you seen the city?"

"Oh, yes, just this fall. It was a wonderful time. So much to see!" replied Poma.

Batu suddenly filled the doorway. He was a thick, dark, heavy-set Mongolian man with greying hair and black eyes. His moustache curled up at the sight of Arle.

"Well, cousin, welcome! How long has it been?"

The men exchanged a bear hug, Arle just holding his own in the embrace of the older man. "And who's this pretty little thing?"

"This is my wife, Poma."

"We heard of Dorinda's death. Did you ever find out how she died?"

Arle's face turned white. "No, actually, we didn't." he said. He glanced at Poma.

"So glad you found a new wife. A man needs a good woman to keep him warm in the winter." He grinned a big bear-like grin at Poma. Poma smiled back politely. She stared at Arle for a moment, then looked away.

"Where did you find that nice dapple grey?" said Batu.

"Poma rode in on him. Fortunately, she decided to stay with us."

"Nice horse. And how are Narmet and his family?"

"They are well."

Anad motioned for Poma to join her as the men discussed old times. Poma smiled at Anad and sat down beside her in front of the rug loom. "How long have you worked at this?" Poma asked, feeling of the soft rug.

Anad picked up a small sharp knife and her fingers worked the knots quickly. The knife flashed, and another knot was done, and then another. Tie and cut, tie and cut. Anad seemed to know which color to work next without even thinking about it. "Well, the boys help out quite a bit now, and it gives me time. It's been a few moons now. If it turns out well, it will go to market next season."

Poma couldn't wait to ask. "And how do you get the beautiful purple?"

Anad smiled. "The only thing I do differently from my mother is, I swear by my big iron pot."

"Iron?"

"Yes, and then I use some potash and acid to brighten up the purple."

Iron! She felt as if she had suddenly learned one of the great secrets of all time. "And no indigo?" she asked.

"No, it's just madder. I just soak it for a moon, and then cook it only gently. In the summer I don't cook it at all, because it sits in the sun."

Poma thought it best not to mention that the rest of the family thought this process to be secret. But after remembering Ru's comments about iron pots, she thought Anad's recipe would be hers alone for a long time. She added another reason for her secret smile.

Anad was a gentle woman who worked hard and supported her husband's belief in their farm. "We have the winter wheat planted, and

I've dried enough vegetables for most of the winter. Sometimes we go down below to get early vegetables and fruit because the winters up here are so long."

"Then you've seen the Taklimakan up close?"

"Oh, yes, we visit a small village where the merchants come through. They say the middle route is more dangerous because of fewer water holes, but it takes a few weeks off their trips."

"How interesting," Poma said. She remembered the dark little silk merchant and the stories of how long it took to get the silk to its destinations.

"Can you sell rugs there?"

"I'm going to try. If I'm not successful, we'll come back to Marakanda or Tashkent or even Kashgar."

The family sat down to a meal of fresh vegetables and lamb, and slice after slice of crusty fresh bread. Batu produced a prize bottle of Greek wine to enrich a very satisfying meal.

Later that night Poma stared at the ceiling from their bed in a corner of the great room, and was reminded of the Egyptian temple. The quiet house was warm, but she felt as though the walls were too close. She fell asleep telling herself she was safe from the snow leopard.

Poma was spinning by Anad's great hearth. As she reached for some wood for the fire, one of the logs turned into the tail of the giant snow leopard. She whirled around to meet with red eyes in the dark corner of the room. Her spindle became an arrow, but she could not find her bow. The leopard spoke to her. "Our children must play together," he said. "Our children must be friends." Poma watched as the arrow in her hand became a spindle again. She started to spin, and then saw the leopard through a familiar halo of smoke. His eyes had turned from red cat's eyes to black buttons, and he winked at her.

Poma awoke with feelings of confusion. She silently repeated the dream to herself and since the room had grown cold, snuggled closer to her sleeping husband. The grey light of dawn crept into the room and focused on the large stone hearth. A small movement caught Poma's eye. After her dream it was a small moment of terror. She held her breath and watched as Anad moved silently out of the shadows. Poma's relief caused her to laugh at herself. She got up, chattering in the cold, to help her cousin start the fire.

"I'll get the fire going, Anad." The women busied themselves with the start of the day. Poma watched the comforting flames, and thought about her dream. There seemed to be a rift inside her about her nomadic way of life. Certainly as a child she had had her share of the dangers that befell her original family, but she always felt safe because of the loving adults around her.

She also felt safe with her present family. Except for a few minor raids, not many folks bothered them. They were wealthy, but had no cities. And they were good soldiers, even without a country of their own. But the thing that Poma pondered most was why the leopard had told her their children should be friends. And at the last, the leopard had begun looking like Tigrax. *Tigrax.* Poma wondered if the old woman had seen this dream.

Her musings were interrupted by Anad's two sons. The youngest was being pushed forward just a bit by his elder brother.

"Cousin Poma?"

"Yes, dear."

"Cousin Poma, we'd like to know if we could maybe ride your horse, just around the yard."

"Why of course, boys." Poma was amused. She remembered when she and Taki had ridden around and around in another yard a very long time ago.

By this time Arle was up. "Be careful, boys," he said. He frowned at Poma, and followed the young pair out the door. Poma felt a small stab of doubt. Why the frown? It was the first time he seemed angry with her. With a heavy heart, she turned back to the fire and helped Anad with the morning meal.

The men came in, rosy-cheeked and tramping mud from their feet. Poma felt grateful for the warmth of this family. The task of their visit was at hand, so the men again disappeared to talk of sheep, hides, and the price of winter wheat.

Later that night, Poma and Arle talked quietly together of the day. "We got the ram we needed, and two ewes in the bargain. We'll have a head start." Arle's eyes were shining.

"Arle . . ." Poma twined her arm in his. "Were you displeased at something this morning?"

"Well, perhaps cautious is a better word. Narmet has entrusted the safety of Estwynd to me—to us—and since the future of our clan is tied up with the horse, I feel a great responsibility. I know those boys are learning to be good horsemen, but Estwynd needs to rest, just as we do, for the trip home. I'll use the pack horse to ride, but now, since we don't have Old Crow . . ." He fell to silent brooding.

Poma instantly understood, and in that moment, became a wife. "I'm sorry, Arle. From now on, I'll know to share our decisions."

Arle's face relaxed into its usual carefree grin.

In another day, they made ready to ride back over the mountain. The weather was much more cooperative, but they had the sheep to herd back to their winter home. The older ewe had a bell around her neck which helped the whole process.

Divining

A few days after they arrived home, winter decided to set in for good. The snow became thick and heavy in the high mountain peaks. The winter pastures shortly became green and muddy. The nomads spent a good deal of time gathering wood in and a few built yurts for their families.

Poma and Arle stayed in their wagon and made do with an outdoor fire. Poma found the camaraderie of the other women to be comforting during the winter days. Along with spinning, weaving and needlework came the gossip and stories. She became something of an instant legend when she told the others about her encounter with the snow leopard.

"And then he just turned and walked away. It was a very frightening moment, but amazing at the same time."

Spindles had stopped momentarily.

"Then I found Arle up the trail, but we lost one of the horses. She took off, and we never did find her."

Tigrax's eyes narrowed through her usual haze of pipe smoke. "Old Crow will be just fine. She was probably very scared," she said.

Later, when Poma was alone with her, she relayed her dream to the old woman. "And what do you think it means?" Tigrax said.

Poma frowned. "I'm not sure about our children being friends," she said. "Why does this dream seem to have more than one meaning?"

Tigrax's eyes snapped through the smoke. "You are becoming a wise woman for one so young. The so-called children of the snow leopard have to do with his heritage, being a cold, ruthless animal. Ancient wisdom tells us the snow leopard represents those in other tribes who might want to harm us. Your so-called children, by the same token, are your aspects of purity, tenacity, patience, and even your anger. These qualities combine into a very formidable human being. In other words, your leopard friend was perhaps saying you can use these qualities to help those around you. But—it's your dream."

"How do I use these qualities?" Poma asked.

"It's a process, child, a process. Making use of anger as the energy to solve problems and not eventually using it against others takes time. But anger will be your protection. Let your dreams help you. Come to my tent each morning, and we'll talk."

"I'm grateful for your wisdom, Tigrax."

"And I for yours. My granddaughters are well schooled in the herbs, but show no signs of having the sight, as you do. I'm an old woman, and I want to leave my family safe with someone who has these powers."

For the first time, Poma saw the vulnerability of this old lady. "Certainly Ru could be taught things . . ." Poma said lamely.

"She will someday make a resting place for many, but the old ways of seeing rest here." Tigrax poked her pipe stem at Poma. "I love those girls," she continued, "and I have given them all I can. But I feel a need to share more. And it was like the Goddess was smiling at us the day she sent you here."

Poma felt these small victories were stepping stones in her life, and gave thanks silently with Tigrax.

Each morning she talked of her dreams with the old woman. One morning Tigrax declared it was time for Poma to learn divining with the mirror. They sat side by side in front of her altar; mugs of tea staved off the cold. Tigrax put her pipe down.

"The first thing you must do is remember that seeing has to do with knowing that you can. The next thing is to exercise that power like you would muscles in your legs by walking. You must believe it; you must use it. Here, look at this." She drew a short dagger out of a basket. The little knife had silver leopards crouching along its handle. The blade shone in the low light. "Hold it in your hands and close your eyes."

Poma obeyed the old shaman. As she touched the cold metal of the dagger, she felt a chill move up her spine and spread into her hair at the back of her neck. She opened her eyes and dropped the little knife.

"Tell me, what is your first thought?" Tigrax whispered.

"I . . . I . . ."

"Don't hesitate. What picture comes to your mind?"

"There is blood on fur . . . ermine. The fur is ruffled by a breeze. There is a flickering candle. More red blood. There is evil here. Evil." Poma surprised herself with this instant knowledge.

Tigrax's eyes shone. "This dagger was involved in a murder. Many years ago, my brother was killed with this very blade."

Poma sought to see who held the knife. The picture was gone.

"We never knew who killed him," Tigrax said.

Poma was excited in the face of discovering her abilities.

"How do you feel?" Tigrax said.

"I feel good about knowing I am capable of such things," Poma said, "But at the same time, it's such a big responsibility."

"That's because these gifts are not given to those who will use them in an evil way. Some day this will be clear to you. Keep this gift in your secret place."

It was Poma's turn to feel vulnerable. But she knew to only smile. "What about the mirror?" she said, finally.

"The mirror holds scenes like you just saw. It is only a tool. Trust your sight, not your tool. It serves only as a space for these images to reflect back at you the things you already know."

"Then why use it?"

"Because others see only themselves in the mirror. They will know at once your power is very real."

The women finished their tea in silence. Tigrax re-lit her pipe.

"I must go now, Tigrax. Thank you so much."

Poma made her way back to her own wagon. She sat on the wagon seat, thinking about her new-found gift. The grey winter provided quiet that morning, and the clan matched that quiet.

Arle came up carrying an armload of wood. "Are you alright?" he said.

"Yes, of course, why?"

"You look a little peaked."

"If talking with Tigrax makes one peaked, then that's what happened," she said.

He dumped the wood, brushed himself off, and reached for her hand. "Come on, let's go for a walk. Help me get some more wood."

The drop back into reality forced Poma out of her reverie. She tucked the precious morning away, promising herself to practice what Tigrax had taught her. It would be awhile before her practice became tied into reality.

Targitaus

It was Madga who first noticed that Poma was with child. Poma sat in the midst of a hillock, surrounded by early crocuses and grape hyacinth. The sun shone on her long curly hair, and her serene expression mirrored the pastoral scene. The women had gathered early that day to warp a loom together. Many hands made the task go faster.

The measurement of the warp, or lengthwise threads, was estimated, and two wooden stakes driven into the ground this distance apart. One of the women walked back and forth and wrapped the yarn continuously around the posts. Two other women, stationed at the posts, inserted small lengths of yarn of another color between each warp thread. The sequence was kept, and when all the required threads were around the posts, they were slid into smaller rods that were lashed onto the beams of the loom. Poma never cared for warping; she preferred the freedom of the more imprecise art of spinning. Although her threads were even, an occasional slight irregularity was tolerable. Later, as she sat by the fire with Madga, she felt Madga's sharp gaze and met it with laughter.

"I know what you are thinking, Madi, and it's true," she said.

Madga kissed her smooth cheek. "Does Arle know yet?"

"No. I just feel such a secret should belong to me for a while, anyway, before the world knows."

"That's what all the women say," Madga said. "I will keep your secret, if you wish."

"Only for a short time. When Arle knows, then we can share."

The two hugged, sealing the secret for the time being.

Within a few days it was warm enough to ride into the hills. Poma and Arle found a place where the Daphne bloomed, making the hillsides appear red. The springtime scent was awesome. Poma jumped down from Estwynd and threw her hood back. She decided right then and there that Daphne was her favorite flower. The rich, heady scent filled her senses and her soul at the same time.

"Oh, Arle, isn't it beautiful?"

Arle watched his young bride blossom along with the spring scene before them. "It certainly is."

She looked back and saw him staring at her. As usual, she melted. "My sweetheart, how would you like to have a son?"

Arle was instantly off his horse and almost threw her into the air. She had never seen him happier. She felt a stab of guilt at the thought of only partially rearing a child and then going off and leaving it behind. And the biggest part of this dilemma was that she knew about this beforehand. She somehow knew that this knowledge had to be kept secret, so as not to interrupt the flow of life among these people. Also, she knew, despite the superstitions, they would never believe a word she might say about her true identity. The God and Goddess would guide her through her life, and this she could trust.

The sky momentarily blackened with undulating chevrons of geese in animated goose conversation about the northerly direction. The grandmother goose in front of one of the long lines was as white as snow. She flew confidently, saving her voice for warning the other geese of danger when they stopped to stand, hundreds of them at once, goose-knee deep in the great wetlands below the surrounding hills.

Poma was thrilled at the white goose. "Look at that!"

Arle broke into a big grin. "We must tell the others. A white goose is a good omen. We will have the grace of the Gods with us."

Poma was warmed by the thought of her little one being so blessed.

Later, Arle made her a mirror to match the comb he had made for her. She stared in it and saw herself smiling her secret smile.

When the word got out about the baby, it spread through the camp in a matter of minutes. Much of that day was spent in talk of children, babies and childbirth. All the mothers seemed to have a story of some kind to tell. The young girls of the tribe grew up with all the talk and seemed to understand it as a part of the procession of life and death experienced by all the nomads. Poma did not have an immediate knowledge, but drew upon far away childhood memories of Ashar in times of childbearing. She consoled herself with her inner strength and knew that, between herself, Boot-Ru and Madga, all that was known about childbirth was at their capable fingertips.

As the spring progressed and the snows receded, the nomads moved their animals farther north. There was an occasional village along the way, but no big cities. Poma wondered to herself if Enash had been to these places. In one of the villages lived an old sage who welcomed Tigrax warmly. Tigrax invited him to the camp. They sat by the fire in animated conversation. Soon the clan gathered around to listen.

"Namaz, tell them what you told me about the Gods," Tigrax said.

Poma's spindle came to a halt. Namaz was a male version of Tigrax, only his beard completed the fuzzy halo into a circle. His thin beard danced up and down in time with his kindly brown eyes. Tigrax's smoke only added to the illusion of dancing grey as he spoke with great passion about the Gods and Goddesses of his lifetime. His eyes brightened at the crowd of people.

"Thank you, Tigrax. It is indeed, good to see you all again. I've been telling Tigrax the news of these parts. When were you here last?" he said to her.

"It's been at least two seasons," she replied.

Namaz had a great following in the village, and they were gathering with the nomads to listen.

"I have seen many things in my life," he began. "Wars, times of peace, many people. I was once a wanderer such as you." He looked directly at Narmet. "I have seen the great sea and traveled around the Taklimakan. My path has been crossed by many Gods and men of wisdom who speak of them. Only a season or two ago there came a young man who was wise beyond his years. He told of a God that is an old God of people who lived a long, long time ago, before our ancestors."

Narmet shifted on his log seat, scowling through his beard. Tigrax glared at him.

"I asked him, 'What of our Gods who provide for us and protect us?' and he very carefully pointed out the human aspects of these many Gods, and how we use these Gods to explain our own behavior."

A murmur went up in the crowd. Poma drew her shawl up around her mouth.

Tigrax got to her feet. "It can do no harm to listen!" she shouted. The whispering subsided. She resumed her seat.

"Look at the beautiful springtime," he continued. The Goddess Api creates life anew. And isn't that what happens to the earth, to the trees, to the animals, and to you?"

Poma felt her babe moving within her. It seemed as if the child and the old man were conspiring.

"Then, when you learn compassion, what God is right there? Tabiti. Yes, that's it. For every season there is a God. Why not give all these attributes to one God?"

The crowd murmured again. Narmet jumped to his feet. "That is blasphemy!" he shouted. "No one God could do all that." The nomads loudly agreed with him.

"That is why He is God," Namaz retorted.

Now the crowd muttered.

Poma watched in awe as they grasped the implication of what this little man was saying. Some in the back turned to leave, but most of them looked thoughtful. In a few moments Poma was able to make her way to where the sage sat with Tigrax.

"Excuse me, sir—may I ask you a question?"

"Why, yes, my dear."

"The young man you talked to. Can you describe him?"

"Well, let me see. He was very tall, brown hair, and—oh, yes, a scar that started over his eye and curled around on his cheek. Have you ever heard him speak?"

"It's been a long time ago," she managed. "Did he say where he was going next?"

"Well, let me see," he said again.

Tigrax squinted at Poma.

"Oh, yes. He was headed east . . . Yes, to the east."

Poma was shocked. She drew her shawl up again. "Thank you, sir," she said. She got up and stumbled back to her wagon. Arle was inside, asleep. She poked up their small fire and sat down to watch the dancing flame. She could no longer hold back the tears. *What had she done? Why couldn't she be totally happy with this good man who was her husband?*

Suddenly a strong arm was around her shoulders. "What's wrong, Poma?"

Poma looked at a worried Arle through her tears. "Oh, nothing important. I'll be alright." She tried to smile at him.

"Are you sure?"

"Just woman and baby stuff," she said.

He put his hand on her growing tummy. "He's putting you through a lot, and he's not even here yet."

"Oh, he's very much here. And what if it's a girl?"

Arle's eyes softened. "If she's as pretty as you are, she will be the second love of my life."

Arle had unknowingly said just the right thing. Poma sighed a big sigh and snuggled up next to Arle to watch the glowing embers.

The steppes were now filled with flowers. After the daphne came tulips, sedge grass and green moss. The spring was like a fairy story. There was bitter pea vine, iris, and snowdrop anemone. Little lambs jumped and played in the amazingly colorful meadows.

Poma felt this pulse of life and was happy to be part of it. The women gathered and shuttles flew to achieve the weaving before the great herds moved on. Single needle knitting wrought mittens and socks. At times the women's conversations turned from men and weaving to subjects more ethereal.

Boot-Ru was chopping herbs.

"And so what Goddess do you think I am?" she said to Poma.

Poma put down her mirror. "Do you like to cook?"

Mint filled the air, just in time for lamb stew. "Yes."

"And you treat the sick. And dance with the children."

Boot-Ru stirred thoughtfully. "Yes."

"So what Goddess is that?"

"Oh, I see. But how come she is a Goddess and I am not?"

"Who said you're not?"

"Oh."

It was the most thoughtful Poma had ever seen Boot-Ru. The rest of the stew preparation was quiet that evening. Poma began to understand the impact that Enash was having on these people. How lucky the God and Goddess knew just where to send him. But there was still that little twinge of longing. She looked back in the mirror and saw two children, a boy and his younger sister. *"Hello, Mother."* And just as suddenly they were gone. Poma stared at the mirror. For a moment she couldn't breathe.

"Poma," said Boot-Ru. Poma was startled. "Honey, are you alright?"

Poma set the mirror down and looked around at Boot-Ru. "What did you say?"

"I said, are you alright?"

"Oh, yes, Ru," she said, snapping back to reality. "Is Tigrax back from the village?"

"Yes. She's been back since the middle of the day."

Poma found Tigrax in her wagon, asleep in a stack of furs, and was about to turn and leave when the old woman spoke.

"Yes, dear, I've seen them. They came to me in a dream. A rather thin young man and his little sister, dark, like you. They are quite handsome, those two. Did you notice the difference in their ages?"

Poma was still almost too stunned to speak. Tigrax was right; the children seemed to be quite a few years apart. Tigrax watched Poma closely.

"It was amazing. I saw them in my mirror," Poma said.

"Not so amazing. I saw Ru and Madi's mother long before she was born."

Poma smiled and sat down with the old one to listen. "Her father was a tall, dark-haired man, handsome, like Arle."

"Did your daughter speak to you?"

"She told me a lot of things that took a long time to understand."

"Did the children today tell you anything?"

"The little girl began to tell me a story about a flying dragon and a search for a golden toe," said Tigrax. "And she was carrying a flute."

Poma felt her mouth open. "A golden toe?" She whispered.

"It's an old story. Have you heard it before?"

"It sounds like a story I heard long ago."

Tigrax frowned. "She also said there was more written down somewhere," she said. "None of us write things down. I don't know where we'd find such words."

But Poma knew. She quickly thanked Tigrax and jumped down from her wagon. After a big meal of lamb stew, it was not long before Arle was asleep. By candlelight Poma pored over her Egyptian scrolls. Some of the writings were difficult to understand. There was a long treatise about chariots and wagons, and references to strange stars in the sky. Finally she came to a passage about life traveling in a circle. The accompanying glyph showed a seated woman with a circular hat, her folded arms formed a circle, and a cart wheel sat in front of her. Even her face was round. What did this mean? Who was the lady in the round hat? Why was she concerned with a cart wheel? A poem came after the picture:

That Dark Place

The God of the day rows our boat,
Dip down and back,
Shining like silver.
The sun is born;
Is eaten by the night.
Dip down and back.
Moons go and come,
Shining like silver.
We come to that dark, dark place,
And must go back.
Deep, deep down and back.
Our babies come from that dark place,
And must return,
Shining like silver.
Deep, deep down and back,
Deep, deep down and back
Soaring like eagles.
Shining like silver,
Dip, deep down and back.

Poma felt a small pang of fear. She had seen much of the cycles of life, but had always wondered how mothers could give up babies who never lived long enough to see their first birthdays. *What a morose little poem.* She shuddered. Even the love she felt for Arle paled beside the love she felt for the little one she now carried. And it seemed it would indeed be a boy, with a sister to follow. What a glorious thing.

As the spring turned to summer and the herds were moved to the north, the flowers became more abundant, and Poma grew bigger and bigger. June brought forget-me-nots, salvia and large yellow daisies. Poma had Arle pick the daisies for her dye pot; she could not bend over.

She visited with Madga and attended all the births in the tribe that spring. There were two healthy girls born quietly, and a pair of twins. One was healthy, the other died within hours of birth. Witnessing these events made Poma aware of the work of birth, of the energy it takes to push a new life into the world. She saw the wordless love these women felt for their little ones, and their joy became hers. She assisted with hot water and herbs. Madga knew, as Hamora had known, that raspberry leaf tea was helpful for women about to give birth.

Poma also spent much time embroidering appliqués on small blankets. Tigrax taught her that the small birds depicted on the blankets were symbolic of the souls yet unborn. Poma delighted in this and studiously sewed birds and flowers in every available space on the little blankets. Arle watched in amusement as his beautiful bride blossomed into a beautiful woman.

One day some Scythians rode into camp. They came in from the west to consult with Narmet about an impending threat from the south. News of the road tax had spread far and wide, and Narmet and his best guards were needed as a show of strength to some Mongol tribes to the east. The euphoria and peace of the summer days were interrupted while the men counseled among themselves around the great fire at night. Tigrax made sure she was included in their talks. She was the one voice of peace and soon became a thorn in Narmet's side.

Early next morning, Poma's water broke. She decided to wash her hair, as she wouldn't be able to do this for a long time. While she was drying off on the bank of the stream, a pain seized her whole body. She made her way to Boot-Ru's wagon, and woke up Madga.

"I think it's time, Madi," she said.

"Go back to bed and I'll be over shortly," Madga said.

Poma obediently got back in her wagon and began combing her long hair so it would dry. Suddenly she was shot through with another pain. As she cried out, Arle was on his feet.

"Poma, are you alright? What should I do?" She tried to square her shoulders. Arle was out the front of the wagon. "Madi! Madi!"

Madga appeared, frowning. "I'm coming, Arle. Build a fire, please." Arle looked grateful for something to do.

The sun was high on a warm summer day when the baby was born. Poma was fearful, but with Madga and Boot-Ru there, and the other women helping, the new little Saka baby was soon welcomed into the world. His newborn cries echoed down the steppe, past the horses to the sheep where Arle had gone to be out of the way of the busy women. He came running. "Poma, darling girl!" he said. Poma smiled at him. She was tired, but the little one was nursing. Her sojourn as a bride was complete. Arle kissed her brow, and watched the boy for a moment.

"I'll name him after our first great leader, King Targitaus." He said. Poma smiled. It was a distinguished name for one so small. When he was through eating, she wrapped him in the little purple blanket and he indeed looked like royalty. His dark curls framed his fat little face. The next day Arle rode off with a group of the other men and joined the Scythians to confer with other Saka tribes. Poma tried not to cry when he left, but the tears streamed down her face. It was great solace to turn her attention to the little one.

At the point of high summer, the clan turned south again and slightly west. This year's market stop would be Tashkent. The herds moved at their usual leisurely pace, the animals enjoying lush grass and many small streams cascading out of the mountains. Poma occupied herself with Targitaus, but as each day passed, she became more worried about Arle.

Some of the older boys helped Poma with her wagon, until she was strong enough to handle the oxen. At times she rode with Madga and Boot-Ru.

"Where do you think they went?" Poma said one day. The talk was that they wouldn't see the war council party until market time.

Boot-Ru clucked at her oxen. "Probably as far as the Aral Sea. They will come down the Syr Darya to Tashkent. They know we will be there this year instead of Marakanda."

Poma felt restless. "How far is this sea?"

"About as far away as we are from Tashkent."

Poma missed her big, smiling husband. Targitaus kept her full attention, however, and grew into a smiling, happy baby who had many aunties looking after him.

Old Friend

Tashkent was bigger than Marakanda. The bazaar was located within the city, in a very large square. There was a well in the center of the square, where water was plentiful for the whole city. The caravans came in from the desert, the nomads from the steppe, and merchants from the seas to the west. Poma had two fat lambs to sell for Arle this year, and they sold quickly, allowing her enough for some grain and a little left over. She knew Arle would be proud of her. She carried the sleeping Targitaus through the stalls to hunt for indigo from the east.

". . . Once your inner spirit truly understands this, that allows the transition. This creation is an illusion . . ."

Poma knew that beautiful, silken voice. She caught her breath and whirled around, awakening the sleeping baby.

There was Enash, a little taller, but still talking with his hands. Poma was elated. At the moment their eyes met, his furrowed brows rose in surprise.

". . . an illusion . . ." He stopped. "Excuse me." As he made his way through the people, the crowd opened a pathway right up to Poma. She could only stare at him, hoping this was not an illusion, that he was real, for the first time in—how long had it been? Five seasons, six? For them, it was six. For the rest of the world, it was a very, very long time.

He embraced Poma and her baby in one big hug, and kissed her forehead. "How good it is to see you!" he exclaimed.

"I've been hunting for you!" she grinned a wide, happy grin. "You disappeared so quickly that day. I've searched and searched. I knew you were close by somewhere; they saw you two seasons ago at Marakanda . . ."

"And who is this?" Targitaus was staring up at Enash in apparent mistrust, his big brown eyes wide in wonder.

The present came back to Poma like an arrow. "Oh, this is Targitaus, my son." How could she explain about Arle? "I had no way of knowing if I'd ever see you again." His eyes rested on his scarab amulet. Then his eyes softened as he looked at her and she felt the old longing.

"I—I have a husband, Enash, and he's gone away right now, but I'm here with some nomads. We live in wagons, and . . ." Somehow she couldn't cram it all in.

"Sit down over here, and tell me all about it," he said.

Targitaus obligingly fell asleep again and she told Enash all that befell her in Egypt after he had gone, and about the war that forced her to flee, and the wild new land she had come to, the chase with Estwynd after her encounter with the Mongols, and her life with Arle and the nomads. And he told her about his wandering on the steppes, preaching, and his encounter with people who were not ready to hear about the one God.

"Oh, but you'd be surprised," Poma said with excitement. "My family heard your words through Namaz, the old seer to the north. My Auntie Ru was definitely intrigued."

Enash seemed surprised. "Well, it's nice to know my words have meaning to someone," he said, smiling.

Poma remembered the strange poem from the scrolls. "Enash, explain this poem to me. I read it in the scroll you left me." And she recited it for him.

"Dip, deep down and back . . . I have what these nomads call the sight. Targitaus and his small sister, who has not been born yet, came to me in a vision and hailed me as their mother. What will become of these babies of mine?"

Enash took her hand. "I have a feeling we will be asked to give back to our own circle of special souls," he began.

Poma felt the tears well up.

"Do you remember what your mother told you about how you came to her? No one knew where you were from, or how you got there?"

The meaning of what he was telling her settled on her heart like a great weight. "Must I give up my little Targitaus?" she whispered.

"I don't think so. His father is not one of us, is he?"

"No, no, he would have told me."

"Have you told him about yourself?"

"Well, no, I don't think it is fair to disrupt . . ." She couldn't breathe.

"At any rate, one who travels through time must be born of others who do the same."

Poma started breathing again. Then she searched his face for an answer to her next question. "Does that mean that you and I . . ."

"Perhaps one day, Poma. But not now. You must focus on your family and establish Targitaus in a good situation. The God and Goddess will always give us earthly work to do first. I am headed west to consult with sages. It is safe to bet that you have things to teach this young man that he couldn't learn from anyone else. What he accomplishes may affect all history. And in about five seasons, I will move on through time once more. I know you well, and I know you would choose well when selecting a husband."

They fell into an uneasy silence. "Enash . . ."

Her name came crashing around her and fell in pieces on the sand. "Poma!" It was Arle. Again she whirled around. There stood her happy husband, his arms outstretched.

"Arle!" Targitaus awoke and started whimpering. As she looked back at Enash, she felt her lip quiver. Enash nodded at her, his eyes wistful.

She turned and stepped into the waiting arms of her husband. The smell of campfire smoke brought her searing back to reality. Targitaus reached for his father for the first time. Arle's attention turned toward his son.

Poma turned back again to Enash. He had disappeared into the crowd. Then she saw him approaching a string of horses. He would be gone again, and this time on a westward quest. Arle put his arm around her shoulder. As they walked away, he said, "Who was that?"

Poma took a deep breath. "It was someone . . . someone I knew as a child. He is a preacher . . . . from a long time ago . . ."

Arle glanced back in curiosity. Then he looked deep into Poma's eyes. "Just as green as the day I left. I have much to tell you."

Poma stole one more look back. She could not see Enash.

"Poma? My dearest one, I have missed you so."

She took a deep breath. "And I have missed you, too. I am glad you have returned in safety."

"And this little one seems happy to see me, though I don't think he remembers me!" She smiled at them both. Her tears would wait until later.

Back at the camp, she built up their fire and warmed Arle a meal from the cauldron. "Now, tell me about your trip," she sat on the ground and rested her chin on her knees.

"We never made it to the sea. We met with some Scythians—you should have seen their horses. They had masks of bronze and gold, with antlers, like deer."

"The horses?"

"Yes, it was astounding!"

"Did they speak of peace?"

"The horses?"

She laughed and pushed his shoulder. It was the Arle of old. "No, silly, the Scythians."

Arle frowned. "They did until Narmet got to bickering about the taxes. But we did have the weight of the confederation behind us, so there was little they could say right now. They will have to pay more for silk and spices from the east, and they were not happy about this."

"Well, it's a changing world, I guess," Poma said. She dished out some more dinner for him.

"Narmet got sick while we were there, and the men voted for me to take his place in the conference."

Poma was surprised. "Is he well again?"

"He was well enough to travel."

"What about Solok?"

"The other men felt he is young and perhaps too brash. He is good in battle, but really lacks an understanding of peace."

"I am so proud of you!" Poma was genuinely pleased to see Arle taking a peaceful place in the clan hierarchy.

Suddenly Arle reached into his bags and pulled out a small rounded cauldron for Poma. "Here, I brought you this for your dyes," he said.

"Oh, Arle, it's beautiful," she whispered. The cauldron had a handle made of a deer. Its feet were implanted firmly on the side, and its stylized head and horns formed the rest of the handle. "Thank you so much—I have much dyeing to do before winter takes away all the things I need to harvest. It is a busy time." She looked at his tired face and saw love. It filled up her being. She ran her fingers over his brow.

"You cannot know how I missed you," he said again.

Soon both he and the baby were asleep, side by side. Poma gently slid into bed. Targitaus lay between them. She smiled as she remembered her little brother, sideways in the big family bed. But her smile was salted with tears. She let them flow for just a few moments, then, looking at her sleeping family, wiped her eyes, took a big breath, and tried to put her inner world right once more. Perhaps some day she would see Enash again, and be free to be with him. But her being ached. Not many people had the opportunities she was blessed with. Or how much of her life was a curse? Somewhere deep inside the answer came into focus, and she knew she would follow her calling and do the best she could. But what was she to do with the next eight seasons? Concentrating on her son was to be the major part of the plan, but raising a son was something she would be doing anyway. What else was to happen? She had found the secret to the madder purple, and Arle had brought this iron pot to her as a gift. Now she could show the other women how this purple was achieved. Surely the God and Goddess had something more important than this. She remembered her search for the purple in the little blanket and the distaff. Would she ever find it? Would she ever see the great sea again?

She had exchanged knowledge with Boot-Ru about the herbs. Certainly this knowledge would never be lost. She brought one-needle knitting to the nomads. Would something that basic and simple resound in the world? She wondered if Tigrax really knew about her mission in life. Everything she had learned with these people would be taken with her when she moved on. Was it important for her to plod along and be true to her beliefs? She would have to just trust in the Goddess. *Perhaps some day* . . . Poma shed a few more tears and drifted off into a fitful sleep.

The Amazons

Poma labored in the birth of her baby, and Madga wiped her brow. Five long, black arrows sunk into her huge tummy, and caused the baby to cry.

Poma awoke in a pool of sweat. Targitaus was sleeping peacefully. But something was wrong. It was not a baby crying; it was a woman screaming. It was still dark, and there was no moon as she peered out the front opening of the wagon. Arle was on his feet. Boot-Ru was screaming. Arle pushed Poma out of the way and jumped from the wagon. Several others of the clan ran toward them. Poma threw her shawl around herself and followed Arle to the screaming Boot-Ru, who was bound hand and foot. Madga was missing. She took Boot-Ru in her arms to calm her down.

Boot-Ru was untied and finally managed to tell her story through sobs. "There were three of them. They all wore masks. The biggest one threatened us with a knife . . ." She sniffled, and started crying.

"There, there, dear. What happened then?"

Boot-Ru sniffled some more. "They tied Madga up and carried her awaaaaaay . . ." Now she was crying again. Tigrax appeared, announced by her halo of grey hair which stood in stumpy shocks. She took her granddaughter by the hand. They both held Boot-Ru close, soothing her as best they could. One of the other women was building a fire to heat some tea.

"Let's go," said Arle evenly. By this time a sleepy Narmet and Solok were there in the shadows. The men started gathering their gear together when Poma remembered her dream.

"Wait. There are five of them," she said.

"No, only three," said Boot-Ru.

"Five. Dressed in black," Poma said stoutly.

Tigrax looked from the astonished Arle back to Poma. "You are correct, little owl." The old woman looked back at Arle. "Five," she whispered. "Now go!" the last was an order. Arle jumped down from the wagon.

Narmet glanced at some of the gathered crowd. "You there, get your brother!" Solok and the younger men saddled the horses. The clan came together under a banner of need: many women might be dispensable, but certainly not the midwife. Madga had long held a place of high esteem and must be found at all cost. She had often made the difference for the life or death of the new babies and sometimes their mothers, not to mention that she was kin to the most powerful shaman in recent memory.

Search parties went out, and the only thing they found was her shoe, a short way up the hill. Hunting parties kept vigil. Stray travelers were questioned. It was as if Madga had stepped off the earth and vanished. Two moons passed. It came time to move the herds and a heated discussion ensued about what might happen if Madga came back and found everyone gone. Boot-Ru, bereft and sad, only found comfort from Tigrax and her deep insights into the lives of them all.

"If she comes back, how will she ever find us again?" She had eaten very little in weeks and had grown almost thin with worry.

"I will see her," Tigrax maintained.

"I wish you could see her now!" Boot-Ru snapped at her grandmother.

"Hush, dear," said Poma, taking her in her arms. It began another round of tears.

Nevertheless, the animals needed to eat, and it now became Boot-Ru's job to care for the pregnant women for the clan. There were three births that summer, and Boot-Ru and Poma learned more from each one. Thankfully, they were easy births and the clan rejoiced with three new little ones. Tigrax kept telling Poma Madga was still alive. Poma gazed into her mirror every night, hoping to find a clue. At last she saw Madga holding a small blonde baby. She frowned, not understanding what that meant. Madga had not been gone long enough to have a baby of her own. Poma kept this news to herself, not yet fully trusting her abilities. It was hard to keep this secret, and the decision to do so weighed heavily as she went about her days. Nearly everyone else had given up hope.

The day Madga came home, a whoop went up from the far side of the herd. One of the men gathered her up on his horse and rode into camp, shouting to everyone. Poma looked up from her dye pots. Madga, in men's clothing, was muddy from head to toe, but her long red hair announced it was really her. And she was clutching a small bundle to her breast.

"Madga! It's Madga! She's back!"

Everyone ran and gathered around the disheveled but relieved midwife. "I found you! Thank the Gods!" Madga whispered.

Everyone had questions all at once. Boot-Ru was glued to her muddy sister in a big hug. Tigrax pushed through the crowd and hugged them both. Poma pressed close to take her turn.

"Are you alright?" Tigrax asked.

"Where did they take you?" Boot-Ru asked.

They heard cries from the small bundle in her arms. Tigrax peered under the blanket. "Who is this?" she asked.

Madga finally began telling her story. Everyone fell silent to listen.

"They wanted me to help them with their newborns. They were far away, up in the mountains. I've spent many nights hunting for you after I escaped. They were so big; it was hard to get away from them."

Poma was curious. "How many men took you away?"

"Five. And they weren't men. They were women."

Everyone drew back. "Women?" They all echoed. The air was thick with disbelief. Madga's bundle started crying.

"That's why they sent five," said Arle softly.

"Yes," Madga said. "Women who needed a midwife. Their queen was expecting a baby. And they wanted me to help with the birthing. And the girls they kept, but the boys—" Madga's face screwed up into an agony of despair, and her voice rang with rage. "The boys—"

Boot-Ru took her sister into her arms as the crowd melted back so she could take her to their wagon. Poma started the fire to make tea.

Tigrax asked again, "Who is this baby?"

"Two of the women had babies after I first got there. The boy was killed immediately, and there was nothing wrong with him." Her shoulders shook as she sobbed out her story.

"When the Queen finally had her child, I was told to take it away; she never wanted to see it again. So I took him and ran. I got away. We got away." And she gently rocked the baby. "I had a goatskin of milk for him. We did just fine." Her thin smile shone through the mud on her face.

Poma knew it would take more than chamomile tea to mend these sorrows. "Tigrax, Madi needs a smoke," she said.

Tigrax looked up, and her vacant eyes snapped to the present. Quietly she went to her wagon to find her stash of hemp.

Poma had heard stories of these big women and their war-like ways. Now she saw the stories were true. It was rumored these warrior women kept the baby girls and killed the boys. Poor Madga! What a horrible time she must have had. But now they had the son of a Queen to rear. She brought Madga some tea and took the little one to her breast. He looked a bit shocked, then settled down to eating hungrily. Madga was happy to have a wet nurse for the little boy.

The men gathered around the fire outside Madga's wagon.

"The son of a Queen?" said one.

"Surely they will hunt her down," said another.

"No, this is not their way. You heard what Madi said. They kill the boy babies. They are a clan of women."

"Then how come they are having children?" said the first one. There was a low murmur and some snickering.

"I heard they came years ago and some of them mixed in with the western tribes. But they didn't get along with the Scythian women," said Arle.

"Nevertheless, I think Madga and the little one should have guards at night," said the first.

And so, although things were quiet, Madga, Boot-Ru and the new baby were given guards. Madga named the little one Tarim, and Poma nursed him for his first year. No one ever followed after Madga, but the clan was more watchful after the kidnapping.

Poma enjoyed nurturing Tarim and it gave Targitaus a small blonde brother to play with. Targitaus walked and talked quite early, and, to Poma's delight, was his father's son. She got out some of her pomegranate skins and stewed them down to make black ink and drew pictures on cow hides for the little boys. Targitaus was fascinated with his pictures. Tarim was not so connected.

When, after a few seasons, it came time for Targitaus to learn to carve wood, Tarim seemed more interested in the knife than in the wooden animals Arle taught Targitaus to make. The boys gathered herbs with their mothers and got very excited about any of the animals they saw. The graceful deer were especially wonderful, because one had to be stealthy and quiet to get a good look. The stags with their large antlers were quite impressive. Targitaus showed as much enthusiasm for the animals as Poma did with the lichen and berries she found to dye with.

One morning early, Poma, Boot-Ru and the boys were in a large grove of walnut trees, gathering nuts from the ground. The hulls made warm browns in the dye pot, and the nuts were saved for winter sweets.

"Look, Mama!" whispered Targitaus. He pointed with a stubby finger toward the adjacent meadow. Three deer moved cautiously toward the open, their heads bobbing forward with each step. One of the does sniffed the air. Satisfied, she grazed on the green steppe grass. The early morning sun cast a golden light.

Behind her was one of the biggest stags Poma had ever seen. His antlers glowed as they pointed his way forward. Targitaus, speechless, pointed again. The little boys hid behind some bushes to watch. The women stood very still. The children were of one accord in their excitement, but Poma knew when they got back to camp, Targitaus would draw what he had seen, and Tarim would count his arrows.

The Heritage

Those seasons passed quickly and peacefully and Targitaus was soon learning to work with metals. He carved fanciful animals and covered them with gold. His cunning animal forms began selling at market, and for a boy of 8 seasons, he was gaining a reputation as an artist. Tarim followed along and was patient until Targitaus seemed to ignore the younger boy and spent more time with his art. They both learned to ride horses from an early age, but Tarim took more to riding and hunting with the older boys. And so the giant steppe and surrounding misty mountains nurtured them both.

It was a happy time for Poma. When some of the women complained that the madder they found was not producing a good red as in the old days, she remembered what Lila had told her about madder.

"The madder has to be growing for at least three seasons before it can be harvested," she had said.

So Poma and the women set out to make a treasure map of where the madder grew and when it had been picked last, so they could find madder that was either virgin or had not been picked in at least three seasons, and preferably about six. The nomads loved the red dye and used it not only for clothing, but horse trappings and rugs, and other decorations for their tents. They had no way of knowing that the knowledge Poma passed along was thousands of years old. She also taught them about using an iron pot to obtain the madder purple, and it was this knowledge that spread at market time to the other tribes in the area. Soon garments of the dark brownish purple became quite the fashion. She smiled her secret smile, and felt very satisfied that she was instrumental in the conveyance of her arts.

Now and again she would dig the small tapestry out of her basket and examine the royal purple which was still the richest and most vibrant of all the purples. Some of the purple-making lichens came close to that purple, but the dye baths were small, for these kinds of lichens only grew in small patches on the rocks. She still had a great longing to find those tiny seashells and make the perfect purple robe. Then she would sigh and pack the tapestry back next to the small purple blanket, which, in 29 seasons, had faded little. She knew that Enash had long since disappeared into the future and as she stared at her mirror, occasionally she wondered as to his whereabouts. She was comforted that Arle was a good father to Targitaus, and had gained recognition in the tribe as being an excellent herdsman and shepherd. And their son was well on his way to becoming a famous artist.

On a hunting trip one fall Targitaus came home excited about a snow leopard they had seen crossing a snowy meadow, stalking the very same herd of deer the men had been hunting for two days. His eyes shown and his black curls bounced as he told about the deer, and his voice lowered as he described the leopard.

"And he moved so slowly he seemed to float over the snow like a giant fish," he said, his black eyes squinting.

Poma sat at her loom, her shuttle waiting for the story to end. She was proud of her small son, and smiled as he described the scene. "How big was the leopard?" she asked.

"Oh, he was huge!" Targitaus reached up with his small arms and stood on his toes. His eyes grew big. "And his tail was this long!" And he reached his arms out and danced in place to keep his balance.

Poma remembered back to her big snow leopard. "Did he catch the deer?"

"We didn't know how to scare him away without scaring the deer, so like father said, we all went hungry. But the next day we caught up with the deer and got two to bring home." His chest puffed out just a bit. "Mama, can I have some more ink to draw the leopard?"

"You'll have to use charcoal until I can make more ink."

And he ran off to find Tarim and some cow hides. Poma thought back to her school in the temple with a touch of nostalgia. Targitaus had a much different education, but it was one that would sustain him in this wild land of mountains and animals.

The young boys grew bold. They loved to ride with the men as they hunted for ermine and fox for the warm furs. Targitaus came back from one such foray alone, leading his horse, which had pulled up lame. He was embarrassed having to tell his story to the women and old men. Madga went out to see about the horse and Ban the old story-teller sat Targitaus down to talk by Poma's wagon.

"And how is the hunt going?" Ban said.

Targitaus was dejected. "Well enough, I suppose." He put his chin in his small hand.

Ban patted the boy on his knee. "You did the right thing by not riding that pony home. His leg may have been worse if you had."

"Will he be alright?"

"Madi will take good care of him."

After Ban was gone, Targitaus was comforted by Poma with some dried fruit and bread. "I'm glad you thought about your horse well enough to bring him home before he was too lame to walk. That was a good thing you did," Poma said.

"Mama, how come Ban always wears a yellow cloud?"

"A yellow cloud?" Poma never ceased to be amazed at this child.

"Yes, yellow. Your cloud is light purple, and Tarim's is light brown, and daddy's is green. How come Ban's is yellow?"

Poma hadn't noticed. "I suppose it's because he's so happy all the time. He's happy to tell stories and make folks laugh."

"Oh, I see. His stories are good ones, Mama."

"Your ability to see these colors around people is a good form of protection, little one. Always guard that way of seeing. And always be leery of folks with very dark auras. They may mean you harm."

Targitaus' eyes widened. "You mean like Solok?"

"Does Solok carry a dark cloud?"

"Sometimes. And sometimes it is red." He munched on his bread.

"Then it is good to be cautious."

"Cautious of what?"

Poma didn't want to frighten the young one. "Just be aware of what he is about. Sometimes people with dark or red auras can become angry. It is best to stay out of their way."

Targitaus frowned. "Should I hide?"

"No, no need to hide. Just go somewhere else and leave them alone."

"Oh." He seemed satisfied with that explanation.

"What about the white auras that don't have people in them?"

Poma's spoon stopped in mid-stir. "No people?"

"No. Just a thin white aura."

She remained as calm as she could, and carefully set her spoon down. "I think maybe those are folks who have gone to the afterworld."

"Oh, I see." Targitaus looked thoughtful for a moment, finished his milk, and then jumped down and ran out toward the herd. "I'm going to check on my horse," he called over his shoulder.

Poma smiled her secret smile, and added a motherly sigh. Later she told Tigrax of this conversation with her son.

"I was surprised. I didn't know he had this ability."

Tigrax puffed thoughtfully on her pipe. Her hair was white now in the front, but seemed to stay grey from the pipe smoke. "This is a special child, little owl. Never discourage a different way of gaining knowledge. You were very wise to tell him he would be protected by being able to read the emotions of others."

"I saw auras as a child, but I lost that ability when I got older," Poma said.

"Why do you think that is so?" Tigrax asked.

Poma was puzzled. She could only shrug.

"Where did you go to school?" Tigrax said.

"How did you know I went to school?"

Tigrax leaned forward and looked Poma in the eye. "One always knows a prize mare in a herd of ordinary horses. Besides, you have always been well-spoken and well-mannered. School does that."

Poma felt a little embarrassed. She couldn't remember learning manners in school. "Thank you, Tigrax."

"And your teacher came to me in a dream."

Poma gasped.

"He told me to wait until the appropriate time, and then give you a message. He said, 'Tell Poma to get the cobwebs out of her hat.'"

Poma was overcome. She knew at once what Enash meant. There was another poem on the bottom of the first scroll. "Why did you wait to tell me until now?"

"Because now you know, as I do, that your legacy will live on here behind us both."

"I shouldn't even ask how you knew . . ." She hugged the little shaman, who seemed now more like a sister. Tigrax had evidently known all along that Poma would soon be gone into time. The only thing the old woman seemed to want was the spiritual protection of her people.

Later that day Poma sat down with her scrolls. She cleared her mind and read the poem on the bottom of the first scroll.

> When the color comes
> You may go.
> When the white comes
> You may go.
> When blue leads to purple,
> You are there.

Whoever in the world wrote these gentle words? Poma saw clearly it was almost time for her to move on. She knew she would have no choice in the matter, the God and Goddess had work for her in another time and place. But to leave Her little Targitaus . . . With a great effort, she turned to the task of re-packing her basket.

Changing of the Guard

Screams punctuated the calm afternoon air. Poma grabbed her gorytus containing bow and arrows, and jumped down from the wagon to find everyone in camp running toward Narmet's wagons. The chief, sick for days, had stayed behind from the hunt, and now there was a great commotion coming from his tent. Narmet's shrieking wives wrung their hands and beat their breasts.

One of the younger ones stepped forward. "Narmet is dead!" She said. Her face revealed fear instead of grief.

The women gathered outside the chieftain's tents, and the mourning continued in earnest. Poma watched as the women rocked back and forth, their faces contorted in grief, their chests pounded by small fists. She knew it to be a show of respect, but it was the howl of terror that touched her heart. These wives were now faced with their own deaths, to be buried with their husband, as was the custom. It was only these howls of fear that could match the sadness she felt at having to leave her son behind.

Poma and Ban sat together at the edge of the crowd. They were the only ones who saw Narmet's youngest wife ride off from the far edge of the herd and disappear down the steppe. Poma looked at Ban, saw his wise old smile, and realized that part of the burial custom included, in some instances, riding away for one's very life.

Poma and Madga took care of the younger children while Boot-Ru did the sad search through her herbs to prepare for the burial. The men came back from the hunt to the howls of the women and soon the preparations were underway. Solok dashed about and barked orders at everyone. Three of his friends followed close behind him, reinforcing his shouts with gruff growls of their own.

Poma saw Tigrax take him to one side. "We are all sad about Narmet's death. Everyone knows what to do; what will happen . . ."

Solok glared at her. "Narmet will have a grand burial, and no one is going to stand in my way." Solok already had Narmet's gold scepter and waved it around like a sword.

"We all know what to do." Tigrax said.

"He should be buried in the best robes, and with all his horses and wives!" Solok shouted.

Poma moved closer.

"Of course, of course," Tigrax said. "That will be done; just leave it all to us. We will bury him . . ." She waved her arms around in frustrated description.

"And I will become chief, since he had no sons."

Tigrax drew herself up and wrapped her red shawl closer. "You know perfectly well it will be a vote of the council that elects a new chieftain," she said.

"I am doing away with the council," he snarled. The old woman's mouth fell open, then clamped shut. Her brows shot up and she stepped forward as her tiny hands became fists.

Poma grabbed the startled Tigrax by the shoulder and led her away. "Don't worry, dear, we'll tell Arle and the other men. This young one is deranged," she whispered. "He's been too concerned with himself since he was very young." Poma ensconced the angry Tigrax with Madga and the children and went in search of Arle.

She found Solok first, took a deep breath, and tried to confront him before the men could deal with him. He was sharpening his knives by his wagon. The blade he was working on flashed in the late afternoon sun. His eyes seemed to flash at her as well.

"I want to talk to you about Tigrax." She tried to maintain a soft voice. Solok did not even look up. "She's an old woman now, and . . ."

"Can't you see I'm busy?"

Poma tucked a loose curl behind her ear. "You can listen for just a moment. I won't take long."

Solok's eyes narrowed. He laid his polishing cloth to one side. The rank smell of rancid oil wafted her way. It was the smell of battle. "What is it then?"

She pulled herself up to her full height, which was only a bit taller than this stocky young man who would be chief. "As I was saying, Tigrax is an old woman now, and she has taught me the art of the shaman so this tribe will be protected after she's gone."

"Protected?" Solok's stance became more mushroom-like, even with his arms akimbo. "Protected, is it? And who is it that protects the shaman?"

His bushy brows lowered. "Who is it who protects you?" He pointed at her with his long knife.

Poma did not expect such venom. Just for an instant it was quiet enough to hear a bell from the midst of the herd. She looked him in the eye. "We need to work together for the good of everyone," she began.

He sneered at her, snatched up his rancid oil cloth and continued polishing. She could see this was going nowhere. "Solok . . ." she implored.

"Be gone, woman, go back to your pots."

Poma felt the heat rise into her face. She stomped off, deliberately in the opposite direction, away from the glowing fires. She saw Arle cutting trees in a small grove and took another deep breath, so she wouldn't be growling and hissing at her husband.

The men were digging a huge hole in the earth to build a new kurgan for their chief and his entourage. The trees were to be used as timber supports for the large tomb. Poma took Arle to one side. "Solok is causing trouble. He says he is going to be chieftain and do away with the council."

Arle's face registered disgust. He lay down his ax. "Couldn't he even wait until Narmet has a proper burial?"

Poma agreed. "He was very rude to Tigrax," she said.

Arle's mouth became determined. He picked his ax up again. "We'd better put a stop to this right now." He gathered the other men, told them the latest turn of events, and they all strode into the camp, an angry force.

Poma followed the men back to the camp, and helped to round up the children and put them in the wagons. She and the other women watched as the men gathered.

"Solok!"

The mangy young man appeared by the fires, a knife in each hand. "You cannot take what is rightfully mine!" he shouted. His three friends gathered behind him, hands on sword hilts. Some of the animals sensed the confusion and moved away from the wagons in a small cloud of dust.

Arle moved closer. "Nothing is rightfully anybody's until the votes are cast."

"I'm abolishing the council," Solok shouted in a rage. His face was red and he brandished the knives about. One of the young men behind him walked backwards toward his wagon.

"The last one to try that ended up in the Taklimakan," said one man. A murmur of agreement swept through the crowd.

"Get him!" Someone shouted. Solok backed away slowly at first, and then turned to run.

The men gave chase. As he ran past the fire, Poma stuck her foot out in one stabbing motion. Solok tripped and fell into the fire. His head cracked with a sharp thud into the iron cauldron full of indigo, which spilled all over his head. With one short shriek, the shaggy beast was dead. The smell of burnt flesh arose in the still air. Poma watched in horror as Solok's contorted face gradually turned blue and his brown hair turned black from the dye. His fat, limp body almost completely covered the fire, and what little wood left burning was put out by the last of the contents of the cauldron. The steam was the only thing left moving. Solok's other two friends ran to the herd to find their horses.

Arle ran over to Poma and helped her up. "Are you alright?" he said.

Her first thought was of the blue man from the indigo pot in her dream of so very long ago. Was this a fulfillment of that dream?

"I—I guess so. I didn't mean to—I only meant to stop him. I didn't mean to kill him." She couldn't keep back the tears.

"It is done. We probably would have killed him anyway." Arle held Poma close until she stopped shaking.

The next day, Narmet and Solok were buried together with the remaining two wives and six of his best horses. The council met, and Boot-Ru and Poma tried to keep Tigrax distracted. They sat near the wagons, spinning. It helped pass the time.

"What did they think?" Tigrax said. "What did Arle say?" Tigrax leaned close to Poma so any gossip could be shared.

"I don't know. But Arle's been chosen more than once to represent them. I'm very proud of him," Poma said.

"Arle is a natural leader. He's calm and just. And he's a compassionate person. He will be a good chief," Boot-Ru said.

The spinning was not progressing very well as the women waited. The air was filled with tension.

"What's keeping them?" Tigrax got up and started pacing up and down in front of the other two. Poma was getting a worried look from Boot-Ru when a mighty shout came from the council circle. The men had proclaimed Arle as their next chieftain. Then the celebration began.

Poma ran to kiss her beaming husband. "Chief Arle!" she said, smiling at him.

He grinned his sheepish grin. "It's a big responsibility. But I will do my best to protect my people."

Their feasting and drinking and dancing went on far into the night.

It soon became time to turn the herd southward. Targitaus and Tarim were old enough to help with the animals. Poma was finally an expert with the oxen now, and guided them down the big steppe. It was an early fall and the leaves had turned. The nights grew chill.

One evening, as the council met to determine the path to take the next day, the women sat by the fire. Poma pulled her shawl around her.

Tigrax, pipe in hand, sat down next to her. "Tell me, child, have you found some new goals for yourself?"

Poma had, indeed, been thinking about the next move into time. "I guess it depends on where I end up, and what the world there has to offer," she said. She thought for a moment, and then shared one of her inner-most dreams. "I'd love to find my mother," she said softly.

"Yes, it is time for that to happen."

"How do you know?"

Tigrax took Poma's chin in her hand. Her fingers were warm on Poma's face. She whispered to her through the smoke. "Because I'm your grandmother."

Poma could not believe what she was hearing. Tears welled up. Her heart pounded. She searched Tigrax's face. "My grandmother?"

Tigrax grinned at her. "Yes, owlet."

Poma fell in her arms. Their embrace held all the longing of history: to belong, to love and be loved. Poma looked at her face again. "Then how—Then why—Aren't you going somewhere too?"

"No, child. When your tasks are done, the Goddess gives you the choice of where you want to be to live out your life."

Poma understood why Tigrax had chosen these people. They had a simple way of life, they laughed a lot, and the energy and movement in their art spoke of their keen perception of their world. "Tell me what my mother looks like."

"She looks so much like you I thought when you first came it was her. If you look in your mirror, you will see her."

They hugged again and talked until the fire was gone. Poma's future seemed brighter to her than it ever had before.

Market time came and went, and the tribe prospered. By this time, Estwynd had fathered enough foals to populate the horse herd with a good stock of big, beautiful horses. Some were traded every fall, and the herds over the entire steppe were blessed with these dignified animals.

Targitaus' art was such that his reputation was almost as widely admired. He secretly made his mother a small knife with a gold handle in the shape of a crouching snow leopard. Poma was thrilled, and packed it away in her basket.

Tigrax got forgetful. In one of her more lucid moments, she gave Poma a small, fat pouch of gold. The tribe was wealthy, she said, and wouldn't miss it. And so Poma's basket was quite a treasure trove. Aside from the gold and the knife, the small purple blanket had been packed into its accustomed place beside the scrolls and her poem for Enash. The Egyptian tapestry was still like new. Poma had used Lila's spindle, and she now returned it to the basket, and added her mirror and comb.

She wore her purple distaff on her wrist, handy for spinning in spare moments.

To Arle's delight, they made love almost every night, and Poma made sure Arle would never forget her. When he slept, she would shed a few tears for this gentle person with whom she had spent the last ten seasons.

She rode with him to round up strays that winter at the foot of some very tall mountains. Madga minded the boys while they were gone. Every time she was separated from Targitaus now, Poma gave him a big hug and told him how proud she was of him, and how much she loved him. He took all this love and attention in a stoic manner, as would any boy of nine seasons. She always looked deeply in his eyes and memorized everything about that small face and the black, curly locks which surrounded it. She thought about that beautiful little face as she followed Arle into the mountains. The snow had been excessive that year, and the horses had difficulty making their way across the large meadows. At the base of the mountains, they were careful not to make any sharp noises, for fear of starting an avalanche.

The forest at the base of the mountain was not so cautious, however, and a large branch snapped and broke and fell to the ground in a shower of sparkling snow. That one snap was all the snow needed, and the next thing Poma knew, she and Estwynd were again running for their lives. Arle was safe in the trees ahead. She could not hear anything but a gigantic roar, and then it was on top of them. Poma felt like a tiny vegetable being stirred in a giant cauldron of stew. The sound was strangely dimmed by the darkness and finality of a mountain's winter shifting with such great speed down the slope that it could not be outrun by man or beast. She lay in the suffocating darkness and cold, thinking more and more how nice it would be to sleep. She could not feel Estwynd anywhere. She smelled the dying gardenias. Just as her uneven breathing consumed the last of the air around her, the familiar white light surrounded her. She was moving on. The beautiful face of the Goddess appeared, and the rushing waters called her name. "Poma!" The Goddess took her hand once more. The familiar purple light surrounded her. Time snapped. She smiled her secret smile, and her hand was dropped.

Arle mourned for his beautiful wife and in time took Boot-Ru and Madga as wives. He ruled peacefully for many years and was buried alone in a beautiful valley overlooking the great Taklimakan. Boot-Ru and Madga escaped the usual funeral and became innkeepers on the northern Silk Road. Targitaus was the most famous artist and shaman of his day. Some gold pieces like his can be seen in the Hermitage Museum in St. Petersburg. Tarim became a great warrior and he and his family moved to the far north. The Vikings may some day trace their lineage to him. Tigrax wandered off into the forest and disappeared. Batu and Anad traveled the Silk Road far to the west and lived a long life at the edge of a great sea. The ghost of Ban the story-teller still haunts the misty Tien Shan. Poma and Estwynd were said to have died in the avalanche, and her basket mysteriously vanished.

Part IV

The Silk Road

c. 1447A.D., Japan

"Before the end of my journey
may I reach within myself
the one which is the all,
leaving the outer shell
to float away with the drifting multitude
upon the current of chance and change
—Rabindranath Tagore

The House of Yakimoto

Poma felt cold water drip on her face. She opened her eyes and looked up. Snow melted from a tree branch and plopped all around her. The meager sun shone bravely on her own private snow bank. She shivered, sat up, and looked around. A narrow creek rushed down a mountainside, creating a noise that almost covered the sounds of children playing. The pungent smell of cooking fires drifted in the air. A small, peaceful village climbed up the far hillside. Small wooden houses, framed by gardens lying fallow in the pale winter sunlight, sat snug against the hills. The smoke from their fires matched the sharp rise of the scraggily pine trees.

The children saw her first. Gradually, people emerged from the houses, moved slowly down the hill, and lined up along the road to stare at Poma. They reminded her of the Mongols she had seen at market, but their faces were generally longer and features sharper. A short old man, hunched over a walking stick, pushed through them and took a few faltering steps toward her. When he spoke, his pointed beard emphasized his words. She could not understand him. He squinted at her face for a moment, and then spoke again. This time she understood.

"Are you lost?" he said.

Poma was used to adjusting quickly. "I am on my way to the city," she said. City folk would perhaps not be quite so curious.

The old man squinted up at the sun. "You'll not make it today. You must stay here. This is the village of Otoma. Do you have a horse?"

Poma's smile faded. Where was Estwynd? "I think he must have strayed . . ." she said, looking around. Why was he not here? Wasn't he going to be with her here? Her heart sank. At least her basket lay under the tree next to the snow bank.

"You will stay at the house of Yakimoto." It seemed to be decided, so Poma picked up her basket and followed the old man up the road. The whole entourage followed, curious. They paused at a small shrine by the side of the road, and each one in turn bowed to a squat stone statue, and seemed to recite some sort of prayer. The old man continued up the road. When Poma passed by the shrine without stopping, she found herself surrounded by the murmuring people.

The old man came back down the road. "They think you are not grateful to the ancestors," he said.

Poma's heart was pounding. Would these people attack her? She thought back to the three civilizations she had experienced. All three had venerated the elderly, the ancestors. "I—I don't have ancestors buried here." She said. She looked around. Most of the faces did not change expression. What were they thinking? He repeated what she said to them. Very slowly, the way parted so she could follow the old man up the road once more. She decided the safest way from now on in this place was to be much more respectful of whatever shrine she found herself near. They reached the last house under the hill. The old man said something to two women on the wide porch, bowed to Poma, and turned to make his way down the road.

Poma was afraid this old man was the only one who spoke her language. "Excuse me, sir. Can you tell me, who is Yakimoto, and which way is the city?" she asked.

The old man stopped only long enough to bow once more. "I am Yakimoto, and we will show you the way to the city tomorrow." He bowed again and was off down the road. The neighbors returned to their homes.

Poma turned and smiled at the women. They returned her smile with bows of their own. *If nothing else, these folks are polite,* thought Poma. She was invited to sit on a small mat on the porch, where tea was being prepared. More family gathered on the porch. She watched in awe as the tea was carefully measured and the water brought to just the right temperature. A beautiful white porcelain pot with small matching cups appeared from within the house. The set was painted with delicate pink blossoms. Soon everyone sipped the bitter tea. It warmed her as she watched the family. The women wore dark blue gowns of finely woven wool. Poma's baggy red pants were different, but no one stared at them. They seemed more interested in her face. Almost everyone had a sash that appeared to be silk. The children wore colorful pants and coats and the little girls wore braids. The boys had short hair. The two youngest of the children stood shyly behind an old woman who sat in a special nook by herself, spinning with a small spindle supported in a tiny wooden cup in her lap. The thread was the finest Poma had ever seen. The sound of—what was it? Mice, perhaps, chewing—wafted through, as soft as a breeze, but no breeze was blowing.

The children shouted. Poma looked up to see Estwynd in his gold mask and trappings, calmly munching on the part of the Yakimoto garden that held the winter vegetables. She jumped up, spilled her tea, and ran down the steps to the garden. "Estwynd! Oh, Estwynd, no! How could you?" The big horse hung his head. Poma was so embarrassed. One of the women came running up, took the reins away from Poma and led the animal toward a small shed on the other side of the house.

"Oh, I am so sorry!" Poma said. No one seemed to hear her. They were enthralled by the appearance of the horse. The trappings and mask seemed to astound them. The children's eyes were big. The level of talking spiked into shouts and some of the neighbors returned to the last house on the hill to behold the big grey horse with the gold mask. They watched as Poma took all the trappings and put them near her basket. How happy she was to have her old companion with her. Some of the immobile expressions had turned to smiles.

The evening passed with much bowing and a meal of fish, rice, and winter vegetables, mostly squashes. Poma was treated as an honored guest, and was later ushered to a tiny room with a mat for sleeping. Her bed had wool and silk covers, and was quite comfortable. The night brought, in addition to the soft chewing sound, the sound of a band of crickets interrupted only by the soft voices of this nice family. Poma would always be grateful to the house of Yakimoto for its hospitality.

When Poma awoke, someone was watching her. She looked around carefully at the bare room. Opaque screens kept her privacy. Her blue shawl was over her feet, ready for the chill of the night mountain air. Two small forms were silhouetted against the morning light. Smells of cooked trout came from the small kitchen on the porch. Female murmurs emanated from the porch, completing the peacefulness of the sturdy little house. She could still hear the soft undercurrent of whatever was chewing on something. Rising to one elbow, she explored the two small forms. She was amused by their curiosity. She remembered Targitaus and Tarim at about that age, and ached for home. Suddenly the silhouettes bobbled and disappeared as high, childish laughter crashed through the sunlit hallways. Smiling, Poma reached for her shawl and slid the screens open to a new day on the mountain.

The small children hid behind their grandmother as Poma approached the kitchen shelter. The stoic grandmother acknowledged her presence only by adding a small trout to the others in the pan. The children eyed her curiously as she bowed to the grandmother and the other women on the sunny porch. Bowing seemed to be the major way of greeting people, and was refreshing in its civility. The women were busily engaged with a fire and a large pot containing silk cocoons which were being carefully unwound in the boiling water. Were they killing the inhabitants of those cocoons? The silk formed long, winding threads, as thin as spider threads shining in the sunlight. Poma watched with wonder as the silk was wound into a single strand on a small wooden reel. The silk was now ready to spin into threads for weaving, as soon as it dried. Off to one side in a small room there were large flat trays with small compartments. Poma heard the distinct munching sounds coming from the room. To her amazement, the trays were alive with beautiful, translucent green worms, busily eating from a spread of broken dark green leaves. Poma examined a pile of cocoons. So this is where the silk came from! It was the worms. Some of them were even making their cocoons, extruding the silk from their bodies, as their heads wove back and forth in a cadenced figure eight. What a wonder!

The children stared at her as she sat with the women to eat of the fish wrapped in cabbage. A strange sauce pot sat at the grandmother's right hand as she deftly scooped out a dark liquid and dribbled it over the small package of breakfast. Poma obediently ate a few bites and was delighted by the tangy flavor.

Mr. Yakimoto appeared, bowed to the old woman presiding over the breakfast, and took his place on the porch where he was served his meal. Poma sensed that conversation was not allowed until everyone had eaten.

After much bowing and ceremony, Poma was finally on her way with Estwynd down the road toward the city. She had stowed the horse's mask in one of her robes. Yakimoto rode ahead.

The mountains plunged quickly to the sea, and Poma could smell the salt air. It brought back memories of the night on the Mediterranean and the ship wreck. Although the climate was mild, the wind was sharp. The trail wound back and forth, lower and lower to the sea and the small port city at the bottom.

Yakimoto stopped and gave Poma a letter to carry to a friend who spoke her language. "Her name is Kim Su. She will help you find your way," he said. "This is a map to her house." He bowed and turned his horse back up the path toward the trees and the mountains.

The Teahouse

Poma felt the urge to stop Mr. Yakimoto once more and have him explain to her more clearly where she was to go. But he had done enough. She thanked him and took a deep breath. She looked closely at the map and path ahead. With all the steepness and winding down the mountain, it would take well into the day to reach the little port. The boats were flecks on the blue water.

Here she was at another crossroads. What was her destination? She thought about Enash and the purple, both so far away. She must look ahead now. Being all alone in the world seemed like a big responsibility. All through her life there were people who loved her, people she had taught things, and who had taught her. Where would Estwynd take her next? Almost as if her thoughts were blowing in the breeze to be inhaled by the big grey, he started off down the path without being directed.

"Yes, go, big fellow. We will find Kim Su. She may have some answers for us. We will get to Canaan this time. No one will stop us."

And so of one mind, the horse and his precious cargo headed down the long trail. At the bottom of the hill there stretched farm lands and small farm houses, and big sheds. Poma came to another roadside shrine, and stopped to pay her religious respects to what God she knew not, but it didn't matter. It was a simple thing to do to keep the peace in this new place. As she mounted the horse again, a strong breeze came up and with it the familiar sour scent of indigo. She rode past a large shed, and the stench was almost overpowering. The smell of indigo was unlike any other, and in the past it was tolerated because it meant that Poma would soon have a nice batch of blue yarn. This smell was so pungent she could only think that someone wanted to paint the entire world blue. Perhaps this would be a good opportunity to buy some of the dyestuff to use in trade on her journey. In any case, she could use it herself.

She pulled Estwynd up under a tree and jumped down and walked toward the big shed. A small woman emerged, her hand shading her eyes from the sun. The woman spoke to her, and when Poma asked her if she had indigo to sell, the woman frowned. Poma reached in her pocket for a small amount of gold, and the meaning became clear. The woman motioned her inside where the indigo was processed. As her eyes became accustomed to the dark, the smell of fermenting indigo leaves was at its height. Great vats, recessed into the ground, held the rotting leaves and water. There were long shelves on the other side of the shed which stretched out into the sun, where balls of indigo were drying. Poma could tell this dyestuff was not from the woad plant, the kind of indigo she had used all her life, but rather an indigo which was much more powerful. The woman pointed to some wooden boxes which held the dried dark blue indigo balls. Poma held out a bit of gold, and the lady pointed to the boxes and held up four fingers. Poma tried not to show her amazement. All that indigo for just that tiny bit of gold? She knew she could get ten times as much gold back if she were to take this indigo to market. Of course, she told herself, she didn't know how far away market was or how much the prices might have changed. She decided to take the plunge.

Poma paid the smiling woman, who bowed, and motioned at two young men to load the boxes of treasure into two large bags to tie onto either side of the horse's saddle. She bowed to the woman, which brought more bowing all around, and was off down the path, satisfied with her purchase. Now she would find Kim Su and ask how many days it would take her to get to market.

Poma led Estwynd down the narrow streets. The city of Tottori was filled with people of all descriptions, most of whom spoke their native Japanese. Poma could better understand the very small scattering of occidentals. There were the older and sometimes better educated among the Japanese who spoke her language, but they were few. It seemed to Poma that the diversity here lay not in peoples from differing lands, but in occupational differences. The more serious merchants and staid-looking housewives mingled with roaming bands of sailors and stoic monks. The thread which held this disparate group together was the reason they were all there: the sea. The air was at once filled with the smell of the fish market and the fisherman's voices hawking their wares. Small carts of vegetables completed the scene near the waterfront. Along the roads leading down to the water were shops with treasures from over the sea: fabrics and jewelry, and all manner of household goods. Poma sensed this wonderful market was here year-round, for it was permanent, and there were no nomads on the outskirts of the city. She wanted to visit all the little shops, but the first business at hand was finding a place to stay.

Following Mr. Yakimoto's map, she finally arrived at her destination. Kim Su was the proprietress of a busy waterfront teahouse. A wide porch overlooked the harbor. People sat on small mats by squat tables, sipping tea and eating cakes. Poma tied Estwynd to a pole just inside the large gate to the teahouse. As she approached the establishment, she saw the porch lined with shoes. She deposited her deerskin boots alongside the more delicate shoes, and was greeted by a smiling young girl who ushered her inside for tea.

"I have come in search of Kim Su," she said. One could not tell by studying her features if this girl was oriental or not. But she understood Poma.

"Follow me, please," she said.

Poma followed the girl to the kitchen in the center of the building. As they approached, Poma could hear a woman shouting at someone. The girl waited until the tirade was over, and then ventured through the door.

The woman, about Poma's age, was large and raw-boned. She had round dark eyes and her fair skin and brown hair was in sharp contrast to the Japanese girls in the teahouse.

Her voice was still in battle mode. "Yes, Nik, what is it?"

Nik pointed to Poma. "She wants to see you." She said, and dodged behind Poma and disappeared.

"Yes?" said the irritated woman.

Poma pushed the letter from Mr. Yakimoto at her. "Are you Kim Su?"

The woman frowned at the letter. She read a few lines, and then looked up to examine Poma more closely.

Her face relaxed a little. "Yes, I am Kim Su. When can you start?"

"Excuse me?" replied Poma.

"When can you start work? That's what you want, isn't it?"

Poma was faced with another lightening-fast decision. Mr. Yakimoto evidently thought she wanted to find work. "Well—yes." Then she added quickly, "I know the herbs, and I can cook, and—and—"

The larger woman cut through to the crux of the situation. "I need a scullery maid," she said. "You can have meals here, and the girls sleep upstairs. I'll expect you to be ready to work tomorrow morning. What is your name?"

"Poma."

"Alright, Poma. Nik will show you where to put your things."

"Is there a place for my horse?"

"Horse? You have a horse?"

"Yes. He's right outside."

Kim Su glanced through the window in the narrow hallway. "Hmmm. There's a stable just down the street. Nik will show you."

"Thank you, Kim Su."

"Call me Kim," she said, and finally smiled at Poma.

Nik and Poma took Estwynd to the large stable next to the teahouse. A big man, filling the doorway, met them as they approached.

"Poma, this is Ashi. He is Kim Su's brother."

Poma bowed to Ashi, thinking to herself that Ashi was almost as tall as Enash. He also had brown hair and fair skin.

"Hello, Poma. This is a beautiful horse you have here."

"Thank you, sir. He's been with me for a long time."

"Bring him in here."

In addition to stalls for horses, the stable housed small living quarters for Ashi. As Poma unloaded and unsaddled the horse and made him comfortable, she noticed a large piece of paper on the wall. It appeared to be a map, and down in the lower left-hand corner was an icon of an Egyptian Pharaoh. The spaces that symbolized the seas held large, ferocious-looking dragons.

Poma was drawn over to the wall and stared, astonished, at the map. "Ashi, excuse me. Is this a map of this land?"

"This is a map of the world." He pointed with a stocky finger at the right-hand side of the map. "This is our land. You are here," he said, pointing to the west coast of the Japanese island.

Poma tried to contain her excitement. "And where is Marakanda?" she asked.

"Marakanda?" Ashi frowned. "I don't know." They both scoured the map.

"Then where is Canaan?"

"Canaan? Let me see. Here is Constantinople," he said, pointing.

"And is this Egypt?" she said, drawing him away.

"I think so. And where are you from?" he said.

"I've traveled so much, I'm not sure where it is on this map," she said. He eyed her curiously.

"How many days is it to Egypt?" she asked.

It was his turn to look astonished. "Days? Oh, no, dear Poma, it is more like years." And he turned and went out of the stable, shaking his head.

Years? "It couldn't be . . ." and she felt the tears stinging. She looked over at Estwynd. He seemed to be watching her. She ran over and threw her arms around his neck. "Oh, Estwynd, whatever should we do?" The big horse nudged her with his nose. "We've only got a short time," she whispered. "We must leave here soon." Oh, how she wished for some sort of home. Perhaps if she found Enash—

She forked some hay into Estwynd's stall, and then Nik helped Poma carry the indigo up to her room. She was delighted to have a small room to herself. She decided to go to work that day. Nik showed her what was expected of her in her job. The teahouse filled up quickly with men for afternoon tea. She worked hard to keep up with the washing of tea cups and pots and the dishes which held the small cakes. When the teahouse empted out, Nik and Poma cleaned up the kitchen and then went for a walk along the waterfront.

"You came along just in time. Kim Su was in bad need of help," Nik said. "The last girl we had ran off with a Korean sailor.

"Korean?" asked Poma.

"Yes. He was very handsome, with curly hair. She regarded him as a way out."

"Way out?" Poma echoed.

"Well, she didn't like to work much, and Kim Su was always yelling at her. Kim Su is a good lady, but she likes to yell a lot."

Poma felt uneasy. "Does she yell at you?"

"Oh, once in a while. I just keep out of her way."

Poma and Nik stood on the beach watching the sunset. The orange light made a path right to their feet, and the big sun sliced through a dark strip of cloud, and out again, and then disappeared below the horizon. It appeared as if the sun had set twice. The women made their way back to the teahouse, whose orange lanterns glowed a warm welcome. Poma lay on her bed and listened as the teahouse filled up once more. Someone was strumming on some kind of stringed instrument. It had been a long day. Poma fell into a heavy sleep.

The snow leopard sat on Mr. Yakimoto's porch, his head weaving about, spinning a blue cocoon snugly about himself. Poma tried to warn him he would be killed, but he wouldn't listen to her. She let him finish his cocoon and it was suddenly small enough to fit in her pocket, so she put him in there, to be safe.

Nik was shaking her shoulder. The dream faded slightly. *The snow leopard, spinning a cocoon?* Evidently the part of her life that held the snow leopard should not be forgotten. She should keep the snow leopard close to her heart because she needed him for balance. Now he was safe in a cocoon. Strange. It was still dark, but it was time to go to work.

Ramatsu

Poma and Nik cleaned the kitchen and all the dishes from the night before, and made ready for the day. Poma worked very hard. She surely didn't want Kim Su to yell at her. At the end of the first moon, Nik took to her bed with a fever.

"Poma, I need you to serve tea today," Kim Su said. And she proceeded to teach Poma the intricacies of the tea ceremony. Poma learned quickly and was soon a very popular server. Kim Su hired a new scullery maid, and Nik became well enough to join Poma and the other tea servers.

One evening an old customer, a sea captain, came to the teahouse and saw Poma serving tea. He immediately appeared to be intrigued by the beautiful foreign woman.

"Poma, Ramatsu is watching you," Nik whispered.

"Who is Ramatsu?" Poma asked.

"The one over there with the lady in red," Nik said.

Poma glanced where Nik was looking. There was, indeed, a lady in red, adorned in gold and pearls, accompanied by a big, gruff-looking man dressed in a mode of wealth, all in black. Two burly men who had come in with them stood to one side, arms crossed, watching the crowd. Ramatsu's eyes followed Poma's every move. Poma had seen men stare at her before, but never with such intensity. He hailed her over to his table. Poma approached with a pot of tea and two small cups on a tray. She was surprised when this Japanese man knew to speak in her language. She almost withered under his gaze.

"You are new here. What is your name?"

"Poma." Her voice didn't seem to work right under such scrutiny.

"Well, Poma, the spring this year is more beautiful because you are here with us."

She had never heard such flowery language. It was strange, coming from one so rough looking.

"Will you have fruit or cakes tonight?" Poma asked.

"We will have both. And bring honey for the tea, if you will."

Poma bowed and quickly made her way back to the kitchen.

Kim Su already had some oranges prepared, and added the nut cakes and honey to a tray. "Take especially good care of Ramatsu and his wife," she said. "They are good customers." Poma hurried back with the food.

Ramatsu had many small smile lines around his bright eyes. "I have heard you came here from the mountains with a very fine-looking horse," he said. His wife kept her eyes lowered.

Poma busied herself with the service of the food. "I was unaware that my reputation was so widespread," she replied.

"Modesty and westerners usually do not complete one another."

Poma could feel her face flush. She could not tell at that moment how much of that was embarrassment and how much was anger.

Her blush only served to pique his interest further. His smile lines now accompanied a slight squint. "Thank you for the tea, Miss Poma."

Poma bowed slightly and moved away. She noticed the two burly men watching her dispassionately.

"That's his ship," whispered Nik, and pointed at the largest boat in the calm harbor. The orange sunset cast shadows from the tall masts onto the dock by the side of the polished decks.

"Is he a fisherman?" Poma asked.

Nik's eyes got big. "Oh, my, no. He rules the biggest pirate family on the coast. His ships are all over the seas."

"A pirate?"

"Yes. He fights with the Chinese and always wins. They say he is very wealthy."

"Isn't that illegal?"

Nik laughed. "Who's going to stop him?"

That gave Poma pause to think. Greed and power. It was the way of the world all down through time. She sighed. That night, the seagulls were circling. And the air grew thick. It was hard to sleep. Poma turned over and over on her small bed. A strange vibration seemed to have invaded the peace of this place.

Early the next morning, Poma was awakened by a series of loud thuds. The horses were kicking their stalls. She and Nik jumped up and went down the stairs. The air was heavy and unseasonably warm. Everything was too still. Song birds were quiet and even the water seemed too calm.

Poma felt uneasy, but did not know why. She stopped and looked around. The sun seemed unnaturally red. A few thin, creamy clouds hung overhead. Seagulls, usually decorating the rooftops like statues, soared above the harbor. They flew in screeching circles, and then flocked toward the hills above the city. They made the only noise of the morning aside from the uneasy horses. Poma noticed the fishnets hanging from the dock were shivering. What was happening?

As they ran for the stable, Poma first heard a low rumble and then felt the ground rolling underneath her. Her stomach lurched and fear clutched at her heart as she fell to the ground. The earth shifted and then shook. The teahouse groaned like a dying man, wrenched one way and then the opposite, and collapsed completely. Nik reached for Poma and they clung together in terror as the shaking earth first destroyed all the buildings on the waterfront and then went to work on the senses of the survivors.

It was over. Poma could not focus. She coughed from the dust which rose from the ruins. The only movements were from the horses, who galloped down the beach. The teahouse and all the buildings that used to stand there were completely destroyed. Breakfast fires grew larger, fueled by the wooden ruins. She could hear the moans of people trapped by debris.

"Nik, we need to find Kim Su and Ashi and—and all the other girls. Oh, God—" and the tears streamed down her face.

"Nik?" The youngster was shaking uncontrollably. Poma took her by the shoulders. "Nik, look at me!" She finally made eye contact. "We've got to find everyone." Poma got up and got Nik to her feet, and they started the impossible task of moving boards and peering under timbers for anyone alive. Pieces of clothing hung from the ruins like ragged flags, symbols of a new and horrible state of being.

A second shock came with a rumble and some of the wreckage shifted. Nik screamed. Kim Su had been killed by a large pillar. "Mama, oh Mama!" It was the first that Poma knew that the two were related. She took Nik in her arms and held her as she sobbed.

Some of the survivors from the town arrived to help. Soon Ashi's body was found under the debris of the stable. Because the horses had escaped, he was considered a hero for setting them free. Poma found the map, folded it up and tucked it in her pocket. They continued to dig for the other girls. Most of them were dead, but two were badly injured, and were carried away by relatives.

When the third aftershock came, Poma was amazed to see the horses returning up the beach toward the harbor.

That night the survivors built fires on the beach and slept in the open. It seemed to be the only safe place. By the end of the next day,

Poma had found her basket and the indigo boxes. Estwynd was safe and put in a temporary enclosure. Funeral pyres were everywhere. There were bundles of food divided among the survivors.

"Nik, we have to go. We have seen to your dead. There is nothing left for us here." Nik looked at her with a blank face.

"Come on, dear," she prodded. Nik got up, but just bowed her head. Poma would have to take charge of this child.

As she packed up the horse, Ramatsu appeared on the beach. "Miss Poma, where are you off to?" he asked.

"Just away from here," she replied.

"You are a woman of strength and purpose. I have a business proposition for you."

Poma cinched up the last strap holding her precious cargo and stopped to look squarely at the grizzled pirate. "What kind of proposition?" she asked, frowning.

His black eyes pierced hers solidly. "I have a nine-year-old son. He needs a governess. You are obviously from a good family and well educated. Please come aboard my ship and work for me."

Poma looked down the beach at the ocean waves. She glanced up the hill at the devastated city. "And where are you going?" she asked.

"We have a safe harbor in the Korea Bay," he replied.

Poma studied his face. He seemed sincere. She hesitated. Then she reached in her pocket. "Show me on this map where that is." She shoved the map at him.

His brows rose only slightly. "Right here." He pointed with a squat finger at a point on the opposite coast. "We won't come back for another year."

This was the way to the great China. Poma took a deep breath. She didn't have to reveal her plans and dreams to this man. "Alright. We accept."

"We?"

"I don't go without Nik or my horse."

"Oh, I can't take any extra . . ."

"Nik and the horse, or we head—ah,—North—right now."

Ramatsu squinted at her for only a moment. "Alright then. We leave at early tide in the morning. We'll travel up the coast for provisions, and then cross the sea. You and Nik will have your own quarters aboard ship. Your horse must share with two others. My wife unfortunately died in the quake. My son, Himiko, will travel with me from now on."

"Thank you, Ramatsu."

"Mmm," he said, his face becoming passive. "And thank you, dear Miss Poma." He scowled at Nik only slightly, and then strode back to his ship.

The next morning, Poma and Nik ensconced Estwynd in his stall aboard the ship and found their small cabin. Nik had been quiet since the earthquake, but now, as they made preparations to set sail, she broke down and cried.

Poma took her in her arms. "There, there, little one. You go ahead and cry."

Nik sobbed out some more of her story. "My mama and my uncle were all I had. We had no grandmothers or grandfathers alive; there was no one. What am I to do? All my mother taught me was how to clean and cook." And she cried some more.

"How old are you, dear?" asked Poma.

"I am 15 years old." She looked at Poma with searching eyes.

"You and I will stay together," said Poma. "Some day we will find a new place to live. In the meantime, I can be your Auntie Poma." As she kissed Nik's forehead she remembered when she was not too much older, how Boot-Ru and Madga had taken her in.

Nik's tears turned from sorrow to gratefulness. "Oh, thank you, Poma. I'll try to be a good traveler." Poma squeezed her new charge.

The China Sea

Then it was time to meet Himiko. He was small for his age and had to be prodded from behind his father. He examined Poma with a great deal of suspicion. His small mouth turned down and he folded his arms in silent but brave mistrust.

"Hello, Himiko. Are you excited about the big voyage?" Poma remembered another nine-year-old who would have been ecstatic. Himiko stared sullenly at Poma. She tried again. "Would you like to see my horse?" He was pushed by his father, who nodded at him. Finally Himiko took her outstretched hand.

They went below to make friends with Estwynd. The big horse, ever good with children, proved to be the way to Himiko's heart. He patiently waited for the little boy to pat him and hug him around the neck and give him a treat Poma had saved for him.

Soon the big vessel was underway. There was a nice breeze which helped them along. Poma, Nik, and Himiko found a place to sit on the polished deck and watched the coastline slip away, and the ship headed north. The earthquake had created damage far up the coast. Smoke from fires in the aftermath formed a steady haze which was then blown up into the hills. Poma felt the fresh sea air blowing through her hair. The musk of salt and seaweed penetrated her very being. As the boat drifted steadily northward, she could understand why men took to the sea. She watched with admiration as the sailors scurried about in the rigging like squirrels in underbrush. The colors of the sea ranged from green to grey to blue. She wondered how to translate those beautiful colors into an outfit for herself, and decided that silk would be the best fiber to represent the shiny ripples. She decided she must experiment with silk.

The three of them had dinner with Ramatsu that evening. They were joined by Ramatsu's second in command, a Korean physician, who was a tall, slender, pleasant man with a small moustache. He was known simply as Doctor, for he had been aboard ships so long he had "forgotten his name," or so he said. The two big bodyguards stood outside the cabin door.

Ramatsu seemed glad to be underway, and spent part of the evening explaining to Poma the extent of education he expected for his son. He spoke as though Himiko were not even present. The ship's cook and his helper attended the Captain's table, bringing in gourmet seafood dishes that fed the eyes of the diners as well as their stomachs. Nevertheless, the boy picked at his food.

"My son is to be trained to be a fearless seaman, and to this end he will spend his mornings with me." Ramatsu rolled up his sleeves so they wouldn't dangle in the food. "He has much to learn of the ship and the sea," he said. "In the afternoon he must be schooled in things which will meet the requirements of the great scholars, so he will grow to be a wise businessman. For this purpose he will spend time with Doctor."

Doctor smiled. "Himiko and I will concentrate on math and science. Right, Himiko?" Himiko stared at his half-empty plate. His father ignored him.

Ramatsu's black eyes rested on Poma. "Everything else I will leave in your capable hands, Miss Poma," he said.

Poma managed to mask her fear with an accommodating smile. "Everything else" could be almost anything, and she decided right away she could teach her young charge to draw and paint.

While Ramatsu was in a good mood, Poma decided to ask for supplies. "I will need some paper and ink," she said, as confidently as she could muster.

"You will find what you need in that trunk." Ramatsu pointed at a small trunk under a bench at the side of the cabin.

Poma smiled at Himiko, who was frowning at his plate. "I'm sure we will do just fine," she said.

Ramatsu finished his meal and studied Nik for just a moment. "And you may make yourself useful and pour the tea," he said to her.

Nik looked up, surprised, and jumped up to do as she was asked. Poma thought to herself this was perhaps a good thing, to keep Nik busy. It would be a long trip.

When the big ship neared the small port city of Komatsu, they all could see clearly that the earthquake had not touched this place. The usual dockside hubbub was reassuring. Large ornate buildings announced the importance of the town, and the usual temples and shrines presented a face of peace.

Poma and Nik took Himiko and went shopping. Poma decided on a green kimono so she would better blend in with the people here. She bought Nik some baubles and kept the little one from being bored with some sweets. She purchased some silk fabric the color of the sunset and some rich silk which had been processed and combed out to a long length for spinning, and bundled into a brick-like package.

One of the shop ladies, an older woman with her grey hair in a neat bun, showed her how to wrap a short length of the long unspun silk around her finger and pull the fibers off the end to form a short triangle. The fibers were then drafted out and attenuated into the twist to make a slender thread. The shop lady spoke only Japanese, but the lesson was one of soft murmuring and soundless spinning on an almost weightless spindle. The old woman's agile fingers spoke volumes as the two women worked together, and shortly, Poma mastered the silk. The silk seemed to melt into yarn and was soft and warm and comforting while she spun. The thread was fine and even and had a sparkle to it like no other fiber she had experienced. No wonder it was so highly prized. Soft, warm, strong and lustrous. What more could one ask of a fiber? The shop lady also insisted that Poma take the small, light-weight, cross-arm spindle to accommodate the weight of the fiber much better than her old one. It was a small leg bone, probably from a goat or sheep, with a slender iron hook extending from its center. The shop lady was very kind to part with such a nicely balanced tool. Poma thought about balance for a moment. The spindles she had used all her life represented the balance she should weave into her daily living. A thought to be tucked away and pondered later.

Back at the dock, the sailors were busy hauling aboard ship food and water and large boxes of cargo containing silks and spices. There were also boxes of weapons. Poma took Estwynd off the ship for some exercise, and gave Himiko a ride, which made his dour little face light up, even though his eyes were big with fear at first. Poma remembered back to her first ride on the big animal, and smiled to herself. After she had put Estwynd back in his stall aboard ship, she and Doctor were sitting on some boxes watching the busy scene.

"Where are you from?" he asked.

Poma's only attachment to a believable city was the old market place. "Near Marakanda," she replied.

"I'm not sure where that is," he said.

She smiled politely. She needed to change the subject. "Ramatsu's son seems like a quiet little one."

"He has lost his mother, you know. I think he is sad. Perhaps frightened."

"I hope we can at least divert his attention away from his sorrows. And in time he will most likely feel better," she said.

"What have you got in mind to teach him?"

"Perhaps some drawing or painting."

Doctor's eyebrows lifted. "Are you an artist?"

She thought back to her school in Egypt, and the glyphs. That would not be believed. "Not in a classical sense, but I have taught children in arts of sorts."

"Do you have any children?"

Targitaus' face popped into her mind, and her eyes grew wet. She bowed her head. "No, not now."

"I am sorry. I did not mean to pry." He watched her curiously.

Poma collected herself. "And you will teach him math and science?"

Doctor pulled himself up and squinted at the horizon. "If I am any judge of his father, the young man will do best to learn as much of history as he does of mathematics. His knowledge of religions and how men think about themselves will be of far more benefit than adding and subtracting. But it is also important to be a good judge of the young one himself; to learn what his interests are. It is by doing this he will learn quickly and his father will be pleased."

Poma was struck not only by Doctor's wisdom, but by his patronage of Ramatsu. This was a complicated culture. So much to learn in the short time she knew she had with these folks.

Later that night, the ship's inhabitants had settled down to sleep in preparation for an early sail the next morning. The night was a dark one, and Poma and Nik had talked little, being tired from the day's adventures. A wisp of light from the dock stabbed its way back and forth across the cabin's wall as the boat rocked. The motion usually put Poma to sleep. At least this ship did not creak and groan as the one on the Mediterranean had. This vessel, although much larger, was sleek and well-fitted. Its crew seemed proud of it, and kept it well polished.

Poma was at the edge of sleep when the door opened silently and she caught just a glimpse of a dark, shadowy figure standing over her. She froze for only an instant and the incident from long ago with the asp in her bed flooded back and clung to her very breath. She reached for the small gold-handled dagger which she kept under her pillow and had it ready when the shadow bent closer. His breath smelled of the sweets Ramatsu had served that night at dinner. The boat rocked the shadow closer, and Poma had the knife at his throat, her hand shaking.

"Poma, it is Ramatsu!" The voice from the midst of the shadow was unmistakable. But she kept the dagger where it was, as steady as she could.

"Miss Poma, I assure you, I have only come to share something with you. Wake up your friend, and both of you, come with me."

"What is it you want, Ramatsu?" Her words were measured.

"I want you to see a sight you won't forget. I am not here to harm you in any way. I don't mix business with pleasure, my dear. Now both of you get up and come see what's happening."

Poma slowly lowered the knife and she and Nik slid out of the bed.

"Hurry," said Ramatsu.

They felt their way through the darkened passageway and up the narrow stairway to the deck. The black night presented them with an astounding display of stars. Some were falling, blazing across the sky only to disappear. It was as if the entire canopy of night was exploding in all different directions, yet the fallen stars still left behind countless other points of light, some twinkling like the silk she had spun.

Doctor and Himiko were sitting and watching, along with some of the crew. Himiko was ooohing at the fall of almost every star, much to the delight of the sailors. The women sat down to admire the heavenly display.

"I'm sorry, Ramatsu," said Poma. "You frightened me there in the dark."

"I didn't want to ruin the show with a lantern," he said. "But I'm glad you can protect yourself." He lifted Himiko into his lap. "If your hand were any steadier, I might not be here to tell about it." She could tell he was grinning by the laughter in his voice. "What a story my son would have to hide from the world . . . that his father, the most feared sea captain on three coasts, had been killed by a small dagger, and at the hands of a woman!" And he chuckled.

Poma heaved a big sigh of relief. Now she would sleep even better, knowing this gruff man seemed to be protecting them all. Yet she could not stay long with this man and his ship. She would set out to find Enash, and the shells that held the royal purple. And the world was much bigger than she had ever imagined. She had promised to take Nik with her, and that doubled her responsibility. She told herself to be patient, to wait and see what the end of the ocean journey would bring.

The next day they were underway again, this time west, with the morning sun behind them. Poma, Doctor, and Himiko went to Ramatsu's cabin in the afternoon to examine the contents of the little trunk. Happily, it held paper, scrolls, ink, and beautiful brushes. There were some dried paint pigments which delighted Poma, for now she could teach Himiko to paint. He was enamored with the brushes, and Poma examined the scrolls. The Japanese writing was lovely to see. The elaborate characters marched down the page with authority, but nonetheless retained an almost feminine grace.

Ramatsu appeared at the cabin door. "Ah, Miss Poma, here you are," he said. "I see you are beginning with the lessons."

Himiko brandished the brushes at his father. "Papa, look! I can learn to write!"

Ramatsu's grin almost swallowed his eyes. "I am very happy for you, my son." He said.

Poma flinched, and then hoped Ramatsu hadn't seen. "Thank you for the supplies," she said. Somehow she would have to learn the Japanese characters herself. Perhaps she could practice copying from the scrolls.

"Come, my son, I have something for you to do," said Ramatsu. Himiko reluctantly put down the brushes and followed his father out to the deck.

Poma took a deep breath and pulled one of the scrolls closer to look at.

Doctor watched her closely. "My guess is Ramatsu has no idea that your knowledge of the Japanese characters is as new as tomorrow," he said.

She glanced at him, and then back at the scroll. She felt her face flush. "I certainly wouldn't want him to know," she replied.

Doctor picked up a brush and opened the small metal-lined box of ink. He spread out some fresh paper in front of her. "I will show you. Ramatsu doesn't care how the job gets done. He's only interested in results." And he quickly brushed some black strokes onto the page. "This is man. And this is woman. And this," he said with a flourish of the brush, "is a ship."

Poma grabbed a brush.

"Here, like this," and his hand guided hers through the motions. "Support your hand with your little finger on the page, like so," he continued.

And so the lessons began. Himiko, eyes shining, patiently copied what Poma taught him, not knowing she had learned the same things only days before. The weeks at sea passed peacefully enough, although Poma was a little restless to see something other than a seemingly unreachable horizon. The Japanese characters were all-absorbing, and Ramatsu was pleased with the boy's progress. Poma broke up the boredom by writing another poem.

Furies

I take my breath from warm spring winds
Descending in grey furies beside me,
All around me. The grey furies,
The blue and gold furies and winds
With breath and life, stalking through
Sea and sail. Bending, rising,
The grey furies of blue and grey and gold.

What breath of life takes one
Whose sun and beauteous grey furies
And blue and gold, are nigh?
What breath takes he?

What sun is breaking 'round, what
Furies has he, walking, stalking,
In front, beside him, swirling there?

What yellow wordless sunset makes
His clouds seem clouds of frail,
Real, fleeting gazelles
On the face of mother night?
What lone star shines there
In fading day,
To take the watch of bluest night?

Oh, love, how dost thy heart
Wing back to other suns and furies,
To the flaming furies,
To the flame-blue passion furies
In clenched fingertips submerged?
Oh love, how dost thy heart within thee
Whisper to thee of me?

She wiped a tear off the page before it smeared the ink, and tucked the poem with the other one she had written so long ago and stored them back in her basket. This felt good; she would get through this time of searching. The poetry temporarily mended a large hole deep inside her—the longing for Enash.

The Dead Calm

One morning Poma awoke to the muffled sound of a drum. The air was very still, but worst of all, so was the ship. The accustomed rolling motion was strangely absent. She and Nik went above and ran to the rail. Nothing moved. The only noise was the drum. Then the oars appeared through small slits in the side of the ship. They dipped and swung in unison, in time with the drum.

"What's happened?" Nik whispered. Her face bore both fright and awe.

"It's a dead calm." Doctor was behind them.

"How can that be?" Poma said. She had never heard of such a thing.

"Some say the Gods are responsible," Doctor said. "So we must use the oars."

Poma frowned. "That could take time," she said. "How long will it stay this way, with no wind for the sails?"

His face was grave. "No one knows. Sometimes these last for days and days at a time."

Poma squinted at the water. It was like the lakes she had seen in the Tien Shan. There wasn't a ripple. And the sun was growing warm.

Ramatsu burst onto deck. His face was dark. His eyes narrowed at the scene. He glanced at the useless rigging, mumbling tersely through clenched teeth in Japanese. Nothing moved except the oars. The big ship was slow to respond.

Poma felt a pang of fear. She hoped there was enough water on board, and grain for the horses. Estwynd! She turned and ran down below to check on the horses. They seemed a little skittish, so she stroked them all gently and whispered reassurance. It seemed to calm them a bit.

The drum became nerve-wracking, reminding them at every beat that they were at the mercy of the sea just as surely as if there were high waves washing over the decks. Poma had never felt more helpless. She looked around for Himiko, and finally found him in a niche under the stairs. His eyes were big and his small face stained with tears.

"Oh, Himiko! Come, little one, come with me. We will find something to do. Let's go look in the trunk again, and see what we can see," she said.

Poma discovered this day that her small student had an aptitude for art that far exceeded anything she had experienced. *And this sensitive young man is destined to take over an empire of pirates?* She almost cried. *Not if I can help it.*

In the next few days, Himiko made painting after painting of delicate blossoms, stylized trees and mountains, and even fighting Samurai that danced in almost romantic steps across the page. Although a bit primitive, the paintings showed great promise. Their plight in the calm sea would have been forgotten if it were not for the monotonous drum.

Himiko was so absorbed in his work he rolled up his sleeves, and Poma gasped. There on his arm were big, ugly black and blue marks.

"Oh, Himiko, what happened to you?"

Himiko put down his brush and slid his small arms under the table in front of him. "Nothing," he whispered. Surely his father didn't—they were interrupted by Ramatsu, who found the two painting together. Himiko held up one of the paintings and beamed at him.

Ramatsu brushed him aside. "If we ration the water, we have a better chance of making it to the Chinese coast," he said. "Therefore, everyone is rationed to three measures of water a day." He looked sternly at Himiko. "Everyone. That includes you, Himiko. I know you can be a good example for the crew."

"I thought we were headed for the Bay of Korea," Poma said.

"We are closer to the Chinese coast at this point, and although it's not as safe, we have to take the chance." He frowned at the pictures and hurried out. Himiko looked stricken.

"It's alright, little one. I'm sure the Gods will send us wind soon." Poma said.

Himiko burst into tears. "He didn't like my pictures," he sputtered.

"Oh, Himiko, I'm sure he'll like them when he has time to look at them. Right now he's worried about getting where we're going." She took the boy in her arms. He felt like a tiny, shaking bird. "Your pictures are wonderful. Truly, you have made things of beauty. Don't worry; there will be many people who will like what you do. Nik will love them. So will Doctor." And he finally stopped crying, picked up his brushes and went back to work. But before he did, he carefully rolled his sleeves down.

Poma was sick with grief. Was Ramatsu responsible for the bruises? She would have to get close enough to the child to find out.

Later, after dinner, when Ramatsu had gone back up on deck, Doctor took a look at the boy's work, and congratulated him with a clap of his big hand on Himiko's back. They smiled together at the colorful work. Doctor looked at Poma and his smile faded. The two moved into the passageway. "You have a real job ahead of yourself," he said.

Poma let out a big breath. "I know. Ramatsu is sometimes a difficult person to please." Her gaze transferred to Himiko.

"I will be taking my turn with the rowing team during the night," Doctor said.

"How far do we have to go?" Poma said.

"We are about two weeks away, under sail, but much longer by oar. It's not a good picture, and we will run very short of water."

She touched his arm. "What about the horses?" she whispered.

"They will have their own ration, and I am watching them closely," he replied.

Poma was relieved. She vowed to herself to pray to all the Gods, even the Japanese ones whose names she didn't know. She never thought in all her life she would be praying for wind.

The next afternoon Poma and Himiko brought the paints on deck to escape the heat of the cabin below. The air was thick with the smell of rotting fish. The sea was uncompromising. She didn't know which was worse, the air here or the heat in the cramped cabin. Himiko's face screwed up to cry. She could tell he was trying not to cry, but the heat evidently had gotten too much for him. His skin was dry. She decided to share just a bit of her water ration with him. Ramatsu looked over just as she was holding her cup to the boy's lips. He rushed over and smacked Himiko with the broad side of his sword, knocking the water to the deck. Poma slid to one side, her arm defending her head.

"Go to my cabin!" he shouted at Himiko. The boy ran below, crying and holding his head.

"You are not to give the boy extra water," he snarled at Poma.

Out of her fear there came anger. "You are treating him worse than an animal. He is your son!" she blazed.

Then she knew she had said too much. He raised his sword back over his head, and then stopped, stock still, and looked up. One of the crew members was shouting from the rigging. The drum stopped. The boat rocked for the first time in days. Ramatsu ran to the side. Poma followed. A great cheer arose from below. Sailors scrambled onto the deck and into the rigging. Everything came alive. Poma felt the breeze on her face. She could smell the salt and feel the cold. The sea again had silver ripples. The sails furled amid shouts above and below. Thick ropes were tied in place. They were moving at last. From the east came grey clouds. Poma's tears of fear and anger became tears of joy.

Ramatsu barked a few orders at the men, and then turned to face her. "Never disobey me again," he whispered, and then turned to the business of the ship. Poma couldn't help but think that this man's dark energy was much closer to the surface than even he realized. He was like the sea he lived in—unpredictable and treacherous. She would have to get far away from this man as soon as possible.

The Escape

She ran to find Himiko. He was with Nik, who was comforting him. She gathered the two children in her arms. "Until there is a better way, and while we are on this ship, we will have to take great care to obey Ramatsu's wishes," she said. "And some day, we will have wonderful stories to tell our grandchildren."

But she was thinking a little differently. She had grown to love this little boy she shared paper and brushes with. The little one looked at her with trusting black eyes. And Nik was fighting her way through a lot of fright. As the three bonded in a big hug, Poma knew she would have to somehow take charge of both of these children.

In a few days, the wind blew them to within sight of land. For the sailors, it only served to increase their anxiety. Now the enemy became the unknown. The Chinese, their age-old foe, might dart out from one of the many bays or coves and attack.

For Poma, the land was a huge relief. She drew Nik to one side and whispered instructions. "Listen carefully, dear. As soon as we are safely in a harbor, it is vital that we pack up three things and load up Estwynd and that big black horse."

Nik's eyes grew big with the realization she was about to become a horse thief. "That's Ramatsu's horse . . ." she began.

"I am leaving some gold behind in payment," Poma said

"But that's not . . ."

"For all these many days I've been schooling his son," Poma's voice was soft, but urgent. "I thought at first I would only get to China and then get away, on my own journey, follow my own plans, but now things have changed. We must get Himiko away from him. And we are going to have to have both the horses if we are to escape this man. He will have only one horse to follow us with, and besides, he was ready to let all of them die back there in the dead calm. He's mean and cruel. He loves only his ship and his gold. He made you into a servant. He almost killed me. No, we deserve a horse out of the bargain." She was gripping Nik by the arm.

"Alright, Poma, whatever you say. I can see you are right." And Nik's face relaxed.

"We need to remember the basket, the indigo, and the small trunk. And you have your bundle. We will need blankets and water. I'll see to some food, and we will ride hard." She looked into Nik's face. "Alright?"

"Alright." Nik's face was white, but her mouth had a new determination.

All at once the drum interrupted their conversation. "What now?" Poma said. They ran to the rail and looked toward the land. Two large, flat ships were approaching. Ramatsu shouted orders. The ship turned into the wind as the oars assisted in running away from the flat boats that were giving chase. Doctor appeared from below. "Those are Chinese ships. We'll be able to outrun them," he said.

Within a short time it was apparent the Chinese were far behind and could not catch up. The coast made a sharp turn, and Ramatsu headed for the safety of a large bay. The bay was barren except for a small town with a dock. There were only a few small fishing boats. Ramatsu and Doctor took the ship's small boat and rowed slowly toward the dock. Poma could hardly stand the wait until they returned with the good news that they would be able to dock. The town was not much more than a fishing village.

Ramatsu let Poma and the children exercise the horses just outside of the town. They left them hobbled in a small pasture. The sailors set about re-provisioning the ship. Then Ramatsu strode back and forth, barking orders and attempting to keep a tight reign on everything, but some of the crew found a brothel and spent the day getting drunk.

Poma went below to pack everything up. She heard Ramatsu grumbling. "We must hurry before we're trapped here," he said.

Doctor tried to keep him calm. "They'll be back in the morning," he said.

The agitated captain paced up and down the cabin. "I want a double watch. And where did those abominable women go?"

Poma appeared at the cabin door. "I'll go and get the children," she said.

That night, Poma managed to get the small trunk, her basket, Nik's bundle and the indigo on the deck, and hid everything among the newly acquired provisions. Late in the night she heard Ramatsu shouting at Himiko. Soon it was quiet. She and Nik were up and dressed, ready to slip away. As they neared the stairway Poma's heart was beating like a hammer. How could she get Himiko away from his father? Perhaps she had not thought all of this through very well. She stopped and tried to collect her thoughts. What would she say to Ramatsu? Would she and Nik be safe? As she tried to formulate a plan, she heard a small sniffle. Suddenly it became very simple. There he was, curled up in his stairwell hideaway, and except for the sniffle, sobbing silently. She scooped him up and they went onto the deck. She set him down. He clung to her, weeping.

She took a deep breath. "Himiko, listen to me. What is wrong?"

The boy saw that Poma was dressed for travel. He sniffled again, his eyes widening. "Poma-san, where are you going?"

She got down on her knees in front of him. "Little one," she whispered, "we are leaving. We have a long journey; it may take many years . . ."

Himiko crumbled and sobbed at Poma, "He hates me. He beats me. Don't leave me!"

Just then there were dark shadows running across the deck. The side of the ship was suddenly alive with shouting Chinese, brandishing swords. They had boarded from their ship which had silently moved into the harbor from the sea. Poma grabbed Himiko's hand and Nik's arm and the three of them hid behind some boxes. The dock side of the ship was empty. She grabbed the small trunk and shoved it at the little boy. Nik had the basket and her bundle, and Poma lifted the indigo, and they ran for the ladder. The children were over the side and onto the dock. Poma lowered down the boxes of indigo into Nik's waiting arms. She glanced back at the battle opposite her. The Chinese had torches. She saw Ramatsu staggering back from two of the Chinese with a sword through his side. She did not hesitate, but jumped down, grabbed her precious boxes and the three ran toward the waiting horses. As soon as everything was ready, they rode off, away from the water and the doomed ship, and up into the hills. In a small pine forest, they stopped to look back. The ship was now ablaze. Himiko had a look on his face that neared relief. Nik's mouth was still set in determination. Poma wondered for only a moment what became of Doctor. They had made their escape.

The Spy

The moon had risen. "Let's get out of here," she said to the other two. She was reminded of that time long ago when she had ridden with two other dear friends away from a whole town afire. And they rode, the children on the black horse, followed by Poma and Estwynd. They skirted the forest and rode toward a dip in the mountains. The full moon cast long shadows through the trees, making them appear larger than they should be. It soon seemed to Poma that there might be monsters behind every rock. She took solace from a sure-footed Estwynd, who trudged with loyal dignity up the path. A big waterfall met them and offered respite for the horses.

Himiko looked frightened again. "Poma-san, don't leave me." He looked as though he were going to cry once more.

"Don't worry, Himiko. You've got a new family now," Poma said, smiling at him. They dismounted so the horses could drink, and she took him in her arms. "I'll take care of you," she said, and embraced the child along with the responsibility.

Suddenly they heard horses coming. Poma glanced around. "Quick, behind the waterfall," she said, and they led the horses behind the water. Some Chinese on horseback pulled up at the big pool. One shouted and pointed down the path. And they all rode off. Poma cautioned the children to silence, and they waited for a few moments, and then made their way back to the trail and continued on. The rising moon made the going easier. They seemed to be on some sort of path that cut through the surrounding grasses and trees.

She was about to take a breath of relief when she was knocked off her horse by a small man who lunged at her, pinning her to the ground.

Struggle as she might, she could not move. He yelled at her in Chinese, and she could only understand what he was about by his actions. Think fast. He would not understand their language.

She shouted to Nik, "I'll meet you at the waterfall!" And Nik and Himiko rode off safely with the horses. The last thing she saw was the man's fist coming at her face.

When Poma awoke, she hurt all over. Her face was throbbing. The thin light of dawn cast a grey shadow from the small, high window of a colorless room onto the straw-covered floor where she lay. Two men sat braced against the opposite wall. One was snoring like a pig. As she rolled over, she discovered her hands were tied. She pulled, but the rough cord held fast.

The door burst open, and two more men crammed themselves into the small room. One bristled with finery and two swords. The other was an elderly peasant. Two Swords spoke with authority to the peasant. The old man looked passively at Poma.

His brows raised only slightly, his eyes shifting from her to Two Swords and back. "He wants me to translate. He wants to know who you are working for. He says he knows you are a spy."

Poma tried to frown, but her battered face wouldn't let her. Her tongue was swollen, but she managed to speak, her voice raspy. "I work for no man," she whispered. "And I am not a spy."

The old man translated into Chinese for the big captor. Two Swords stepped nearer and glared at her. He issued an order, and the peasant ran out of the room and returned shortly with a wooden bowl of water. Two Swords lifted up her head and fed her some of the water. His Chinese seemed a song to Poma's ears, but she knew better than to think it meant anything more than another command. The peasant looked at Poma once more. He moved closer to her. Two Swords stood behind him, arms crossed.

"He wants me to tell you, if you don't tell him what he wants to know, he will kill you. And I have left something for you in your water bowl." His black eyes were impassive. Poma instinctively knew not to look at the bowl. And she knew her face could not betray her; it was too swollen.

She replied in as nasty a tone as she could, "I am not a spy. And thank you."

There were sudden loud shouts outside the room. Two Swords shoved the old man out the door, and the other two followed him out. Poma was alone. She inched her way over to the water bowl. She could see nothing in it. She reached for it, her hands shaking. As she lifted it to her face, she saw something which made a shadow on the side of the bowl. Her head snapped back as she focused. A small sliver of bamboo was neatly stabbed into the side of the wooden bowl. She listened for just a moment. It was too quiet. She sat, frozen to the corner of her cell, when one of the guards slammed through the door once more. She put the bowl down by her side away from the greasy little man who was out of breath from running. The only other thing that broke the silence was what sounded like fighting in the distance, then horses galloping away.

The morning grew long and the room grew warm. Flies buzzed around her shifting, scratching guard. The stench of this disgusting place announced that it had been used as a prison for a very long time. Something told her to horde the water in her bowl. It would protect the small bamboo sliver hidden there. Soon she found herself drifting in and out of sleep. She became fully awake when the guard threw some bread at her. She propped herself in the corner once more, and took a tentative bite out of the stale crust. Old, but it would have to do. She could ill afford a choice. Soon the guard fell asleep. When his snoring became measured, she picked up the bowl and carefully pulled the bamboo sliver out of its place, drank the rest of the water, and began sawing at the cord around her wrists with the bamboo. It was awkward, but effective. Soon her hands were free. She tucked the sliver into her waistband, and crawled to the door. Watching the guard, she gently slid it open. She was on her feet and running for her life. She made it up a steep hill and behind some houses. She thought the whole world would hear her heart beating. At least all of China.

She peeked around a corner. There sat the old man who had given her the bamboo sliver. He motioned her into his house, where she collapsed onto the floor. She looked around. The old man lived simply, but had some luxuries that spoke of days gone by. A very old rug which had seen better days covered the floor of the small room with a faded glory. Some ancient pillows adorned one of the corners. Their thread-bare corners attested to many years of wear. A few wooden dishes were stacked neatly on a shelf in back of a low table. The table top was worn and scarred, but well-scrubbed. As she sat up, he grinned at her.

"Thank you!" she gasped.

"No one as lovely as you could be a spy," he said, and they smiled at one another.

"Which way is the waterfall?" she asked.

"When it is nightfall, I will take you there," he replied.

Poma closed her eyes in relief.

After a few minutes, they could hear shouting and the sounds of several men running through the streets. The old man lifted up a corner of the rug, revealing a trap door. He pulled it up and motioned Poma down into the darkness. The cellar was totally black as the door eased shut. She could only sit, helpless, and listen. She wished her heart would slow down. She breathed through her mouth so no one would hear her. The cool cellar added a few ripples of shiver down her body. She wished she were a mouse in a corner with a small hole to hide in.

There was insistent pounding on the outside door, amidst much shouting. She could hear footsteps overhead as the old man's house was searched. Soon the outside door slammed and all became very quiet. After what seemed an eternity, the trap door opened, and the silhouette of the old man appeared. She climbed up the cellar stairs cautiously, and finally, with relief, saw that the peasant's house was empty of the soldiers.

"Thank you again," she stammered. "What is your name?"

"We need no names." The old one said. "We have learned to live in silence here." The old man pointed to the cushions in the corner. "Sit here, and you can be comfortable while we wait. It is nearly time to go." And he offered Poma some rice and goat's milk. She gratefully accepted.

"And where are you going?" he said politely.

Poma did not want to endanger this nice old man any further. "We need no places," she replied.

He squinted at her in another smile. "You learn quickly," he said. They ate in silence. At long last the night was dark. The old man reached in a basket and pulled out a dark grey hooded shawl for Poma. "This belonged to my wife," he said. "She's been gone two years now." He fingered the shawl for a moment, and then put it over her head. His smile was forlorn. He lit a lantern, and they set out up the street and into a dark wood. They came to a rushing stream and followed it down the mountain to the waterfall. As they made their way under the falls, they found the horses standing alone in the semi-darkness of a small fire that was mostly embers.

Poma called out to the children. "Nik! Himiko!" No answer. She thought maybe she couldn't be heard above the rushing water. "Nik! It's me. I'm here!" Far up in the back of the cave, they found them, hugging one another, their eyes wide.

"Oh, Poma, what happened to you? Your face . . ." Nik said. Her eyes showed her concern.

Poma hugged them both. "I was on the receiving end of a powerful fist," she said. "But I'll be okay. This kind gentleman helped me get away and . . ." she turned to introduce the old man, but he was gone. The last of his lantern could be seen disappearing under the curtain of water.

"We were going to leave," Nik said. "We didn't know how long to stay here."

Himiko clung to Poma.

"I'm glad you stayed and waited," she said. "The old man said we'll be safe if we keep traveling to the west. There is one more village before we get to the big mountains. We are to find a woman named Chan-Li. We can purchase food from her for our journey." Poma looked at the disappearing light. "We must remember him in our prayers," she said.

She washed her face in the cold water, built up the fire and they ate the last of the bread from the small stash of food. Poma was frightened at the thought of the other two being hungry, and she tried gallantly not to show it.

"Tomorrow we will re-stock our food," she said confidently. Himiko seemed satisfied, but Nik's worried expression did not dissolve into sleep so easily.

Poma slept fitfully. *Two Swords walked in circles around her. She tried to move, but her feet were buried in sand. The big man circled closer and closer. Poma saw something on the ground, and realized it was a tooth. She felt in her mouth. It was her tooth. There were teeth all around her, and Two Swords was laughing at her. Two Swords had turned into Ramatsu. The wooden bowl was there, and it rolled into a forest of bamboo trees. The wind blew the bamboo leaves, creating a sound like rushing water.*

Poma awoke, and the wind was still blowing through the bamboo leaves. She lay still, listening. It was the waterfall. *Why the teeth?* Perhaps she had said too much to Ramatsu about his son at the end of the dead calm on the sea. But it wasn't too much, she told herself. She knew she was right. If she ever dreamed of Ramatsu again, she should turn and face him, and tell him again what she thought of him.

The next day they followed the stream back up the mountain, skirted the village, and were on their way up a very long and winding trail. Toward mid-morning they reached the top of the ridge. Poma glanced back and saw a horse and rider starting slowly up the mountain.

Chan Li

The mysterious horseman was very far away, and Poma could not tell if he was one of the soldiers. His horse was traveling at a leisurely pace. Nevertheless, she thought it best to keep ahead. She urged the big grey up over the ridge and didn't even look back at the great sea spread out behind them. The road beckoned them into a broad, green valley with a patchwork of small neat fields. Houses were nestled in occasional stands of trees. The spring had been consumed by the voyage across the sea. It was early summer now, and the grass was high. The crops created a multi-colored panorama. The valley was divided by the stream, marked by banks of burgeoning grass. Occasional fields held brown dots of cattle and white dots of sheep and goats. In the immediate front of the valley were small individual lakes, made by the hand of man, growing green shoots right out of the water. The only thing disturbing the tranquility was the thought of the faceless rider behind them.

"We've no time to waste," Poma said, and they followed the neat trail through the maze of fields toward the ancient village on the far side of the valley. She must find Chan Li so she could feed the children. Nik was telling a story to Himiko, and the two seemed happily occupied during the long ride.

She looked over her shoulder several times, and when she was feeling just a little bit comfortable and began to relax, the horse and rider appeared over the ridge and started down into the valley. Were they being followed? The rider wasn't in any hurry. Poma couldn't tell if they were being followed, but decided it best to get to the village as soon as they could.

At the first house, some children pointed the way to the house of Chan Li. They rode down the main street to the other end of the small town. The crowd of rosy-cheeked children following them grew bigger as they proceeded. Evidently foreigners did not frequent this place. The village was poor but tidy. Each little house had a garden with all the requisite chickens, and there were even a few goats scattered here and there. There were a few horses, and shaggy black beasts that appeared to be like the oxen Poma knew from the steppe. She was afraid to ask what they were, for fear no one would believe she didn't know. Most of the folks here wore round pointed hats woven with reeds, protecting them from the summer sun.

By the time they reached the home of Chan Li, their presence was already known. They were ushered by the children into a courtyard in the center of the villa. The pungent odor of an indigo pot braided itself with scents of breakfast which had been cooked in a garden choked with flowers. Now Poma was hungry, too.

The big house was old, but swept and washed clean. A middle-aged, grey-haired woman with a round, smiling face wiped her worn hands on a dark blue apron, and welcomed her guests. The village children stood staring at Himiko in the curious way only children can muster. A young boy emerged from the house and helped Nik settle the horses.

"Are you Chan Li?" Poma asked, approaching the woman.

"Yes, dear. Where are you going, all by yourselves?"

"It will be a long journey, I'm afraid," replied Poma. Chan Li had no way of knowing that Poma intended to ask her where they were going.

Chan Li motioned to wooden seats in the shade. Poma was reminded of a long-ago Lila and her stone bench. "Have some tea," Chan Li said, and motioned to a young girl in the doorway. The girl disappeared momentarily into the house and re-emerged with a pot of tea and cups on an enamel tray decorated with vivid chrysanthemums and poppies.

"I was told in a village by the sea that you have provisions I might obtain for our trip," Poma said. She sipped her tea.

"Oh, my, yes. I'll show you our storeroom," replied Chan Li. "Aren't you afraid to travel alone, my dear?" Her face looked worried for Poma and the children. Nik, tired from the ride, joined them, and was poured some tea. Her frown faded slightly.

"There are bandits and all kinds of folks who would seek to do you nothing but harm."

Poma thought back to the market towns of the Tien Shan, and the long parades of camels that had come through the great Taklimakan. "I was hoping to join one of the great caravans," she replied.

Chan Li looked surprised. "My, you do have a long journey," she said. "We will have lunch first, and then we'll visit the storehouse." She spoke in Chinese to the youngsters near the house, and they ran into the villa kitchen to help prepare a noon-time meal.

"We are very grateful to you," Poma said.

After they had eaten, they went to Chan Li's warehouse and Poma purchased rice, dried fish and vegetables and fresh fruit for a treat. Chan Li showed Poma the lovely big garden.

Poma recognized the indigo plants and the madder, and after that, Chan Li had to explain the shrubs and trees. "This is Zi Cao. The root gives me purple." Poma frowned at the bush. She had never seen one before. Chan Li tried to translate. "Let me see—I guess you would call it red root. But it gives us a fairly good purple. We also use it for medicine."

Another purple, thought Poma.

"However," Chan Li Continued, "It tends to fade. So I use it for things that can just go back in the dye pot."

Poma thought back to Hamora, who would have done exactly the same thing.

They walked through the flowers. Chan Li bent over to pick a stray weed. "And the best yellow comes from these gardenias. I use the seeds in my dye pot."

Poma was mesmerized. The scent of the gardenias took her directly back to that warm day on an Egyptian cliff, when Enash had disappeared.

"Here," said Chan Li, and she plucked a beautiful blossom and held it up for Poma to put in her hair. Poma felt so happy with such a small gesture. But the happiness was sorely tempered by the loss on that long-ago day, the loss of Enash.

Chan Li's weathered hands had lovingly tended all these plants so she could have color in her life.

Poma felt very connected to her. "Your garden is so very beautiful," she said.

"It lives long after in all that I spin and weave," replied Chan Li. The women smiled at one another.

Then, Chan Li sat down with Poma to show her the way to Chang 'an.

"Chang 'an is a big city where the caravans form for travel to the west."

"Can you mark it on this map for me?" Poma pulled out her map and smoothed it out before the older woman.

"You are here, and you need to follow this road through the mountains and along this valley. The road divides here and you must take the fork to the right and travel north."

Poma watched the woman's finger as it traced the way. She called Himiko. "Go and get your trunk. I need some ink."

Chan Li continued. "The road is well-traveled here and you will come across many people. The caravans start here, in Chang 'an. You must make good time, for the merchants prefer the fall for traveling to the west. It is high desert beyond Chang 'an and not good to travel in the summer."

"How many days to Chang 'an?" Poma asked. She felt excited about the journey.

"I have made it in a little over two moons, but with the children . . ." Chan Li's voice trailed off.

Poma studied the map. She carefully measured the distance to Chang 'an and then quickly estimated the time from there to the great sea. She frowned.

"How far are you going?" Chan-Li asked.

Poma thought about her indigo. "First I'd like to get to Marakanda."

Chan Li looked astonished. "My father crossed the southern route of the great Taklimakan, and he had many stories to tell. I think Marakanda might have changed names many seasons ago."

"And what is it now?"

"I think you might mean Samarkand."

Poma looked back on the map. There was Samarkand. Her road this time would lead from east to west instead of north to south. *Quite a crossroads,* she thought.

Himiko ran up with his trunk, and got out the ink and a tiny brush. Poma made some thin brush strokes to mark the way, with Chan Li's help.

"Please stay a night here with us and rest yourselves and your animals. You have a very long trip."

Before Poma could answer, she saw Himiko running for the doorway in an apparent fright. Then Nik jumped up and ran behind him. What was happening? Poma turned and saw the horse and rider from earlier in the day approaching the gate. She shivered as she recognized who it was. Beads of sweat broke out on her forehead.

Chan Li smiled, got up, and walked down the path. She greeted the rider like an old friend. "Doctor. How long has it been?"

Doctor got off his horse and grinned at Chan Li. "Far too long. But you are as beautiful as ever." And he bowed to Chan Li, and then kissed her cheek.

Poma was frozen to her seat. It was too late to run and hide with the children. He neared her with a beseeching look on his face.

"Poma, please don't be afraid," he began.

"Did Ramatsu send you?" She got up and looked toward the horses.

"Yes, but . . ."

"I'm taking Himiko far, far away, where he won't be hurt any more." She planted her feet.

"And thank the Gods for that," he said.

"But I thought . . ."

Chan Li watched the two of them with her mouth open.

Doctor moved a step closer. "Ramatsu was badly wounded, although the ship is not beyond repair. I was the only one left of the crew who speaks Chinese. He sent me to bring Himiko back, but . . ."

"Don't come any closer." Poma was trembling.

"Please listen. I can't take Himiko back to a father who beats him. And I can't in good conscience work for the man any more. And I've come to help you get Himiko just as far away from him as possible."

Poma felt helpless. "And how do I know I can trust you?"

Doctor held his hands out to her. "Because I am in love with you. I've loved you since the first moment I met you. Poma . . ."

Poma was confused.

"Please believe me. I have seen treachery in the man for years. But it was against enemies. This was the first time I have seen him alone with his son. I was sickened."

Poma searched Doctor's face.

"And then, when you came on board, I felt alive for the first time in many years."

Poma tried to remember any possible reason to doubt what he was saying. She took a deep breath. "Doctor, I'm—the children and I are going far away from here. It may even take . . ."

"I will follow you wherever you go." His eyes were wet with tears.

Poma felt flattered, but knew she could not return his love. The aroma of the Gardenia in her hair only confirmed how she felt in her heart.

Chan Li's mouth closed, and then opened once more. "My dear, I have known Doctor for, I don't know how many years. He is a man of his word—and a good man at that. Why, if I were any younger . . ."

Doctor's face broke into its accustomed smile. "If you were any younger, I would have carried you off a long time ago." He slipped his arm around Chan Li's plump waist.

"You'd marry me for my money, you fox," she replied

Poma stared at both of them for only a moment more. She decided to take the chance. Now she would have to convince Himiko. "Alright. I'm going first to Chang 'an and from there I'll be—we'll be joining one of the caravans to the west. It is a long trip." She became determined again. "And it is a journey I must make," she said. She wanted him to understand her determination.

"Then west it is," Doctor said. "I've never been any farther away than right here at Chan Li's, and I look forward to traveling somewhere besides the sea." He looked closely at Poma. "Gracious, girl, what happened to your face?"

Poma was embarrassed. "Some time I'll tell you all about it. In the meantime, let's just say I'm glad you are here."

Doctor gave her a knowing look, just a little condescending, and then switched to his wide smile. "I am, too," he said simply.

Poma decided she would reveal her plans only one step at a time. She would be safer that way.

They finally found Himiko hiding under a stairwell just off the kitchen. Poma knew from past experience what kind of hiding place he would choose. It took only a little convincing to assure him he was still safe.

"Himiko," Doctor said, "I hope you will let me be a part of your new family."

The boy stared at him with mistrust.

"I will show you how science relates to your art."

Himiko's eyes lit up. "Really?"

"Really."

"I thought my father was coming with you when you rode up."

"Your father will never hurt you again, I promise." Himiko finally bowed to Doctor, then ran over and took his hand. Nik was ready to do whatever Poma said. And so it was settled. The four became traveling companions.

A long, warm evening beckoned the children to play and the women to spin. Poma got out the purple distaff and her new oriental spindle to practice on the silk. She so admired how the threads could be spun so fine and even.

Chan Li had a spindle with a copper whorl and a slender bamboo shaft. As she made herself comfortable on a large cushion, Poma's purple distaff caught her eye. She did not hide her astonishment too well. Her eyes switched to Poma's calm face.

"That's a beautiful purple," she began. "However did you arrive at that color?"

Poma smiled. This time she could be truthful. "Actually, it was a gift to me when I was a child. I have no idea where it came from."

Chan Li stared in admiration. "Looks like there may be indigo involved," she decided. Poma opened her mouth to correct the older woman, and then thought better of it.

The conversation turned to the children. "The boy seems withdrawn," Chan Li said.

"He's had some bad times in his life," Poma said. "He lost his mother in an earthquake in the spring."

"Earthquake?"

"Yes, it was across the sea."

"We didn't feel it here."

"It destroyed the whole town we were living in," Poma said. "Nik lost her family as well."

"How wonderful of you to take them in," Chan Li said. Her spindle moved like a small whirlwind. "They seem happy with you."

"Well, Nik is almost grown, and Himiko seemed so lost and afraid."

Doctor sauntered over to the placid scene. "Chan Li, your work never ends," he said.

Her brows shot up. "Idle hands don't feed their master," she retorted.

Doctor squatted down to watch the spindle moving. "I have a big favor to ask of you," he said.

Chan Li looked at him steadily. "No more surprises today, Doctor. These old ears have already heard too much."

"They need to listen to one more thing," Doctor said.

Poma knew that Doctor would be better at explaining their predicament with Ramatsu to his old friend.

"If Ramatsu or anyone else comes here and asks you about Poma or the children or me, you must tell them nothing."

"You need not even ask, dear one. I had that figured out already. We are a household of secrets."

Poma smiled in relief.

Chan Li drew more fiber out of her basket. "These are hard times we live in. Sometimes it seems as if the whole world is upside down."

Doctor rose and patted her shoulder. "Thank you," he said simply.

The next morning was a warm one. Poma could well understand how Chan Li could love this peaceful valley. Small yellow-breasted larks called out their long and equally colorful songs. Children's voices could be heard laughing in time with the narrow brook that gurgled its way through a meadow dotted with bright purple flowers. It was a scene Poma would never forget. Perhaps she would have such a home, some day. It was also a spiritual longing for home that emanated from an unsettled heart. But each bend in the road offered up new possibilities along with new scenes to look at. Doctor's profession of love had only served to sharpen her determination to find Enash. She still had a very small doubt about Doctor flirting with her sense of security. And so it was with mixed feelings that she took leave of Chan Li and her flower-filled gardens.

Bandits

The road meandered through a rocky canyon and up a steep hillside to a wind-blown mesa. Far off mountains would soon be shoulders for the pathway. Rows of hills only announced more rows of hills. Trees were sparse here; huge rocky bluffs were at once inhospitable to them and to the men from before time who had tried to tame them. Man had long ago sensibly left drawings behind, glyphs to inform and entertain their offspring. Himiko was especially fascinated with them, and they would show up later in some of his art.

Poma was confused and upset by Doctor's advances, and decided they needed a long talk. The children fell asleep as the campfire crackled into the quiet night.

"I need you to know—" she began—

He looked up at her and his black eyes caught the dance of the fire. "I know you still don't trust me completely," he said.

"I guess I have no reason to mistrust you, but, I am on this journey hunting for someone I knew long ago—" How could she explain something that sounded so irrational, hunting this big world for one person? "I have reason to believe he may be in a certain location—" *Did that sound odd?*

Doctor's brows rose in apparent condescension. "You make it sound like a fairy tale," he said bluntly.

"I know it's—well, that it sounds unrealistic, but I have my reasons."

His face sank into a look of sadness. "At least I can help you find the way, and perhaps protect you and the children."

And perhaps I can learn to love you, but I am not free to do that, she thought. All she could respond with was her secret smile. And so blossomed the tacit agreement between them that romance, if at all, would have to wait.

Their journey became a daze of riding over a well-worn trail through rocky hills, and nightly campfires with warm rice and vegetables. Small villages evoked nothing more than patient, staring people and a few barking dogs and curious children. An occasional group of travelers passed by them with nods to Poma and Doctor and an exchange of waves among the children.

Although Poma was usually tired from the long days, in the evenings she spun enough silk for a head scarf. The yarn's transformation into a scarf would have to wait for a time when she wasn't traveling.

On a hot morning some soldiers came up behind them. Poma's heart beat faster. Were these the soldiers she had encountered earlier? She pulled her straw hat down over her eyes. But these men turned out to be strangers. Doctor talked to the soldiers for a few minutes, then told Poma and the children that the soldiers were hunting for bandits who frequented the area. They had robbed some travelers and killed two of the men in the party. As far as the soldiers could tell, the bandits did not get away with much booty. The soldiers cautioned Doctor to try and find shelter at night in the villages along the way, so his family would be safe.

And so, after gaining permission from the farmers, they stayed in barns or sheds at night. In this desert-like world, they mostly found sheds and not large barns, but they discovered that even a shed was better than camping in the open. Occasionally there was an inn and they and the horses could rest an extra day.

It was on a night when they couldn't reach a shelter that the bandits struck. Poma was almost asleep when she was disturbed by the horses. In an instant her knife was in her hand. She looked over at the place where Doctor had made his bed. It was empty. She awakened Nik and Himiko and it was then she saw Doctor next to a big rock, sword in hand. He motioned them to be quiet. Poma's treasures were hidden with the horse trappings. She peered over Doctor's shoulder and into the dark night. Three shadowy figures were sneaking along the road toward their camp. They were about to be attacked.

Poma knew she had to be brave for the children. Nik had all but disappeared into a crevice of the big rock, and clutched Himiko by her side. Poma saw in their eyes that the children trusted Doctor and her to protect them. Doctor was concentrating on the ragged shadows on the road. Where were the bandits? Poma's heart raced. She wondered if Doctor could hear it. Estwynd gave a shrill whinny. Doctor leapt up. A high-pitched scream sliced the night air, and his sword found its mark. One of the bandits was down.

Poma felt the hot breath of the second one, and turned in time to stab the man in the neck before he could touch her. The children were screaming. Doctor finished the man off with his sword. The thud of hooves could be heard as the third man escaped with nothing but the horse he came with.

Poma shook as Doctor put an arm around her. His breath came in gasps. "Are you alright?"

"I—I think so," she said.

"We must go, before the other one comes back."

No time to calm the children. They packed up in a heated rush, and urged the horses down the road.

Before it was light, they came to a small town that had an inn. Their room faced onto a courtyard. The stables were at the far end of a muddy yard. But the room was white and clean, with thick walls. The innkeeper's vegetable garden was near the door. But Poma didn't take too much notice. She was grateful for a place to rest that had a roof. They were all in shock over the attack of the bandits and needed to sleep. When the horses and the children were settled, Poma lay on her bed shivering and couldn't sleep. She could not get the foul odor of the bandit's breath out of her system. When she took a deep breath, there it was. When she closed her eyes, all she saw was the man's ugly face.

"Keep the candle burning," she said. Her voice was hoarse and trembling. Doctor gave her some hot chamomile tea and bathed her face in warm water.

Poma stood on a high hill overlooking the great Taklimakan. Tigrax and Targitaus stood at the bottom of the hill with a crowd of people. She was supposed to speak to them, but didn't know what to say. Suddenly Arle was there with his back to her. His hair had turned white and he was staring out over the desert. She said to him, "Why are you here?" But he didn't answer. He only searched the horizon and waited.

The candle was still burning when Poma awoke. Tigrax and Targitaus—and a group of people to speak to. What should she say to her past and her future? Poma opened her eyes part way, thinking perhaps she must somehow find what it was that needed to be said to these people in her past, but especially what should be said to those in her future. Perhaps it was time to concentrate more on teaching what she knew, thereby preserving her art for those who would follow.

Doctor stood in the doorway watching the gathering light of a new day. The foul scent had faded, and she could taste the high, almost mint-like notes of the chamomile. She gathered her shawl around her and joined Doctor at the small door.

He put his arm around her. "How are you feeling?"

"Much better, thank you. Don't you need some rest, too?" she said. Doctor looked as if he, too, was finally overcome by exhaustion.

"We will rest here for a day or two," he said.

Poma was glad for the time to get back her balance. "Why does evil take such energy to overcome?" she mused, almost to herself. Doctor lifted her face to his and kissed her. His kiss was like that of a butterfly. She rested her head on his shoulder, glad for the sudden intimacy. It helped her to know the world was good again.

The first rays of the sun hit his face. He kissed her forehead. "We had ourselves quite a night, didn't we?" He glanced at the children, then went and curled up in his bed like a baby.

Poma blew out the flickering candle and slept soundly.

The Bell

In another two weeks they reached the big city of Chang 'an nestled at the head of a large valley, completed by a wide river. Many people were on the road. Among the farmers with carts and yaks, and soldiers with horses, were wealthy merchants on camels and what appeared to be ladies of the court, carried in sedan chairs. Among the travelers like themselves, weary and dusty from the road, were colorful monks and peasants in more serious garb.

The outskirts of the city was home to large pens where whole herds of animals were kept, awaiting sale or exchange in order to organize the caravans to the west. Poma was happy the wind was non-existent so the odorous scene did not accost their senses. Large groups of camels were assembled, sitting in dignified disdain of all the bustle around them.

Poma was amazed at the size of the city. It was the largest city she had ever seen. They approached the south gate. A high wall encompassed the city all around so there was no sense of the extent of the massive churning of all this humanity and animals until after they rode through the gate. Then the city came alive. The buildings were all shapes and sizes. Tall pagodas pierced the sky. Somber grey monasteries sat shoulder to shoulder, their only distinction the curved Chinese roof corners of brightly painted wood smiling up at the morning sun.

She was struck by the mix of poverty and ostentation. Child beggars tugged at gold-embroidered coattails. Squalid alleyways led to imperial, manicured parks. It was a scene to evoke multi-layered emotions. The bazaars were divided up by type of shops in long rows. People here were shoulder to shoulder, streaming in and out of the shops. It was breathtaking.

Doctor found a park for them to rest in and they lunched on delicacies from a nearby street vendor. The flavor of these foods, along with the aromas from so many animals, made up a major part of the atmosphere. A small old woman sat nearby, eating her meager lunch. She bowed her head at Poma and Nik. Poma caught her eye and smiled. She smiled back and bowed slightly, a gesture seemingly reserved for strangers.

Poma sat in the shade of a large tree and drank cold tea. Himiko lay his head on her lap and almost fell asleep. She smoothed his hair and thought about Targitaus. Right at that moment there came a sound she had never heard before. At first she thought an animal was brawling. But it shook her whole being. Then it sounded once more with the same deep-throated authority, again reverberating through her soul. She looked around. Aside from a scattering of pigeons, everyone went on about their business. Again it sounded, and its deep music caught her heart.

The old woman must have seen the startled look on Poma's face. She pointed at the bell tower high above the city. A huge brass bell announced to all who heard that it was noon. It seemed to Poma to say much more than the time of day.

The lady smiled at Doctor and explained to him that the bell symbolized the gathering of the great caravans and the lure of the western frontier.

Doctor turned and translated all this to Poma and Nik. "She says that for many hundreds of years this has been the eastern end of a great road that leads to the marvels of the west, great cities such as Tun-Huang, Samarkand, Constantinople, and Rome. The bell calls the merchants and travelers to the beginning of their great journey." Doctor grinned at Poma. "I guess we're in the right place."

Poma could feel deep within her that the bell was re-affirming her longing for home, her search for Enash, and the insatiable desire to know more about the royal purple and the ancient mother-Goddess who made her distaff. The sound of the bell seemed to center her desire to travel down this long road and find her way back to who she really was. In this centering was a peaceful purpose, and it gladdened her heart.

Poma stayed in the city park while Doctor searched out a caravan camp for them to stay in while they found the next group forming for the westward trek. As Poma studied her little map, she began to realize that the Goddess was testing her; each time she traveled through time, she was farther away from her goal. As she had grown older, she felt more and more that she should be at Enash's side. This time she would make it, she told herself. Now she knew how to let nothing stand in her way.

As they gathered in the camp, each merchant or family was given a number. Doctor could tell by the activity in the camel market it would be soon that their number would be called. He and Nik went to look at the camels. Poma and Himiko settled under some trees and built a small campfire to wait.

It seemed to Poma that the entire world was represented here, and that every dream ever dreamt hung in the air and mixed with the smoke of the cook fires. Men haggled, children played, and women stirred pots and watched, as she did. And they were all bonded together by dreams, camels, and campfires.

At prescribed times during the day, the camel drivers and a few others stopped for prayer. The call to prayer could be heard from inside the city walls. The brown sands blossomed with colorful mosaics of lovely old prayer rugs. The haggling was replaced with chants and ancient prayers. Everyone waited patiently. Even the camels seemed to know they were being cared for by other than earthly hands.

Close by was an old woman with the saddest face Poma had ever seen. The deep brown wrinkles framed black eyes that were wells of fear. Poma saw no one around her, so she went over and introduced herself.

"Hello. My name is Poma. Are you traveling alone?"

The black eyes snapped at her for only a moment before tears streamed down her lined face. She began rocking to and fro in the honored tradition of mourning.

"I'm so sorry," Poma said. She sat down beside the woman. "I didn't think . . ."

The old one's face became composed. She brushed a wisp of grey hair out of her eyes. "It's alright dear; you had no way of knowing. My husband died only three days ago." Her face crumpled with the apparent memory.

"I'm so sorry," Poma said again. "Is there anything I can do?"

"Oh, no, dear. I'll be safe with the caravan. This was to be our last trip. We were going home. Now I have to leave Abraham in this foreign place." And the rocking began again.

Poma reached for the old one's slender hand. "Ride along with us. We can at least share a fire."

"Oh, I will be just fine—"

Poma heard the hesitancy in the old voice. "I insist."

"Thank you, dear."

Himiko dashed up to the fire. He had been playing with some other children in the camp. "Where is Estwynd?" he said.

Poma dropped the old woman's hand and rose to her feet. "He's right over . . ." The grandmother was forgotten. She stopped in horror, pointing to the empty spot she had last seen the big grey. She looked all around. Her heart started pounding. She ran toward a small hill where she could oversee the area better.

"Go find Doctor," she shouted at Himiko. She ran, breathless, up the small hill. Tears streamed down her face. Her stomach felt empty. She did not see any sign of Estwynd anywhere. What was happening here? It was not time for her and Estwynd to go; she had not been here for a year yet.

Himiko came running up the hill. "Doctor says to stay at this end of the camp and look, and he and Nik will search over there. And he said to tell you he has the camels!"

Poma stopped in her tracks. Of course! She would almost bet that she would find Estwynd again when he was needed. No use of subjecting a horse to the terrible journey across that vast desert. But she would still look for him, because there was, of course, a chance he had been stolen.

In due time, Doctor waved at her across the crowds of people and animals, and she could see him shrugging. She waved back. He pointed toward their camp, and she and Himiko headed in that direction. Doctor and Nik were there waiting for them.

"Did you see him anywhere?" Poma asked.

Doctor looked very worried. "No, we couldn't find him. And the camel drivers have not seen him. There were a few trades with dapple greys, but none with one blue eye."

"I heard you found us some camels," she said. "How soon must we leave?"

"Just as soon as the trading is complete, probably tomorrow," he said.

"So soon?" Poma bit her lip. "I suppose now I will have to give up some more gold for one of the beasts," she said. Her eyes came to rest on the grandmother. She walked over to her. "Do you have a camel yet?"

The old woman stirred out of her reverie. "What? Oh, yes, yes. It is an old beast, almost as old as I am." She looked at Poma thoughtfully. "Actually, I have two camels. But I won't need one. If your trading is not complete, may I sell you one of mine?"

Doctor overheard the women talking. "Now that we are missing a horse, that might be a good solution for all of us," he said.

And so Poma found herself the proud possessor of a large, satisfied-looking camel. It was with respect to the history of the day that his name was Genghis. Search as they might, they could not find Estwynd or his saddle anywhere. The only thing left from his trappings was the gold mask. They posted the children on the small hill, and while they searched inside the city, the grandmother watched their camp. They all met again that evening and decided that Estwynd was long gone. Although Poma knew she would probably find him again some day, she was nevertheless sad that such an old and treasured friend was gone. But, of course, she could not talk about how she felt sure she and Estwynd were destined to find one another again. Nor could she ever admit that Estwynd had been given to her when she was ten seasons old—and by an Egyptian Pharaoh, at that. No, her sadness was not entirely feigned, but she did feel a certain loneliness, especially when she looked at Genghis. What an ungainly beast! But these animals would get them safely across the great expanse of wilderness they must cross.

That night they gathered around the campfire. Doctor, Nik, Himiko, Poma and the grandmother—a new traveling family in the larger caravan family surrounding them. The grandmother had some fresh vegetables, and they ate well, with rice and some eastern spices. The sun set red and the glow of the evening was a backdrop for the excitement everyone felt to start their journey together. The velvet night displayed diamonds for stars and the evening glow funneled into the campfire embers. Voices were low and lullabies calmed the animals and small children. The grandmother smiled for the first time. Himiko could not sleep for the excitement of setting off with all these people. The children in the camp seemed to love the big camels, and the camels seemed to know it.

Poma had everything packed and sat down to listen to the quiet. The grandmother pulled out a small bamboo flute and started playing. Poma's heart was immediately warmed by the haunting tones. The loss of her horse was the only sad thing in this day, and even that was not so bad, as she knew in her heart they would be reunited. The music was like a song someone could sing from any part of the world and be understood anywhere. The notes took her back to those long evenings in Egypt when she sat with Taki and heard the Egyptian music rise up from the cook-fires along the river. The song became a companion for a dance, which brought back a night on the steppe with a handsome man watching her. The music faded down to a subdued lullaby and brought back the nights when she fell asleep in her fur bed as a small child.

The big bell from the city groaned its last sound of the day and brought a silence to the camp, punctuated only by an occasional soft whining sigh from the camel enclosure. It seemed as if the whole world slept.

On the Trail

Early in the morning, just at dawn, the somber bell sounded once more. It was the call to the journey. All the travelers talked about a new life; some talked about new philosophies, and most knew there were treasures to be bought and sold. The camels were loaded down with spices, dyes, silks and children. One by one they rose, hind quarters first, here and there a whine or a snort, and everyone was assembled in a long line.

The grandmother led Poma's small party of six camels. Himiko rode with Nik. The other two camels carried the grandmother's load of spices, Poma's indigo and basket, Himiko's trunk and some bundles with cooking utensils, food, and goatskins of water. Doctor had purchased some silk to sell in one of the western markets. Fortunately, Genghis was a mild-mannered camel, tall and dignified. He was at home with the dust of the trail, and lumbered along at a good pace. Poma felt she would never get used to sand and dust. She remembered the Egyptian desert held the same atmosphere. But this area of the world smelled different. The dust of Egypt smelled dead, whereas the rocky trail through central China was graced with the occasional scent of pine. *Every forest flavors the desert around it,* thought Poma.

The animals quickly settled into a pace that suited the caravan as a whole. The summer provided no rain, and the days were hot. It was on one of these hot days the peace of the group was ruptured when almost half of them wanted to stop at a Buddhist shrine. The Moslems and others grew impatient. The grumbling made its way back to Poma's small family.

"What's happening up there?" Poma asked.

Doctor reigned in his camel. "I don't know. It is bad to sit here in the midday sun," he said.

A stocky little fellow named Emar was just ahead of the grandmother. He turned and yelled back at them. "They are stopping for a shrine. Some of the Buddhists forgot to pray this morning." Emar had narrow eyes and a large neck. To that he added a sinister giggle, and the full picture emerged of one who perhaps could not be trusted. Poma pulled up alongside the grandmother. "A snake!" The old lady whispered. "His ears are too big. Stingy!" And her eyes squinted at Emar's broad back. The grandmother evidently was not one to mince words.

"Certainly it will not take long to say a prayer," Poma said.

"One can pray anywhere," the old one replied. "But we need to allow everyone his own way of doing," she added.

On this day the Moslems only grumbled. One or two joined the Buddhists at their shrine. The big Persian who led the caravan passed the word along that they would have a meeting that night, and all the men were to attend. Poma sighed. She got out her spindle and took the time waiting to spin. Nik joined in spinning, and the grandmother sucked on a piece of dried meat.

When the grandmother's eyes found the purple distaff, her face became immobile. Her black eyes were studying Poma with a fixation that made Poma blush. Although the grandmother said nothing, Poma knew the old woman was curious. The curiosity would have to be assuaged later, for the trip was resuming.

Soon there was a holler or two and the camels roused themselves back into line. It was on this occasion that Poma and Nik both learned to spin on the back of a moving camel, a feat of no small accomplishment. The textured yarn from that day was later woven into camel bags.

That night at the meeting, the Persian elucidated some strict rules that involved the sanctity of everyone's religion. The Moslems would pray at their noon-day rest, and the only other place they would stop for any length of time was Tun-Huang, where the caves in the area offered Buddhist art painted on the walls and innumerable shrines. It was a very holy place, and some in the group were making it a pilgrimage. But Tun-Huang was many days away.

Himiko played with the other children in the evenings and at every dinnertime, he came back to the fire with stories about Tun-Huang. "Poma-san!"

Poma looked up from the fire. "What now, little one?"

"When we get to Tun-Huang, can we stop and see the caves? Chan Yi told me this is where they are going, and they have wonderful paintings on the wall, and . . ."

His small face was so serious he was almost comical. Poma thought back for just a moment to a large scrap of deerskin with the rude designs of another nine-year-old.

"Yes, dear, we will stop and see the caves. But only as long as the caravan stops."

Himiko's eyes lit up. He immediately turned and ran off to find his new friend and tell her his good news. Poma had never seen him quite so excited.

The caravan's days soon entered into a monotonous system of setting up camp, tearing it down, and packing up the camels. A few weeks before they reached Tun-Huang, word spread among the women that a young Chinese woman was about to have her baby. That evening Poma hurried to the woman's fire. The men had erected a hastily built tent for her.

Poma approached the women gathered nearby. "I am Poma, and I assisted a midwife long ago. Can I be of help?"

One of the women grabbed her hand and drew her over to the makeshift tent. "The baby is early, and the mother is suffering badly. What should we do?"

Poma knelt down beside the young woman. The nearby campfire light caught the woman's face, shiny with perspiration. Poma felt the woman's brow and gave her a reassuring smile. She felt the woman's stomach, tried to estimate the progress of the baby. "When did the pains begin?" she asked.

One of the women spoke in a whisper; her large eyes announced her fear. "Yesterday she did not feel well, and the pains began in the night."

Poma frowned. "Get her some rice water to drink." The woman would need liquid and as much nourishment as they could give her. The baby was not in a good position. Poma wished that she had Madga by her side, but that, of course, could not be. After many hours and many midwife tricks, the exhausted woman finally gave birth to a dead little girl. All of the women turned away except for the mother's little sister. She continued to fan her sister's face and spoke to her in whispers. Some of the older women took the stillborn child away. A buzz went through the group of men gathered outside the small tent. No one seemed concerned about the mother or the child except for the Chinese sister.

One of the older Moslem women took Poma to one side. "Be glad it was a girl. A stillborn boy, and you'd be in danger now." Poma felt shocked, but decided it better not to show it. She thought back to Madga again, this time holding the tiny Tarim in her arms. Back in that place it was the boys who were not wanted.

When she got back to her little family, she was tired and thoroughly aggravated.

Doctor saw the glum look on her face. "You are exhausted. Here, sit down and tell me what happened."

Poma was grateful for his kind face and a place to rest. "The child was stillborn," she said. "I was told to be glad it was a girl, otherwise I'd be in trouble." She sat down and heaved a big sigh. "What is it that is wrong with men when logic dictates they would not even exist if it were not for women?"

Doctor had no answer. He just let her put her head on his shoulder. "Maybe next time you should not be so quick to volunteer," he said.

This irritated her all over again. She drew back and snapped at him, "That's a fine thing for a physician to say!" And she got up and strode away, needing fresh air. As she wiped the tears away, a red dawn broke, promising another day of heat and dust. The grandmother, although awake, kept her own council and fixed a big breakfast for the tired Poma.

For the next few days, the desert got drier and they could see sand dunes. Conversation between Poma and Doctor dried up as well. There was an uncomfortable truce as Tun-Huang grew closer. Poma kept a cold distance between them. In a way, she felt sorry there should be bad feelings, but Doctor had simply been a little too arrogant. He left Poma alone except for communicating about necessary day-to-day activities.

Tun-Huang

As they skirted the large sand dunes, the slightest breeze whipped the sand up on the top ridges of the dunes, creating an ever-changing scene. Poma felt small twinges of fear when the breezes picked up each afternoon. She had heard stories of the great storms, and was happy each day when the horizon was done rearranging itself for the day. They traveled through the Gansu corridor, with occasional dusty brown cliffs on either side of the trail. Tun-Huang was brown for an oasis. Even the green places were dusty. Here the caravan would rest for a few days to re-provision itself for the next part of the trip—the dreaded Taklimakan. Tun-Huang was considered the jade gate, as the mountains of the west yielded the beautiful green gems so precious to the Chinese.

Himiko was excited by the anticipation of seeing the Buddhist cave art. "They say there are a thousand Buddhas," he said. His eyes shone. He got so excited he hardly slept.

Poma sat down next to him. "Tell me, little one, what excites you so about the Buddhist art?"

"My mother taught me we must spend a long time becoming enlightened. We have many Buddhas and other helpers who assist us in this."

"How do you become enlightened?" asked Poma.

"Well, I'm not sure about all of it, but mother also taught me that we must learn to put the desires of others ahead of ourselves. It is very hard."

Poma smiled at him. "That seems a lot for a child to do, but I think your mother was very wise. Don't ever forget what she taught you. Love of others above oneself is a very noble goal." This got his mind on something else, and eventually he fell asleep.

They gathered the next morning with a small group of pilgrims to make the trek to the caves. The grandmother stayed in the caravan camp to rest, saying she had seen the Buddhas. Nik suggested to Himiko that he bring along paper and paint to copy some of the paintings. Himiko looked at Poma with such excitement she almost laughed. She nodded, and so he brought along his paper and paints.

Soon they arrived at the huge cliff, lined with rickety staircases. The scope of the artwork was breathtaking. Some of the painting was fairly new, and the array of colors was astounding to Poma. There was malachite green, pink, azure blue, white, and black on a red background. Niches held modeled clay figures. Walls were painted with many disciples, some kneeling, some flying, some with musical instruments, others making offerings. Some of the cave paintings had a mother-of-pearl background, to catch the flickering lamps of the worshippers. The paintings filled the caves. The Buddhas were everywhere, in every conceivable position of omniscience. Himiko was enthralled. Nik wandered through the caves with him, and then sat down to eat her lunch. Poma sat with her for awhile, and then continued looking with Himiko. Some of the painting was in bad need of repair. One of the caves held a space to one side where workers and artisans were restoring some of the work. It was here that Himiko, eyes wide, sat down, speechless. He got out his paints and started to work copying one of the Buddhas. Finally, an old man, one of the painters, noticed the little boy.

He smiled at Himiko and Poma. "Hello, young man. Are you and your mother pilgrims?" he said.

The usually gregarious Himiko could only stare at him.

Poma smiled at the elderly gentleman. "I guess you could say he's a pilgrim," she said, amused.

The old man sat down across from Himiko. "My name is Jan. And who might you be?"

Himiko finally responded. "I am Himiko."

"And where are you traveling to?" asked Jan. Himiko looked at Poma. It evidently occurred to him that he had never heard Poma mention any kind of destination. He looked a little confused.

Poma spoke up for him. "We are going to the big sea," she said.

Jan saw the picture Himiko was drawing. "May I see?" he said. Himiko shyly turned the paper around so Jan could see it. Jan glanced at Poma for only a moment before turning back to the boy. "This is very nice work, Himiko." He looked over at Poma once more. "May I show him some more of the paintings?" Jan asked.

Poma wanted to rest her feet. "Of course," said Poma. "I will meet him back here when you are finished."

Nik and Doctor wandered in, looking a little lost. Nik wandered to the back of the cave, intrigued by the restoration.

"Himiko went to see some more rooms of the cave with one of the painters." Poma said.

"This is quite a wonderful place," Doctor said. "Artisans will be busy here for many years." He sat down next to Poma.

"I overheard you saying we were headed for the big sea. Will this be the end of your wandering?" Doctor asked quietly.

Poma looked at his face. He wore a frown, and his eyes were searching hers. She smiled. "I honestly don't know. I would love to have a home some day. Perhaps when I am old," she replied.

His frown soured into melancholy. "Poma . . ." Then he stopped, as if he did not know what to say. She waited, her eyes searching his sad face.

"Poma, you know I love you very much, but I can't . . ." He stopped, interrupted by Jan and Himiko.

The boy came running up to them. "Poma-San!" His small face was so serious. "Poma-San, I want to stay here. I want to paint with Jan. He said they will need help to do the—the—"

"Restoration," Jan completed the sentence, smiling. "The boy tells me he wants to show me his work."

Doctor spoke up first. "That would be a good opportunity for him."

Poma felt a mixture of emotions. "Jan, why don't you come to our camp this evening, and Himiko can show you his paintings, and we can talk more." She felt a great pride in Himiko, but at the same time was fearful for him. She felt a motherly protectiveness.

Jan bowed politely and said he would be happy to meet with them that night, and then returned to his work.

Poma spent some time talking with the other artisans. They spoke very highly of Jan, saying he was a master of colors. They had youngsters helping them to mix paints and run errands. "Jan is famous here for matching the new colors to the old ones," said one of the young men. "The reproductions are as faithful as he can get to the old art." His face became serious. "Jan is teaching us to continue the work, because of all the influences you see from both east and west, right here in one spot."

Poma could see why the young artisan was so excited about his work. She had spotted the Scythian-like animal symbols in one of the caves.

All her family soon gathered around her again. Himiko was almost babbling about some aqua blue paint pots, Nik needed some fresh air, and Doctor's expression had changed from sadness to pensiveness. Poma suspected he had an idea.

When they arrived back at the caravan camp, Poma and Nik busied themselves with the evening meal.

As Poma stirred the rice, Doctor became talkative. He was abrupt. "I think it will be best for us all if I stay here with Himiko."

Poma put the lid on the rice pot. Doctor looked serious. "What would you do here?" she asked.

"Jan told me they have no physician here. There was an old man who knew the herbs, but he died long ago. Jan feels responsible for the young artists in his care, and has asked me to stay here for awhile. And I thought if we agree to let Himiko stay, I would stay with him. Of course, I'd love for you to stay, too, but I know how important it is for you to continue your journey."

Poma felt diverse emotions for the second time that day. She was surprised at herself for feeling a certain amount of relief. Was it relief from the responsibility of the boy, or was it relief from the entanglements that Doctor represented?

"Doctor, I—I am sorry if I have offended you. I feel—"

"You have never offended me, dear one."

"Well, I said a few harsh things, and I feel I should apologize."

He smiled at her. "For what? Having the good sense to put me in my place? You are a gentle person, Poma, and your dark energies seem overpowering to you. Actually, you are right on course."

She laughed with him, but couldn't help keeping the upper hand. "So, dark energies, is it? Well, yes, and I sharpen my tongue every day just for you."

They chuckled some more together. Jan came strolling up just as the dinner was ready. Himiko had gotten out his paintings to show the old man. And no one could sit down and eat until he had seen them all. Poma watched Jan's face carefully. She was rewarded when she caught the glimmer of astonishment in the old man's eyes.

"These are beautiful," he exclaimed.

Himiko's grin spread all across his face. The grandmother was also struck by the little one's talents. "Mmmm," she mused, and nodded in appreciation. Jan sat down across from Poma. Nik served up the dinner. The conversation was light as they ate.

Jan reached into his cloak and pulled out a long-stemmed pipe. He looked directly at Poma. "You and your husband can be quite proud of your son," he said.

Poma stopped him. "We are not quite the family we appear," she said quickly. "We are—well, only friends, traveling together. To make a long story short, Nik and I escaped an earthquake, Himiko and Doctor escaped from pirates, and the fates brought us together. We are only related by circumstance."

Doctor put his hand on Himiko's shoulder. "I am prepared to stay here with the boy. I offer my services to the community of artisans, and I will also protect the young man here as he begins his apprenticeship."

Himiko looked imploringly at Poma. "Poma-San, may I stay? Please?"

The last shreds of opposition Poma felt fell away. "Yes, Himiko, if that is really what you want to do."

Himiko got up and bowed to Poma, then turned and bowed to Jan. Then, in boyish exuberance, he hugged Poma, jumping up and down at the same time. He stopped and looked at Poma face-to-face. He appeared to be torn by his decision. Tears welled up in his eyes. Poma knew Himiko had instinctively made the right decision for himself. His talents should not be wasted.

She put her hands on his small shoulders. "You will be happy here, little one," she whispered. "I will never forget you."

He allowed her to give him a motherly hug. He sat beside Doctor and took his hand. And so it was settled. Later that evening, after Jan had left, Nik helped Poma clean up the dinner.

"I'll miss Himiko," Nik said. Poma glanced at her. Her face was wet with tears. Poma didn't realize how close the two children had become.

She put an arm around the girl. "It seems as if you have lost a lot of people in your life lately," she said.

Nik stopped and put her head on Poma's shoulder. Her voice was soft. "Thank you for bringing me along," she said.

Poma hugged her. "It looks like it's just you and me—and the grandmother will help," she replied. Poma was comforted by the fact that she was still needed.

The next morning, Doctor helped Poma pack up four of the camels. He gave her a good price for the silk he had carried across the country. "You can get a better price farther on," he said.

"Thank you for your help," she said. It sounded so weak, somehow. They had traveled far, and even killed bandits together. "I—I won't forget you, my friend," she said.

"Nor I, you," he replied. "I will take good care of the youngster. He will be happy here." The other camel was loaded up with Himiko and his trunk.

Poma could see this was true. As the beast rose to its feet and lumbered away toward the caves, Doctor waved at them, but Himiko never looked back.

Poma smiled her secret smile. She realized this parting was better than the parting which would surely come in another nine years or so. The three women tore down the camp and rejoined the long row of camels heading west into the hot Taklimakan.

The Storm

Some in the caravan joined another large group headed to the northern road across the top of the desert. This road was quicker, but more dangerous. The southern road, although longer, had more water holes. And some from the other group joined them. Within just a few weeks they arrived at the desolate edge of the Taklimakan. The old stories that Poma had heard so many hundreds of years before were still being retold. Some had been refined and disguised by time, but others were basically the same. She even found herself telling some of the stories she heard from old Ban, the storyteller.

One morning at breakfast, Nik told Poma about her dream. "It was so strange. I was in a huge house, and Genghis was there and all these people were expecting me to give a speech. So I started to talk, and then they weren't paying any attention. But they listened to Genghis. Only, I couldn't understand Genghis. It was like he was speaking a foreign language."

"Was the house like the teahouse, or more like Chan Li's big house?"

Nik frowned into her tea. "I didn't recognize the house. It was just big."

"That's a very interesting dream," Poma said.

"Why? What does it mean?"

"I think the stories about the desert have suggested your dream to you, "Poma said. "Your house right now is the desert."

Nik's eyes grew large. "But I've never seen the Taklimakan until now."

"That's why you don't recognize the house in your dream."

"Why did the people want me to give a speech?"

"Your dream would indicate that you have a need to be self-assured. You are gathering courage for the trip into that big house—that big patch of earth that you don't recognize. Perhaps you should learn the language of these people."

"But what about Genghis?"

"Our camels are going to help us through this. Some folks even call them the ships of the desert. We couldn't travel here without them."

Nik seemed to be satisfied with those explanations. "Perhaps I feel that Himiko was much more courageous than I—and now I don't have him here—but I know he'll be happy at Tun-Huang." Her smile was braver than her speech.

Poma sat down next to her and gave her a hug. "Sometimes being brave means simply going along and facing our problems, one day at a time."

Nik's face crumpled into gratitude as the tears ran down. "Oh, Poma, I love you so much. Thank you!"

Poma felt drawn to this girl who was so like her when she was young. But she could see her own growth, and was able to smile her secret smile, pleased with being a little older and a little wiser.

It was deep into fall when they came to the barren reaches of the Taklimakan. There were no visible changes in the seasons here, no leaves to announce the autumn with a blaze of gold and burnt orange. The nights were perhaps cooler, but the desert simply retained its year-round ugly but delicate demeanor. Poma searched the horizon. She knew from her map that she was looking directly toward the area she had been in when she had first seen this mighty desert, so long ago, from the mountains. The desert was so large; however, the mountains were nowhere in sight.

The caravan followed the ever-changing trail at the edge of the great desert. Old villages near this great desert had disappeared. Every now and then a caravan group would have to forge a new section of the trail. The greedy sands wanted to cover the world. The women knew to build fires at night and cook for the next day. The spicy array of food was welcomed as the aromas helped to blot out the acrid smell of the camels. The caravan was up before dawn to travel in the cool part of the day. The high fires helped the sentries at night keep watch for jackals and bandits.

The long line of camels with their precious cargo was interrupted in the second week by a ferocious storm. As the morning sun reddened the sky, not an insect sound could be heard. Sudden eddies of sand indicated the only other live thing in the desert was the occasional breeze that foreshadowed the great winds to come. The Persian ordered the ropes be strung out along the camels, each one attached as if to a long life-line. Poma and Nik piled onto the resilient camels who then rose obediently to their feet.

The caravan crept slowly through the still morning. The grandmother turned and reminisced to Poma and Nik about a storm out of the past.

"I remember one storm when I was very young. We had 50 people on that trip, and only 36 of us lived through it."

Nik's eyes got very big. "What happened?" she asked.

"Someone let go of the rope, and those people simply disappeared into the desert, and were never seen again." She looked knowingly at Poma.

"All of them?" Nik asked.

"All of them." She confirmed.

Poma quietly explained to Nik to never let go of the rope, to stay with the camel and cover herself completely. The sand had a way of being everywhere at once and even on a good day it drifted into everything—eyes, throat, and food. It was relentless in a storm, took charge of one's very soul. Everything on all sides disappeared.

"The sun itself cannot be seen for hours," the grandmother said. "Time and space are gone from the earth and it is said the under-gods seize you by the throat."

Nik shivered. Her eyes were wide with terror. "Do you mean Kitak of the underworld?"

Poma wasn't quite sure who this was, but Nik should be thoroughly convinced of the dangers.

"Yes, that's the one." Poma said.

Nik's knuckles turned white as she clung to the camel saddle.

The men placed themselves strategically down the long line to help keep all the animals together. Poma and Nik were assigned a smallish Turkoman with worried eyes and a narrow mustache. Poma's camels and precious load of indigo and other dyestuffs were felt to be important enough for protection.

Talking halted along with the camels when they first heard the storm. Suddenly the wind howled out of the north, the sky darkened and the great clouds of sand and grit hit like a great ocean wave. The camels, grumbling, got to their knees and Poma and the small Turkoman propped up part of the tent at the side of the biggest camel. Gradually the world and the grandmother's camel disappeared.

"Get under here!" Poma shouted, pointing to the tent. Nik was frozen to the camel saddle.

"Nik!" Poma struggled to the other side of the camel. "Nik!" she shouted. Nik didn't move. Poma grabbed her by the arms and pulled her down from the camel and around to their hiding place under the piece of tent.

Poma clutched at her shawl, covering her head. Even the animal seemed grateful for the shelter. They settled in, breathing in gulps of air when they could, and waited. The new world was red, gritty, and dark.

The Turk clung to the rope. Luckily it stayed taut at both ends, their only indication of other life.

Poma put her arm around Nik. "Are you all right?" she shouted. Nik was crying. She clutched at the tent. "I . . . I think so," she wailed. Poma hugged her closer. Soon her sobbing ceased and they clung to each other through the almost endless whistling winds.

The wind stopped as suddenly as it had started. The camel shook his head and breathed deeply at the fresh air. The sand had piled up along his back. Slowly the animals rose with their loads, and a great shout went up along the line as Allah and some lesser Gods were praised. The next water was a day away, and already half the day was wasted. They would make a dry camp that night, and depend on water in the goatskins.

The camels were unconcerned and moved forward obligingly. They knew the whereabouts of the water even before the humans did. The Turkoman flashed a great white smile at the women, bowed, and ran ahead to his group of countrymen, a large family near the front with a bevy of five camels.

The Persian leader, a man said by some to be wealthy and ruthless, and by others to be honest and fair, pushed the caravan farther that day than they thought the animals capable of. It was vital they reach this oasis, because the one after this was fully a three days' journey.

When the camels had plodded through an endless day, it became apparent to some of the seasoned travelers that the watering hole had been lost. The camels were the only ones smiling. Silly grins, thought Poma. Estwynd had never been quite that condescending.

They camped quietly that night, drinking little of the water saved in goatskins. In another two days they reached a bigger oasis and everyone was relieved when the Persian decided to rest the animals an extra day. And so the traveling went, the very existence of commerce depending on elusive water and grinning camels.

One morning early, Poma arose to pack up her bed, and realized the grandmother was not up. As she bent over the old woman, she could see the pallid skin. Her usually wrinkled cheeks were drawn and hot.

"Grandmother . . ."

The old one's brows furrowed. "The gold," she whispered.

Poma quickly wet a corner of her shawl from a goatskin and wiped the pale face. "Rest now, old one. Everything is safe."

The old eyes searched from Poma's face to the patient camel, and then through the desert camp awakening in the glow of early morning.

"The gold, Poma . . . please take the gold . . . for you and the girl . . . and I want you to have my flute." The death rattle was mercifully short as she sighed her last breath, and left the struggle behind.

Poma felt helpless. She realized she never knew the old one's name. She had seen death before, and certainly this woman had lived a long life. She felt no need for tears, and in a confused way she felt relief for the fragile old woman. The grandmother, in her stern way, was a friend, and Poma felt grateful to her.

Poma called to Nik. "She's gone, Nik. Go get the Persian." The caravan leader would have to deal with death as well as life this day and the final word as to the disposition of the old woman's earthly treasures was his.

Poma quickly looked through the woman's large bags and found the flute and a small sack of gold. Just as she placed the gold in her basket the Persian and his women folk walked quickly past the camels and over to the old woman, now lying still in her bed. One of the women touched her arm and quickly drew her hand away.

"Bury her there," he said, and pointed to a spot near a dune. "Where is the gold?"

Poma stood up and turned to face him. "She wanted me to have it." She said.

The big man scowled at her. "Shouldn't have let her come in the first place," he muttered. His gaze was cold. "The gold is mine for the trouble of bringing along one so old. The gold is mine. You may keep the beast."

Poma looked first at the grandmother's camel and then back at the determined Persian. "She told me to split the gold between the girl and me." She gestured at Nik. Nik shrank back slightly, her eyes frightened. Poma widened her stance, placing a hand on her hip. "It was her wish that we have that gold." She said.

The Persian wouldn't budge. "It's either the gold or your goatskins," he said.

Poma knew this meant being left to die in the desert. She quickly formed an idea. She managed to look contrite as she silently reached into the basket and into the pouch. She grabbed only a handful of the gold, leaving about half of it behind in the little bag.

"Here," she said, pretending petulance, and gave the frowning man a handful of the gold. She stepped back, praying her ruse would work.

He examined the chunks of yellow metal and his brows rose. "Hmmm," he said. "Alright." His lips pursed as he looked at her basket. Their eyes met in a knowing, tacit agreement. He turned to the assembled women. "Divide up her other things quickly." To the men, "Pack up those beasts. The sun is high. It's time to move on." He returned to the front of the caravan.

Poma took a big breath. Now her basket carried another very real secret. She would keep this secret until the end of the trip, when it was time to share the leftover gold with Nik. She wrapped the grandmother's body in its robe and watched as the men dug a shallow grave and lifted her into it. The sand was mounded over her and a few large rocks placed on the mound.

Poma shuddered, thinking the old one's hasty grave not deep enough. But the merciless sun grew higher, and the animals anxious. The desert was a living thing, and those who chose to skirt its edge soon learned that it controlled much of the life and death along the way.

Amidst the tending of children and animals that night, many of the people stopped a moment for a spectacular sunset. Clouds formed into a fan to whisk the sun into night. Gold flared into persimmon, and orange into purple. Although the desert sunsets were colorful, it was not often such an array of colors unfolded. Poma and Nik stared and drank in the beauty.

"Wouldn't it be fine and nice to have a robe of such colors!" mused Nik.

Poma glanced over at her. For an instant she thought of the grandmother, and how she might have enjoyed this sunset as well. But a torch had been passed. It was up to Poma to help Nik channel her appreciation and move toward the creative process that fed their souls, even if it was only to water the seeds of a dream. "Well," she said carefully, "we could do that." She smiled, allowing her excitement to bubble up just a little.

"How?" said Nik, her eyes shining.

"Let's see, the gold will be from chamomile flowers, the pomegranate and oranges from madder, and the purple . . ." Poma's voice trailed off wistfully. Perhaps this new western place could provide her with a full sky of colors for her pots. She sighed, her dark brows furrowed in thought.

Nik adopted Poma's secret smile that night in the dark, as the clouds drifted off and the moon took over the desert sands, creating yet another idea for something silver to wear.

Emar

Without Doctor riding with them, Emar had become an irritant. He leered at the women from time to time, made snide comments, and was generally a nuisance.

One morning before dawn, Poma was awakened by a muffled cry. "Nik!" Poma jumped up and reached for Nik, and then realized Nik was being attacked by Emar. She stumbled over Nik's blanket, which had been cast to one side. She grabbed her dagger, pulled on the back of Emar's shirt, and thrust the small knife so just the tip disappeared into the folds of his fat neck.

Nik cried out loud, "Get off me, you pig!"

Emar didn't move.

Poma shouted at him, to get the attention of others nearby. "Get off her—very slowly—get on your hands and knees."

Emar did what he was told. Poma kept the dagger pointed at him. She hoped he didn't notice her hands shook.

"Nik, are you alright?"

Nik rolled over, crying. Others in the camp began to emerge out of the darkness. One of the women bent over to help Nik.

The Persian was there with some of the younger men. "What's going on here?" roared the big man.

Poma was enraged. "This man attacked my friend." She pointed at him with her knife.

Emar started to get to his feet. The young men held him by his arms. The Persian bent over Nik. She buried her head in the woman's lap and cried some more. The morning light broke. The Persian addressed the crowd. "And what did she do to bring this on?"

Poma erupted. "What did she do? She has done nothing! This man has been making rude conversation."

Emar started laughing. "Oh, I think not, lady. She was parading around in next to nothing, showing her . . ."

Poma was only kept from running the man through with her dagger by the thought she would never see Enash again. She felt her face flush red. Now she shook all over. "If you ever come near us again, I'll—"

"Enough!" cried the Persian. He pointed a stubby finger at Emar. "You! Get to the front of the line." Then he turned to Poma. "And you! You keep your friend under control." Poma realized she may have said too much, but she gave herself permission. She tossed the Persian a snarl, and went to put her arm around Nik.

"There, there, honey. It's all over now. Come on, let's wash your face." They used some of the precious water to wipe Nik's tearful face.

"What did I do?" she whispered.

"You didn't do anything wrong. We'll just have to teach you what a good dagger can do."

The woman who helped Nik brought her some goat's milk, and by then the day was warm. It was time to board the camels and continue on. Genghis provided his loping rhythm to calm Poma's thoughts. She was almost amazed at how angry she had been that morning. But as she pondered it, she thought perhaps some of the anger had been stored up deep inside her for many years, from the night she heard about her mother's rape. She felt like all the energy inside her was gone. She was grateful for this day on Genghis, where she could have her thoughts to herself and the camel could pick his way through the rocky trail. From that day forward, Nik and Poma slept very close together under the same blanket, for protection.

As the days became shorter, the desert became interminable. Soon the eastern reaches of the misty Tien Shan came into view. Poma was amazed at how high they seemed, looking at them from this vantage point.

She remembered the first time she had seen the Taklimakan from the mountains; Arle's arm was around her. It seemed as if he were still there, searching his horizons for her return. As she watched the snow-covered peaks, remembering the glorious fall days on the steppe, she saw the glint of something shine in the sun. Was someone there? What could be shining that far away? A sword? She looked to see if anyone else saw the glimmer from the mountain. The camels moved along, unconcerned. When she looked back, nothing was there but the rising mist, looking like it wanted to lift the snow and whirl it into the wind of her memories.

Starr

Kashgar was the great crossroads between two rivers on the western end of the Taklimakan. The sand dunes packed themselves right up to the foot of the stark Tien Shan, which was covered with snow all year. Although it was winter, the city was comfortable and welcoming. A big new mosque was its gleaming prize. More Moslem than Chinese in design, its yellow and white tiles caught the morning sun and its carpeted courtyard caught the eye.

The caravan settled into an ancient campground near the old city walls. The next part of the journey, the mountain pass to Samarkand, would be delayed until the snows melted enough to allow their passage. Poma and Nik spent their days in the huge market place, admiring goods from the four corners of the earth. Along with the usual household items, pots, rugs and other household textiles, were musical instruments, a spicy array of food, and huge paddocks of sheep and goats. The nomads had developed a fine line of cattle in the many years Poma had been gone. The herders' yurts dotted the barren landscape outside the city.

It was on a special day they found the bird market. Hundreds of songbirds graced small wooden cages and competed with each other in musical messages. Nik's face lit up. Poma had never seen a bird market, and was a little sorry for the birds. A small booth near the end of the row housed bird cages of unusual craftsmanship.

A young boy popped out of a nearby tent to attend to his customers. "Good day, ladies," he said. "Our birds are young and healthy, and we have a special price today."

Poma turned to look at the boy who appeared to be about ten or twelve seasons old, despite his adult-like salesmanship. She stopped in her tracks. The boy looked so much like her Targitaus, for a moment she was speechless. He had the same eyes, and his curly dark hair framed his face exactly as her son's had. His face was only a bit thinner and he was just a bit taller. He stared back at her with a steadfast gaze.

Poma finally collected herself. "Who does the beautiful carving?" she asked.

"I do," he said, standing even taller.

"These are very beautiful."

"Thank you. And today only they are half price." His eyes twinkled.

Poma was taken with the gregarious young man. A taller version of the boy appeared from behind the booth. He looked to be about five seasons older than his little brother. He struck up a conversation with Nik, who was her usual blushing self.

Poma thought a pair of birds would be something Nik would take good care of. "Would you like a pair of these?" she asked, pointing to some noisy birds in a roomy cage hanging just above them.

Nik was enraptured. "Oh, could we?"

"We certainly could," said Poma, and slipped the boy some gold coins. "We are traveling far, and we will tell those we meet about you," she said.

Both the boys beamed.

"And what are your names?"

The older one spoke first. "I am Mohammed. This is Toru. Thank you for your kind words."

It was an inspired purchase. Nik talked to her new charges almost all day long, and they sang back to her. Poma had never seen her quite so happy.

The next morning, Poma left the chattering threesome to sit by a wall near the camp well. She felt like writing a poem, but her thoughts were scattered.

Suddenly she thought she heard someone whispering her name. "Poma!" No one was around her. Some children played across the road, and two goats grazed nearby. "Poma!" The voice, louder this time, seemed to be emanating from the wall behind her. She saw a very small opening between the stones in the wall. "Sssst!" She peered into the small space. She was surprised to see two beautiful green eyes looking back at her. It was like looking in the river at herself.

"Poma! Is that you?"

She didn't know what to say.

The green eyes were piercing. "Come down to the gate. Hurry!"

She got up and walked quickly down the wall to a small gate with iron bars. A woman was waiting there covered by a veil. The woman looked over her shoulder, dropped the veil down to reveal her lovely face, grabbed the iron bars and searched Poma's face. "It *is* you. I know it's you!" she whispered. Poma was astonished. But for a streak of white hair and lines around her eyes, she was looking in a mirror.

Suddenly she remembered what Tigrax had said. "Mother?"

"Yes, Poma. Oh, darling, I found you! It's me, Starr, your mother!"

Poma wanted to be sure. "And who is your mother?"

"Tigrax."

Poma felt her knees become weak. Tears welled up from far below and streamed down her face. "Oh, mother! I'm so glad to find you. I didn't think I'd ever—"

"Sh!" Starr said, looking around. "I'm not supposed to be here. I can't talk to anyone. This is the harem of the Khan. Oh, Poma, we have so much to talk about. Come back to this gate at moonrise tonight. Don't tell anyone." And Starr disappeared into some trees guarding a small courtyard.

Poma looked around. The children were gone. Only the goats completed the scene. She went back to her place by the wall and sat down to collect herself. Her mother! She had not been so excited in a very long time. Why had her mother been so frightened? Was she being held against her will? Poma tried to appear casual as she made her way back to Nik and the birds.

Nik took one glance at her and frowned. "What's happened?" she asked.

Poma sank down on her bed. She had already decided to take Nik into her confidence, with some reservations. "Sit down over here. I have something to tell you, and you must promise to keep it a secret."

Nik's eyes widened. "What's happened?" she asked again.

Poma looked all around, took Nik's hands and said in a low voice, "This is unbelievable. I have found my—uh—my sister." Not knowing where one's mother was seemed a bit far-fetched. "She's being held captive by the Khan in his harem."

Nik gasped. "How did you find her?"

"She found me. I was sitting by that wall over there, and she saw me and recognized me."

"How long has it been since you've seen her?"

Poma had to stop and think how to answer. "Well, it's been a very long time. Anyway, we have to get her out of there." Poma looked around again. "She told me to go back tonight. We have to figure out a way . . ."

"Oh, that sounds dangerous," Nik said.

"I can't just go off and leave her there. Perhaps when I see her tonight, she will have a plan."

That night, Poma put on her grey hood and made her way over to the small gate. She was so excited to know her mother was right there, behind these big walls.

Whoom! In the darkness, two strong arms lifted her up, and four other strong arms rolled her in a blanket. She was thrown over someone's shoulder almost like Arle used to carry the sheep, carried for a long distance and then up some stairs and into a brightly lit room. Female laughter arose, but it was not happy laughter. It was sharp and derisive. She was dumped on something soft and unceremoniously unrolled. The first thing she saw was a faded orange rug. She looked up to see faces worn by age, painted with cosmetics in a vain effort to arrest the aging process. The men who had carried her in hurried out.

"Ooooo, look at this one!"

"My, she's a young one!"

The faces stared at her, and spoke to one another as if she couldn't hear them.

"She looks like . . ."

"Starr! She looks just like Starr!"

Everyone gathered closer to stare at her.

"Starr! Come see—she looks just like you!"

Starr pushed the others aside. "Get out of the way," she said. "Come with me, dear." She reached for Poma's hand. Poma thought it wise to say as little as possible. Starr pulled her to a corner of the room stacked with dusty brown pillows. The other women gathered around them in a semi-circle.

"Shoo!" Starr said. "Otherwise we'll have to have another dancing lesson!" The group immediately disbursed, whispered together and arranged themselves like fallen leaves over the yellowed upholstered couches in a far corner.

"Ptah," Starr said. "The old man wanted me to teach them to dance and you never saw such a bunch of clumsy fools in all your life."

Poma could not help but smile.

Starr's face grew concerned. "Now," she continued, "I was going to meet you as we planned, but we were locked up this evening. Evidently the guards overheard us this morning. I had no way to warn you."

"How long have you been here?" asked Poma.

"About three moons. The Goddess sent me to Tashkent, and I came west with a family of Turkish folks on their way to join some kind of battle."

Poma drew closer to Starr so no one could hear them. "I'm traveling with a young girl who came with me after her family was killed in an earthquake in Japan. She knows where I am. Perhaps she will be able to help us."

Starr's eyes lit up. "Really? Oh, that's good—we will be able to go to the garden once more tomorrow. We're supposed to get you all ready for the Khan, but it's too late tonight. The old man will be asleep."

Poma caught her breath. "You mean, I'm supposed to—I have to—"

Starr suppressed a giggle. "Listen; don't worry about the old curmudgeon. He can hardly lift a finger, let alone . . ."

Poma's fears vanished into laughter. "Then what?"

"He only wants you to dance for him."

Poma remembered when she first learned to dance. "That won't be hard. I learned long ago in Egypt," she said.

Her mother's green eyes grew wide. "Egypt?"

"Yes, I was a temple maiden when I was very young."

"I was in Egypt. When were you there?"

Poma felt relieved to be able to talk freely with someone about her past. "The Pharaoh was the last of the Hyksos kings. His name was Apophis."

"Oh, gracious! I was there years and years later, during the time of Ramesses. He was quite an interesting man."

Poma remembered when Heptle had been sold into slavery. "Those old kings almost had to be both good and bad," she said.

"How so?"

"Well, Apophis was, for the most part, a kind man, but his justice was swift." And she told Starr the story of Heptle and the asp.

Starr was impressed with Poma's fighting courage. "Ho, ho, you are just like me. You are wonderful! You know, it was in Egypt that I learned how I wanted to present a baby to the world. When you came along and I had to give you up, the Goddess helped me make your basket and we put you on that river."

Poma was amazed. "I still have that basket!" she exclaimed. "Who is my father?"

Starr's face darkened. "Your father was a minstrel who could never stay put." She let out a big sigh. "His name is Burdette, and I've lost track of him." She smiled a wistful smile. "Maybe some day we can find him again."

Poma felt sorry for her mother, and was glad Starr knew how to prevail with this apparent loss in her life. "And where did you get the purple distaff?" Poma asked.

"The Goddess gave it to me, along with your spindle. I was happy for that, because I knew you would have tools that would comfort you in bad times."

Poma understood this; it was certainly true. The two talked together until dawn. Later that morning, the women ate and bathed, and the morning was spent in the garden. The women sat in the grassy courtyard sipping juice made from the fruit of the apricot tree. Some were spinning, but it seemed more of a pastime than a necessity to them. Starr and Poma sat next to the gate to watch for Nik.

Soon a young male voice called her name. "Poma! Over here."

Poma looked through the bars of the gate. She couldn't see anyone. "Pssst!"

She looked down the wall to the small opening. When she peered through, a pair of black eyes looked back. She recognized Toru from the bird market.

"Poma! You and your sister meet us at the gate in the front at evening prayer time. Be ready to ride!"

Before Poma could say anything to him, he was gone.

"Mother, we will be rescued tonight at evening prayers. We are to be at the front gate, ready to go. Oh, and I told Nik you were my sister. I hope that was alright."

"Perfect. Oh, Poma, you don't know how happy I'll be to get out of here. Who was that?"

"Our friend from the bird market. One of two brothers. Very nice young men."

Starr frowned. "Are you sure about them?"

"We haven't known them long, but they seemed very well brought up. Right now, we really haven't much choice," said Poma.

The day lumbered by. Every moment seemed like a lifetime. Poma and Starr sat by the wall, away from the other women, talking.

"Do any of the others try to escape?" Poma asked.

"Oh, gracious, no. They have a better life here than they ever could on the outside. They are old, and have no place there. Here, they are somebody in the eyes of the Khan. They would never leave him."

Poma could not imagine living in slavery and enjoying it. But she could understand not wanting to live in poverty, and having nowhere to go or anyone who loved you. Although she hated to think what would happen to these women when the old Khan died, it would still be better to be free.

As the morning dragged into afternoon, the Khan sent word he wanted to see his new acquisition. Poma was suddenly surrounded by the women, who insisted she be dressed just so in as much finery as they could muster. They poked around in an old leather trunk and came up with some wrinkled blue and green silks. She allowed them to apply cosmetics to her face. It would be rude to deny them these small pleasures. When they deemed her perfect, she was escorted to a great hall where the enfeebled Khan was ensconced on a low couch surrounded by gold pillows. Poma was pushed close to the old man.

"Come closer, woman," he mumbled.

Poma obediently stepped closer. The scene from long ago in front of another ruler flashed through her mind.

The old man's brown eyes were still bright. His long nose seemed to announce his authority, and his thin lips pursed as he looked her over.

"What is your name?"

"Poma," she said, smiling.

"Turn around," he said.

Poma felt like a prize horse. She bit her tongue and slowly turned around.

"Hmmmm," he said in appreciation. "And where are you from, my dear?"

Poma wasn't sure how much she should reveal to this old man. "The Ferghana Valley," she replied.

He seemed to accept that. He raised himself up on one elbow. "Can you dance, Poma?"

"Yes, sir," she said. *This evening I will be out of here,* she told herself.

"Music!" the old man roared, in spite of his frail voice.

Musicians appeared and began playing. It consisted of a slow drum beat and the strumming of a stringed instrument. Even the musicians were older men who appeared bored with their jobs. Although the music was uninspiring, Poma started to dance. She kept a frozen smile on her face, but thought of many other things she'd rather be doing. The dance finished in a frenzy of rhythm, and Poma sank to the floor, her breathing heavy.

The old Khan seemed pleased. "Very nice," he said.

Poma studied his face. The thin lips curled into a smile. "It has been a long time since I've acquired a woman quite so young," he said, almost to himself. Then, in a droop of his eyebrows, he looked tired. "I must rest now. I will call for you again this evening." His sidelong look turned to a frown. "Have Starr teach you the latest steps." Then, relieved, Poma was escorted back to the women's quarters. The ladies gathered around her.

"What happened?"

"Did he ask you to come back?"

"Does he like your dancing?"

Poma put up her hands. "All in good time," she said. "I want to remove my cosmetics and all this hot silk."

The solemn call to evening prayers could be heard from the mosque. Poma glanced at Starr. No time. Poma gathered up her grey shawl.

Starr grabbed her by the hand. "I want to show you the back of the palace," she said loudly, so the others could hear. Poma looked around. The women watched her closely as they talked among themselves. They moved as if they wanted to go with them.

Starr swung into action. "Ladies, Poma will show you her dance, just as soon as you all sit down. Here, let's make a stage, right there, and you can be the audience. Just pull those pillows over here, and everyone sit, and Poma will come out from behind the curtains to dance. It will take her only a few moments to be ready. We have to make some minor costume adjustments."

The ladies looked excited. They all gathered together and plopped down on the pillows to wait obediently for Poma's performance. Poma and Starr disappeared behind the curtains, and then took off down the long hallway.

"This way!" whispered Starr. They tiptoed past a sleeping guard and doubled back through some darkened rooms, toward the front of the large building. Poma heard the familiar sound of the small birds from the bird market. The women crouched down in the dark to listen.

Mohammed's voice arose above the twittering. "And we wanted to bring the almighty Khan music to enjoy in his old age."

The deep voice of an older man said something Poma could not hear.

"Well, of course, I know he is not old. He is—well—venerable. I am sure if the great Khan knew we were here, he would want to at least hear the beautiful music our small but mighty birds offer to bring joy to the heart, love to the soul . . ."

The other man spoke. "Wait here."

An elderly guard passed by the hiding women and disappeared down a hallway. Starr grabbed Poma's hand, and they ran toward the great entrance of the palace. Mohammed motioned them to be quiet and whispered, "Quick, there are horses waiting outside by the three pillars. Ride around the back of the great trumpet rock, and if they follow, Toru and I will lead them into the desert. Nik will meet you on the western road with the camels. Hurry!"

Poma didn't look back. The two women ran out the front doors and down the long flight of stairs to a promenade. The three pillars were situated at the end of the pathway. The fourth pillar lay in pieces nearby. It was a crumbling house of a crumbling empire and a dying ruler. Two horses were waiting. They leapt up. Just as they galloped off, they heard shouts behind them. Starr led the way to the big trumpet rock on the outskirts of the city. Two horsemen chased close behind them. Starr led the way through a maze of streets and out into an open area. A huge trumpet-shaped rock appeared. As they rode around to the back of it, the boys were waiting. Starr and Poma pulled up and the boys waved and rode out the other side. The horsemen giving chase fell right into the trap and galloped off after the two boys. Starr and Poma waited until they were gone, and then urged the horses back toward the western road. They soon found Nik waiting with the camels and another small boy who took charge of the horses. It was complete. They had made their escape.

Poma was worried about the two young men. "What will happen to them?" she asked Starr.

"Don't worry about them. The guards will soon give up the chase. Especially since they are going in the direction of the desert. And besides, those guards are the laziest men in the entire town of Kashgar. If I had known it was this easy, I would have left long ago."

Poma smiled at her mother's bravado. They were, indeed, much alike. "I think we must hurry to find the caravan. Let's hope it has not left without us."

The Auction

The trio rejoined the caravan just in time to make the trip over the Terek pass. The great peaks were barren of trees and heavy-laden with snow.

The trail was muddy, but the camels slogged patiently through the mire. "We'll have to get horses soon," Starr remarked. "There's not much more desert left like the Taklimakan. And it will be a long time before we get to Constantinople."

Poma felt a pang of excitement at the mere mention of Constantinople. This city more than any other now represented the end of her journey, her dream come true. Soon she would be able to find the source of the royal purple. Her heart skipped a beat, and she took a big breath. Her smile was not secret this time.

The next stop was Samarkand. The night before they arrived, Poma had a vivid dream. *She was in a large building with lots of people. Tigrax came running up to her, out of breath. Her button eyes were shining. "Be sure to go to the auction," she said, then turned back and ran through the crowd and disappeared.*

Poma awoke to a starry dawn. As she sat up, an unmistakable scent of pipe smoke announced that Tigrax had most certainly been there. Starr aroused and sat up as well, pulling her blanket around her.

She sniffed the early morning air. "Blast that woman—she comes and goes and never says a word to me!"

"She came to me," Poma said.

Nik opened her eyes and looked at both of them as if they were crazy. "What now?" she mumbled.

The older women laughed. Poma stoked up the fire. "It was only Tigrax. That's Starr's mother. She came to me in a dream."

"Starr's mother? And not yours?" Nik squinted at them. "You two are not sisters—you are Poma's mother." She blinked at Starr.

"Alright, we can't keep it a secret. You're right. But we could pass as sisters, don't you think?" Poma said.

Nik was still confused. "But why . . ."

"I didn't think you would believe me," Poma said simply.

Nik looked from Poma to Starr and back. "Of course I believe you. Just look at the two of you!" She got up to dress. "What's that smell?" She frowned.

Starr looked for a moment at Poma, and then said, "Pipe smoke."

Later, on the trail, Poma told Starr about the dream. "What auction is she talking about, I wonder?" Poma mused.

"The auction? She must have meant the horse auction at Samarkand."

The east-west caravan trail to Samarkand crossed over the old north-south nomad trail the next day. Genghis came to a complete stop right in the middle of the crossroads and lowered his head. Out of the corner of her eye, Poma caught a glimpse of gold. She turned in the camel saddle just in time to see the ghost of a grey horse with a gold mask disappear over a small hill, on the northern side of the road. In a flash she knew Estwynd would be here, waiting for her. She remembered coming south on this road and passing through this exact crossroads those many years before. The little breeze of time rippled her robe as it had then. She smiled her secret smile, and urged the tired camel on up the western road toward the city.

Marakanda was gone. Nothing remained but a few stones piled one atop the other. Poma's heart was saddened by the sight. It seemed as if her days with the nomads had disintegrated with the dust. The people had moved on, the buildings burned or destroyed by wars, weather, and the wear of winter upon fall, summer upon spring, over and over until nothing remained, not even in the memory of the old men on donkeys along the dusty path. The newer city of Samarkand was just beyond, overlooking the river, which had changed course over the years.

Samarkand had seen its share of history. Great mosques and other buildings had been erected, and shone in their glory. As in Kashgar, the children looked something like the nomad children, a face or two in the crowd were like the faces of old, and Poma realized that the history and traditions of the people were also alive and would live on. Through all manner of battles the grand mosques were left alone, their blue mosaic tiles gleaming in the late morning sun. Poma had seen some of the great cities of the east, but this one was the grandest of all. The large blue domes were shouldered by minarets which held up the sky like slender fingers. They radiated a majestic presence over even the poorest mud hovels lining the squalid streets, so that everything within earshot of the call to prayer fit together to make the city whole.

The caravan camped by the river, and Poma and Starr went in search of the horse auction, leaving Nik with the camels. They came to a large enclosure, where many unhappy looking horses stood, waiting to be sold.

Poma was about to remark that she didn't know why Tigrax had sent her here when she spied the big grey standing alone in a corner. "Estwynd!" she exclaimed. She ran up to the fence. "Estwynd, I found you! Estwynd!" He trotted over to the women and whinnied a big hello. Poma climbed to the top of the fence and threw her arms around the dappled neck. Tears of joy ran down her face and into the silver mane.

Starr watched, her mouth open. "You two know each other?" she asked.

Poma laughed through her tears. "He's been with me since Egypt."

A squat little man appeared. "The bidding begins in about an hour," he said. "This one will bring a high price. Such bloodlines we have here, but he is an especially great beauty."

It was all Poma could do to not tell the little man that this was the father of all the good bloodlines in this part of the world. She and Starr would have been politely escorted out of the city. "But . . ." she began.

Starr stopped her. "We will think about it," she said to the little man.

Poma was aghast. When the grinning little man was out of earshot, she said, "But Mother, he's my horse."

"Well, you know that, and I know that, but I don't think you're going to explain that to him." She stabbed an elbow in the direction of the little auctioneer.

Poma was devastated. *She would have to pay for her own horse?* Tears filled her eyes once more. Then she became very determined. "We have to go back for the gold."

"Gold?"

"Yes, I have a little, and will use it to buy him back. I can't just let him go to anyone else."

They soon returned with Poma's basket. She traded her gold for ducats. They waited patiently while several other horses were sold. Most of them went to a tall soldier who caught the attention of the whole crowd. He was a big and fearsome man with an almost foppish appearance. He wore a short green tunic and a headdress which to Poma appeared almost Egyptian in style. It was topped off with a long white feather which started at his forehead and flopped over the top of his head. The tip of the feather had been dipped in blue—probably indigo. He was almost laughable except for the ferocious mustache and a long firearm at his side. A large cutlass completed the costume, and his European face was focused on the business of horseflesh. Someone in the crowd whispered, "Janissary," and Poma listened closely and learned he was from the land of the Turkmen, and a member of the Sultan's palace guard. She saw him staring at Estwynd with appreciation.

Her heart was pounding. Did she have enough gold to outbid the frightening dandy? Finally the bidding on Estwynd began with ten ducats. The other horses had gone for about 50 ducats apiece. Poma was enraged that she had to buy her own horse. She tried to contain her anger.

"Twenty ducats!" She and Starr had made their way into the middle of the crowd. The Janissary had one eyebrow in motion as he turned to look at this woman who was bidding.

"Do I hear thirty?"

The Janissary nodded.

"Forty!" Poma shouted.

"The bid is forty ducats. Who will give me 50 for this beautiful animal?"

The Janissary nodded again.

"And sixty? Do I hear a bid of sixty?"

Estwynd stood with his head bowed.

Poma decided to leap. "Sixty!"

Now the Janissary appeared to grow impatient with this woman, and spoke up. "One hundred!"

The crowd murmured.

"We have one hundred ducats," the auctioneer said suavely.

Poma had no more money. Tears streamed down her face. She clenched her fists so tightly she could feel her fingernails marking her palms.

A silken voice spoke behind her. "Two hundred!"

She whirled around. There, in a long red robe, stood Enash. She gasped. The noise of the crowd seemed to melt away. "Enash!" Astonished, she pushed through the crowd toward him.

The auctioneer called, "Two hundred once, two hundred twice—" he paused, watching the Janissary's reaction. The big soldier flashed a frown in Enash's direction.

"Sold for two hundred ducats to the gentleman in red!"

Poma rushed into Enash's arms. She saw his intent look and then felt his warm kiss. Everything around them seemed to disappear as she lost herself once more in his love. The Janissary stormed out of the crowd, his feather bobbing in disgust. Estwynd nodded in approval as he was led toward Enash and Poma by the auctioneer's assistant.

Enash looked at Poma with smiling eyes. "I was told in a dream to be here. Thank God I was," he said.

Poma cried with joy. "How long has it been?"

At first, Starr was wordless. Finally she said with an unabashed look of approval, "And who is this?"

Poma took her hand. "Mother, this is Enash, the temple priest I told you about." She was beaming.

Starr seemed impressed, but at that moment was the only practical one there. "Come, we must pay for your horse and get him far away from that Janissary Guard."

Light and Freedom

Poma took Estwynd for a ride that night. The big horse responded with a gentle gait that soothed away all the hardships of her long trip across the big China. Enash rode along with her and they found solitude away from the caravan for the night. Poma's heart was not at peace; she was too excited with her dreams falling into place. Peace would mean restfulness, but her whole body quaked with energy.

As the moon rose, the two of them stopped their horses to watch. It was an indigo night and the creamy moon gave its light to a turquoise mist just off the desert floor.

"And so I've really been traveling all this time, and now, even though I have found you again, there is still the purple missing." She was answering all the questions Enash had on their ride from the twilight into the early night.

"But what about you?" she asked. "Have you been here all this time?"

Enash got down from his horse and helped Poma down and into his strong arms. "No, I have been traveling as well. I traveled with a group of builders for awhile, until they turned north. I was on my way west, to try and find you." He kissed her. "You are the only woman I have met who could ever keep me grounded." She melted just a bit more into his arms. His brown eyes searched hers. They sat down on his long red robe which he stretched out on the sand. "Poma, the Goddess told me in a dream that there is need for more of us in the world—the ones who travel through time. There are so many more people now, and we are helping to make a difference." He looked pensively at the rising moon. "Man must learn to spiritualize his violence . . ." He didn't finish. Poma kissed him and the conversation came to an end. The warm desert air touched them with light fingers as the love in the night brought them together as one. Poma's dreams that night turned to the soft music of a flute. It rippled through her very being just before she awoke.

Later, they talked of many things, of bandits and pirates, of art and of God. Poma fingered the last ducat she had. It was emblazoned with a ruler on one side and a God on the other.

"Who is this God?" she asked.

"That is Jesus, the Son of the one God."

"And what is he the God of?"

Enash sat up and put his arms around his knees. "He is the savior of all the world. Long ago, prophets told of his coming. Now all men will be saved forever and ever."

Poma sat up beside him. She remembered something the elders of her tribe had talked about when she was a young child. They had said some day there would be a saving God. "And do you believe in this Jesus?"

His face grew serious. "Yes," he said softly. "Yes, I do. This God is a gentle God of peace. That's why I'm going to Constantinople, to help preach about peace to the enemies of the city. If Jesus loses Constantinople, the whole East will be lost."

It was a lot to think about. Poma braided her hair as he spoke again.

"One thing more I need to tell you. The message of the Goddess was that we need to give our firstborn back to the world."

Poma stopped braiding. Give up a baby? *How could she give up another child?*

"Don't look so sad, little one. We will have lots of children. I pray my love for you will not be a burden."

The thought of spending even that much time with Enash calmed her. Still . . . "Is this a proposal?" she asked.

"My wish for you is that my love, like sunlight, surround you and yet give you freedom," he said.

What more could a woman ask for than light and freedom?

"We've been friends for a long time," he continued.

"And?" She finished braiding her hair and stood up.

"And our marriage would be different from other people's, I guess," he said.

Her heart sang. But there was the fact that she would often spend years at a time without him. He would always be that four years ahead of her when he went off into time ahead of her. When she considered it to be better to have him six out of every ten years than not at all, she smiled her secret smile. Light and freedom. This would be a happy choice.

She stepped into his arms once more and kissed him. "Yes," she repeated, almost to herself, "A happy choice."

They mounted the horses just as the sun rose, forcing another pink day into being, and making the soft night just another memory. Poma's heart was filled with the sweet and the bitter, but this time the sweet overruled all else.

As they rode back into camp, singing greeted them. Starr was teaching Nik to dance, and the sight was an amusing one. Starr was still nimble, and Nik was still clumsy, so it was the cause of much laughter. But Nik was good natured and everyone seemed happy, all for different reasons, but with a good life seeming to be in the offing, laughter was the order of the morning. Another day of rest, and the caravan would move on.

Poma and Enash spent the day together. They talked and laughed for hours. The baskets were re-packed and everything made ready for the rest of the trip beneath the Caspian Sea and across the rocky stretches of Persia and Anatolia. Now Poma only had one other thing to make her life complete, and that would be at the end of her journey—the secrets of the royal purple.

Enash and Poma rode side by side. "You have come much farther than you know," he said.

"It has been over two seasons."

"And when you have found the purple?"

Poma smiled. "I don't know. Life goes on, I suppose." She frowned. "What will become of me if I share it?"

Enash was amused. "First you must find it."

"I don't need any more of a challenge."

"I know. It's been your passion since you were—how old? You were almost twelve seasons, weren't you?"

Poma remembered the storeroom where she first saw the mysterious tapestry. "I still have that tapestry. I saved it from the fire during the war when the Pharaoh was killed." She remembered the other treasures in her basket. "I have a surprise for you," she said.

"What kind of surprise?"

"You'll see. I'll show you later."

That evening Poma presented Enash with the poems she had written for him. He seemed very pleased with her poetry. He held Poma's hand, and his eyes danced in the firelight. "Some day I'll build you a home," he said.

"As long as I have a home in your heart," she said.

Constantinople

Poma was so happy she barely noticed her surroundings in the next few weeks. The caravan rested briefly in the dusty village of Tehran. The town was inhabited with small groups of men who seemed intent on every sort of rowdy behavior. It was a crossroads for bandits, hooligans and soldiers of every stripe. The women were happy when it was time to move on. It was far into spring when they reached the western end of Anatolia. The scent of the sea invigorated even the animals.

Poma wondered if this place would offer them a home. It was her first glimpse of the decaying empire that was Byzantium. The warm sun bounced off white stones which formed the classical Greco-Roman facades. Here the roofs were tiled. Here the narrow streets wound through ancient neighborhoods and ended at the lazy shores of the great sea. Here the wind whispered soft words of a long history born in the dim but grand past. Now the city stretched itself like an old man in the blazing sun, to enjoy itself vicariously through the diverse scenes depicting the commerce of the sea. The sprawling, dozing city would soon change forever, and only the carts and donkeys, only the languid sea beating on the shores where no bridge existed, would stay the same. Only the washed cobblestones and small, ancient courtyards which once were opulent, only these small things would remain. Poma was enthralled with the beauty of this place. The blue sea and the warm sun shining on the white city could easily be called home.

What she didn't notice so much were the families who were leaving. At least three or four times a day, a large family with all its possessions passed them on the road, usually with a sorrowful demeanor and frightened-looking children.

At the sight of the beach, Poma spurred Estwynd down to the sand and dismounted at the first pile of shells. Not only did the pile of shells testify to the number of mollusks it took to make a very small amount of dye, but this practice had gone on for so many years that the beach was white with the remains. She fell to her knees and carefully picked up one broken shell and frowned at it. Then her hand moved over hundreds of shell pieces. She sat down and stared around her in dismay. It was, indeed, a sad sight. The purple was simply the most elegant and wondrous of colors, but at what cost? *Where was the balance?* Her emotions ran a full gamut from wonder and elation to grief and guilt. But the old alchemical curiosity rose to the top.

Enash rode up slowly and surveyed the scene. He got off his horse, and came down to where she sat staring out across the waters of the Golden Horn. She glanced up at him. Her face reflected her confusion.

He squatted down behind her and put his hands on her shoulders. "Someone got carried away here," he said. The irony was not lost on her.

She thought back to the steppe and Arle's comments about the fur-bearing animals. "I hope there's shellfish left," she said simply.

His tone became softer. "Do you still want to find out about the purple?"

She only hesitated for a moment. "I think knowing the secrets of any art is just as important as keeping a balance with natural things." She felt good that Enash understood her passion for the color. Her love for him deepened as every day passed. It was a love that had changed from just the passion they first exchanged those many yeas ago. He had become more thoughtful, she more philosophical. And through it all, the respect he held for her was built like a rock altar on the shores of time.

The remnants of the caravan which had sheltered her for so long had melted into the small villages and farms on the eastern side of the Golden Horn. They sold the camels at the camel market. Poma could not help but shed a tear over faithful old Genghis. He remained his dignified self as his new master led him away. The merchants who went beyond to Rome, went now by sea. Poma and her family camped opposite the great walls of the city and she and Enash went together by boat across the narrow water to the Gate of Petrion and the great outdoor markets on the waterfront. Enash carried her boxes of indigo. She had saved out two balls of the blue dye for herself, and was eager to sell the rest. Poma recognized the goods from the east and the big eastern cities. But now a whole new world opened up as she saw the scope of the art from the west. Florentine dry goods and glass shone in the sun almost equally like jewels. The deep colors in the fabrics took her breath away. The array of seafood was just as colorful, and added an unforgettable scent to the entire market. Fruits and vegetables from the Anatolian plateau created another mosaic feast for the eyes.

When they rested for lunch, Poma opened the boxes of indigo and placed them at her feet. Gradually some of the Venetian and Genoese merchants gathered around to admire the lumps of blue. A tall, slender Venetian fellow took a good sniff of one with a long, aristocratic nose. Before he could hide his admiration, his blue eyes lit up and one brow arched slightly.

Poma knew he was interested. "It is true indigo from Japan," she said.

The young man glanced at Enash, then back at her, and then at the blue orbs once more.

He held one up and sniffed at it again. "And what price are you asking?" He had a heavy accent.

"Excuse me?" she said.

"Price. How much money?"

Cautiously she named a price that was ten times what she had paid. He thought for a moment, and then made a reasonable offer. She stuck with her original price. The young man's eyes flickered to the gathered merchants behind him. He made a counter offer.

Poma hesitated for a moment, and then came down to a figure just in between.

"Alright, sold," he said. He took out a small pouch and tossed it down beside the boxes she had guarded for so long.

Poma was amused at herself for not knowing how this man had manipulated her into the exact amount in his pouch. But then, he was obviously more experienced in such matters. As she counted the gold, Enash asked the young man if he knew of any houses for reasonable rent.

The young man laughed. "All the houses are reasonable. About half the city is for rent. I'm sure you won't have any trouble finding something." Then he seemed to have an idea. "In fact, the house next door to mine is vacant. Is there just you and your wife?"

"No, we have two others with us, her mother and sister," Enash said.

"This house would be perfect for you. A big family moved out only three days ago. They even left some furniture behind. I would be happy to introduce you to the landlord."

"We would be grateful," Poma said.

"My name is Carlo Romaginino. Come, it is not far from here."

It was the first time Poma had met anyone with two names. All the people she knew had a given name, and then were divided by the place they were from or their father's name, or their occupation. Having two names seemed almost ostentatious somehow.

"I am Enash, and this is Poma. We came west with the caravan."

"Oh, yes. I purchased some silk only yesterday from a fellow who called himself Emar."

Poma smiled politely. She was glad Emar had dealt with someone who was obviously much smarter than he was.

Carlo led them up the narrow street to his house. The city had shrunk into a collection of village-like neighborhoods clustered around various churches. The area called Petrion was positioned perfectly near the waterfront market place and near the church where Enash might find influential clergy.

So Poma, Enash, Starr, and Nik moved into the house next to the Venetian. There was a bright main room with a cooking area and a large porch with a courtyard. Upstairs were two sleeping rooms with a balcony overlooking the courtyard and beyond the wall to the Golden Horn, busy with boats plying back and forth. A little cleaning, and they could move in. Poma found jasmine by her kitchen door and apricot trees in the courtyard. Finally! A home of her own.

Isaac

She became the queen of her home. Carlo was a good neighbor. He introduced Enash to the officials of the small hamlet, and they quickly became a part of the community. Soon it became evident that a new baby would complete the family. Poma was ambivalent, for she knew this little one was pledged to history. But she also knew that one day they would be reunited just as she and Starr had been. Starr kept reminding her of that fact, and it did make things somewhat easier.

Nik had blossomed into a young woman of great classic beauty. Carlo was immediately taken with her. She spent long hours with him in the market place. Carlo became a part of Poma's household. Her small courtyard looked like a dye studio. A madder pot full of yarn sat soaking in the sun. Other pots sat over a small brazier fire, cooking about four different shades of yellow. And the ever-present indigo would help make its usual blues, eat up the pale yellows and spit out turquoise. A dunk or two of the darker yellows yielded rich forest greens. It digested the reds and burped up purples. Poma's home would soon provide a colorful backdrop for the events to come.

Nik and Carlo spent their time gathering dyestuffs: three-leaf sage, monk's pepper tree, and chamomile for various yellows and golds, and sumac for black. Carlo was fairly knowledgeable about dyes, and told Poma stories of the big dye works near his home in Florence.

"Carlo, do you know where I can find a good dye master here in Constantinople?"

They were sitting in the courtyard sun, minding the various colors and also some mutton purchased that morning at the market. Enash was napping and Starr and Nik were at the market talking with the women there about opportunities for work.

"There is an old man who lives down by the great Church of the Holy Wisdom. You'll surely want to see it soon. Anyway, this old man is rumored to still be producing the purple dye from the shellfish. They say he is commissioned by the Emperor."

Poma felt the old excitement build up. "Do you suppose we could find him and visit his dye works?" she asked.

"I am going to the marketplace this afternoon. They say a boatload of spices has come in, and I need some peppercorns. I know of someone to ask about the old man."

"Oh, Carlo, I'd love to meet this man. For a long time, I've been longing to . . ."

She saw a look of curiosity on Carlo's face.

"to . . . see some of the imperial purple." She would have to hide her purple distaff and make a new one. She knew this was not the place to be showing off the distaff. It could get them all into deep trouble.

The next day Carlo took Nik and Poma over to the south side of the city. Enash visited the clergymen of their small community.

Poma wanted Enash to come with them, but he felt his meeting this day with the Fathers was as important to him as her meeting with the dye master was to her. "I meet today with Father Rudolfo and some others in the church here. They are working to unify the Church of Constantinople with the Church of Rome. It is important that I be there." He kissed her and wished her well in her search for the dye master.

Carlo pointed at the great church located atop a hill near the cavernous cisterns. The Sea of Marmora blazed blue in the distance. The church was open and they wandered into the huge cool marbled interior. Even their whispers echoed here. The walls were covered with large mosaics of Christian saints. It was as Carlo had said, a very impressive edifice. Poma was awed by the spirit of a people who would build such a beautiful church to worship their God.

Then it was time to hunt for the famous dye master. As they rode down the hill, Estwynd attracted his usual crowd of admiring children.

Carlo stopped to ask directions. "We are searching for Isaac Ivanovitch, the dye master."

Two of the children pointed down the hill.

One of the older ones spoke up. "It's the last house at the bottom of the hill, on the right." Poma felt her heart beat in her throat as they approached the old, ornate building. It was all she could do to contain a lifetime of excitement. *Would he be home? Did he truly know the secrets of the purple? Would he even speak to them?* Carlo knocked at the beautifully carved door several times. No answer. Poma's heart fell. They were about to leave when at last, the big door swung open. She felt her face flush with excitement. A big man with a large moustache glared at them with piercing black eyes. Nik backed up a step.

Poma had to screw up her courage to even speak to him. "Good day, sir. Are you Isaac Ivanovitch?"

"Who wants to know?" he roared.

Carlo interrupted. "I am Carlo Romaginino of the Romagininos of Venice. We are cousins to the Medici. My friend Poma here, wanted an introduction."

The old man's glare softened somewhat. "Romaginino? Are you related to Gaspar Romaginino?"

"Why yes, he's my uncle." Carlo said.

Now the old man seemed almost cordial. "Won't you please come in. My housekeeper is on a short holiday, and I'm afraid I wasn't expecting company." The old man shuffled through a hallway to a small library where there sat a large desk heaped with scrolls of every description.

When his company was seated, the old man sank into a big red velvet chair with a grunt. "Your uncle Gaspar and I went to school together. This old world seems to shrink every day."

Carlo's eyes lit up. "Uncle Gaspar will be glad to hear about you."

"Now tell me—Poma, is it? What brings you to visit an old curmudgeon such as me?"

Poma was almost overwhelmed. "Well, you see, sir, that is—" She took a big breath. "The purple—sir. I have wanted to see the imperial purple all my life, and to learn more about it."

Isaac's bushy brows shot up. "Well, certainly I can show you the results of the process, but as you know, the recipes are all proprietary. I am the only one left in Constantinople who is authorized—"

"Oh, I understand, Mr. Ivanovitch. Certainly I would do nothing to disturb the law in such matters. However, I do know much about the herbs and I have studied with—well, studied quite a bit about some of the ancient recipes." It was the best Poma could say about her credentials in the ancient art of dyeing, and although she knew the recipe to be a secret one, she felt slightly annoyed by the patronage of this big mountain of a man.

Again the old man seemed intrigued. "Well, my dear, come with me, and I will show you some of my samples." Poma was equally intrigued by this old scholar. They followed him down a long hallway which ended with another quite ornate, carved door of dark wood. It was graced by a big, well-polished silver door handle. But the ornate woodwork was immediately forgotten when Poma stepped through it and into the darkened laboratory of Isaac Ivanovitch.

The Mediterranean sun attempted to beam through a high, barred window and was diffused with grey dust and blue smoke which arose languidly from an enormous brazier just under the window. The stone walls were lined with dusty shelves which were choked with every shape of glass container filled with every conceivable type of mysterious powder Poma could imagine. Her jaw fell. Huge vats lined the wall next to the low fire. Boxes and barrels, holding mysteries begging to be solved were stacked everywhere. A strange combination of scents accosted her nostrils. Indigo? Stale urine? Or was it the mold which grew over fermenting rhubarb leaves? Poma wasn't quite sure. She jumped as a big fluffy white cat rubbed up against her leg, purring in pleasure. A pair of yellow eyes glared down at them from a cob-webbed corner. As her eyes grew accustomed to the dark, she saw an owl blink from a high perch. Dried bundles of herbs hung from the beams, connected by slender spider webs.

Carlos' nose moved in an offended way. Nik's eyes grew big. Poma thought heaven must certainly have at least one room just like this one.

"Please excuse the dust," Isaac said. "My housekeeper refuses to enter this part of the house. Now let me see—where did I put those samples?" He searched through an old faded leather chest in a corner and came up with a small, flat wooden box. "Oh, yes, here we are." And he produced fabric swatches in the loveliest shades of purple, violet, pink, and red that Poma had ever beheld.

"Why, they are exquisite!" she said. "And the imperial purple? My guess is it's this one," and she pointed to the deep dark purple that she imagined would match her purple distaff.

"Right!" the old man said proudly. "And the other colors are achieved with different mordants and after baths." He waved his large hands toward the shelves. Poma was entranced.

She and Isaac got into a long conversation about such things as the length of time needed for good madder roots to grow, and the way to build a fire in order to evenly distribute the heat under the dye pots.

"I can see you have a passion for color," Isaac said.

Poma gazed steadily into the old man's black eyes. "Color is my life," she said.

"Color should be the life of everyone. Our world is filled with light, and color is the child of light. Mankind would be better served to array itself in color and thereby keep the Heavenly light in the surroundings of us all."

Poma had never heard anything quite so beautifully said. She immediately became very attached to this bear of a man.

When it was time to go, Poma could hardly tear herself away.

"You have an unusual understanding of our art," Isaac said.

Poma felt herself blush just a little. "I have traveled widely," she replied.

"Please come again," he said.

As they made their way home, Poma talked and talked to Nik and Carlo. When they reached their little house, Enash was there to hear about their adventure.

"I found him! I finally found the dye master. His name is Isaac and he lives in a big, beautiful home, and you should have seen his laboratory— and the scrolls, and he's a well of information, and—"

"Whoa, little one. It sounds as if you had quite a day."

Nik and Carlo came in from putting the horses away. "What a scary place!" Nik said.

Carlo laughed. "It was an adventure, alright. Poma is certainly a happy lady," he said.

Starr arrived home with good news of her own. "A troop of entertainers will be here for a few weeks, and they want me to help them with their new play." She was beaming.

Enash sat down in his place near the courtyard. "Everyone has such good news, perhaps we should celebrate."

The Party

And celebrate they did. Starr brought in her musician friends from the troop of entertainers, Carlo invited his friends, and everyone brought food and there was dancing and drinking and eating far into the evening. Poma could not remember being happier.

Then, to top it all off, in the midst of the festivities, Enash whispered to her, "I've arranged for us to be married next week."

"Next week!" She was about to say that was too soon, but immediately thought better of it. Isaac would help her dye fabric for a wedding dress, and Starr was handy with a needle.

"Your eyes are sparkling," Enash said. "That must mean yes."

"Yes, oh yes!" And she could not help but grin from ear to ear.

Enash turned toward the crowd. "Everyone! I have an announcement to make."

Conversation died. Dancing stopped. The only things moving were the brazier fire and Poma's beating heart.

"I'm pleased to announce that my lovely Poma has agreed to be my wife."

A cheer went up, and the dancing resumed. Now she was in his arms and her heart was dancing. He kissed her with a tenderness that matched his silken voice.

Just then there was a loud knocking at the door and men shouting outside their house. Carlo opened the door. A burly soldier with a long, evil-looking spear was there, and several of his fellows behind him. Poma recognized them as being from the Emperor's guard.

"We have come for a lady named Poma. She is wanted at the palace."

Poma felt her mouth open, but nothing came out.

Fear crept up her spine and spread into her breath. "What for?" she whispered. How could they come here like this and ruin her perfect evening?

Enash stepped to the door. "By whose orders have you interrupted our celebration here?"

"By orders of the Emperor's Minister and Consigliore."

Poma took Enash's arm. "I'm sure it is nothing," she said. She attempted a brave smile.

The soldier nodded to her. "Are you Poma?"

"Yes." She held her head up proudly.

"The Consigliore wants to see you right away."

"But I don't know who . . ."

"I will accompany the lady," Enash said with authority.

"Very well. We are sorry to disrupt the festivities." The soldier was at least being polite.

Poma turned to Carlo. "Please see to it that our guests are entertained. I'm sure we will be back shortly."

Carlo looked as if he would protest, but Poma patted his arm. "I'll be fine. Enash is with me." She was going to give every energy to having nothing ruin this wonderful evening.

The palace was nearby, up a short hill from their house. People stared at them as the soldiers marched them around the hill and through an inauspicious back gate. Although Poma had seen palaces in her time, she would never feel comfortable in them. This one was no exception. They usually housed tyrants or men who used their power to pretend to be tyrants. Either way, these leaders were generally not good news. Poma had heard that Constantine, the Emperor who bore the same name as the founder of the city, was a fair and good person. It was rumored that this Emperor was in the midst of personal and political turmoil, and had gathered around himself a diverse group of advisors. Poma and Enash would soon find out if the advisors were as generous as their Emperor.

They were ushered into a small room off a hallway. The room was covered with scrolls rolled up on shelves and spread out on a large desk. Poma had learned long ago that people who kept too much order were difficult folks to deal with, and she was grateful for the disarray. Clutter was easier to understand. Three men were gathered in a corner engaged in a whispered conversation about a scroll before them on a table. The dim candlelight obscured their expressions somewhat, making it difficult to gauge their thoughts.

The guards suddenly deserted them, but from the lack of footsteps, must have taken places outside the doorway.

One of the men stared at Poma and frowned. "And are you Poma?"

Poma stepped forward. "Yes, sir."

The man disengaged himself from the other two. He was a man about Poma's age with blonde hair which fell to his shoulders.

"What is your last name?"

Poma had never thought about such a thing. A vision of Tigrax flashed through her mind. She was about to reply with another question, as the old woman used to do, then thought better of it. Then she remembered what Isaac had said about color being the child of light.

She quickly translated. "My name is Poma di Biondo."

Enash glanced sideways at her for only a moment, and then looked back at the small man, barely hiding his amusement.

"Well, Poma di Biondo, perhaps you can enlighten us as to what you were doing at the house of Ivanovitch today."

Suddenly one of the other men who had been surveying the scroll stepped out of the shadows. He wore the long red robe of a cleric.

"What is the problem, Consigliore? This gentleman here is Enash, the holy man I was telling you about."

Enash stepped forward. "Good evening, Father Rudolfo. This is Poma, soon to be my wife. Poma, this is Father Rudolfo. I met with him earlier today."

The Consigliore seemed embarrassed. He looked from the priest to Enash and then at Poma.

"I can see we have made a grave error. Miss di Biondo, my apologies. So sorry to have disturbed you."

"Quite alright." Poma nodded to the man, and smiled at the priest. "How do you do?"

The Consigliore turned his attention to Enash, stepped forward and put his hand on the taller man's shoulder, continuing the previous conversation, something about unifying the churches. He turned his back on Poma.

Poma was at once relieved that trouble had passed her by, and astounded that a visit to Isaac would have gotten her into trouble in the first place. But mostly she was angered by the actions of this pompous little man who had almost ruined the happiest day of her life, then ignored her. And she also was getting the idea that being rescued by the males in her life was definitely a double-edged sword. She sat down by the desk and waited patiently for the men to end their conversation. Finally, Enash excused himself and took her hand.

They made their way down the hill toward home. "Thank God for Father Rudolfo. I'm afraid it will pay to select our friends carefully," Enash said.

"Does that mean I must stay away from Isaac?" Poma was almost in tears.

"Oh, no, I'm sure it will be alright now. I know how much he means to you. And certainly Isaac is part of your mission here. I will go with you whenever you want to visit, then we won't have soldiers banging on our door anymore."

Poma breathed a sigh of relief, and hugged Enash close to her. When they returned home, the party was a little more subdued, but everyone seemed to want to congratulate Poma and Enash all over again.

The Flute

With Isaac's help, Poma had a beautiful light blue wedding dress to match the lapis in her scarab. His eyes filled with tears as he presented her with some lace trim that had been his wife's. Poma kissed his cheek, and wore the beautiful lace proudly. She and Enash were married in the small Petrion chapel. It was filled to overflowing with friends and neighbors. Then they partied in an outdoor café. Enash gave Poma a gold velvet robe, and she gave him a wide red sash and another poem:

The Paradox

At once dignified, yet wistful.
He is as the slender moon and morning star
Rising together, fading in the chase,
Losing to the day.

He frowns, concerned, makes noises
Like the bright bird singing orders at the dawn.
Then he is elusive,
Scattering his thoughts as rainbows
Through his crystal hanging there.

A practical romantic, he works
In cold of winter
Remembering the warmth of summer
On his brow.

He is gentle but intense,
Like the windstorm which settled
Into soft breezes like fingers
Curling over our sleeping form.

I see his graceful walk
And remember autumn leaves.
I hear his voice
And so rise the butterflies.

He is a mystic
Who slept while lightening
Played havoc with the night,
But he remembers his dreams.

He is all of these:
He is mine,
Yet never will be.

Poma knew that their life together would be intermittent at best. But to have small amounts of time with someone she loved was more important than constant reassurance of his love. They had established a friendship and a good base for their love many years before. Now the happy days flew by. The women turned their attention to the coming baby. Poma set out to make a small blanket with the one-needle knitting.

Starr cut her short. "Oh, no, dear, no. Here, sit over here and I'll teach you something much faster. Look here." And she pulled out a long, slender wire which curled around in a big circle. Both ends were pointed. "Give me that yarn." She showed Poma how to do two-needle knitting with a circular needle. Poma was delighted with this new technology and was soon knitting her baby a blanket and a small robe.

The night before Sophie was born, Poma dreamt of the Goddess. *She spoke to Poma from the rushes beside a wide green river, which reminded Poma of the Nile. The Goddess taught Poma how to weave a basket. The Goddess spoke to her. "Your babe is to have your flute."*

When Poma awoke she kept her eyes closed and went over the basket making process in her mind. When she opened her eyes, she felt queasy. She forced herself up and in the first light of early morning, she bathed.

Then she woke Starr up. "It's time," she said. She woke up Enash. He was immediately on his feet. She let Nik sleep and Starr started a fire as Poma went back to her bed. Enash kept the fire going. Her labor was not long, and soon a beautiful little girl was born. Poma looked at the baby and thought about its future. *Somewhere in history there is someone who can teach this child much more than I can. She needs to sit at the feet of this great musician, whoever he is, so she can learn what I cannot teach her.* A long baby with brown hair and eyes, she was a picture of her father.

"I want to name her Sophia," Poma said. Starr frowned. "They may not name her that where she goes next," she said.

"What did you name me?" Poma asked.

"I didn't give you a name, but I was close enough to hear what Ashar named you. I thought it quite appropriate."

"Well, I will always think of her as Sophia, regardless of what her new mother thinks."

Nik came in, rubbing her eyes. "You should have awakened me," she said.

Starr patted her arm. "It all went very quickly, my dear. If I had needed you, we would have awakened you."

"Oh, Poma, what a beautiful baby! I hope I have lots of beautiful babies just like this one."

Poma smiled at Nik. "Is there something you want to tell us?"

Nik blushed. "Carlo wants me to marry him."

"Why, that's wonderful! I can't think of a better husband for you. And how do you feel about this?" Poma said.

"I love him so much. He wants to take me to Venice to meet his family."

Poma felt happy for Nik, but at the same time there was a certain sadness. She knew that Sophie would soon be gone into time, and if Nik left, her motherly responsibilities were on hold again. But Nik was an appropriate bride for the world she would find herself in. Carlo was outgoing enough for the both of them, and would be a good provider.

The next day, Nik packed up her few belongings and prepared to go with Carlo.

Poma kissed her and said, "Don't ever forget your mama and your uncle."

"We've had wonderful adventures, Poma, and I won't forget you, either." She hugged Starr and Enash, smiled at Carlo, who kissed Poma's hand and said, "Don't worry about her. I will take good care of her." And they were very suddenly gone. They would go to Carlo's home by boat.

It was in the night a few days later that the Goddess came for them. She told them this time they would go back in time instead of forward. Poma held the baby close and held Enash's hand. He held the old flute. They went out and stood in the garden. The scent of Gardenias arose, and the purple light enveloped them. Time snapped, and they were standing on the banks of the green river. Poma was not sure where they were, or when. A fog had settled in the midst of the water and made it difficult for the sun to warm up the scene. A big, dark forest was interrupted only by the river. Enash held the baby while Poma deftly wove a basket from the wet rushes as she had been taught in her dream. Enash kissed his little daughter and gave her to Poma. Poma kissed the serious little brow. Tears streamed down her face as she placed Sophie in her basket and tucked her small blanket around her. Then they placed the flute next to her. She remembered the beautiful flute music she had heard in her lifetime, on the banks of the Nile, and around the campfires of the markets near the Tien Shan. Could it be? Poma now was sure little Sophie had probably been nearby her whole life through. It was comforting.

"Goodbye for now, little one," she said, and placed the sleeping baby on the water. The basket floated away, and Poma cried as Enash held her close. She looked up at him and saw that his face was also wet with tears.

Suddenly they heard voices. Around the bend of the river on the far side came a group of people. There was a man on horseback dressed in armor which caught the morning sun, now seen in patches through the fog. A group of women followed a short distance, and then stopped. He waved at them and then urged his big horse off through the woods. One of the women sobbed into her apron. An older woman tried to comfort her.

Poma and Enash watched as their precious basket floated over to the other side of the river and bumped along the shore until it washed up on the beach where the women were sitting. A little girl saw the basket first and ran down to see if it held anything.

"Mama!" she cried, "Come look—it's a baby!"

"Nonsense," said the older woman. The little girl's mama stopped crying and came down to the edge of the water. The women seemed very excited by Sophie. They looked all around, but could not see Enash and Poma, who were hiding behind the rushes.

"What's this?" said one of the women. "It's a flute!"

Sophie and her flute were being admired all around. She woke up and started to cry. Poma felt a tug at her breasts, but clung to Enash's hand. One of the young women took Sophie to her breast, which calmed the baby down. The man in armor had been quite forgotten as Sophie and her flute were accepted into this group of women.

"What should I call her?"

"Ophelia," said one.

"Deidre," said another.

"Sophie," said someone.

"Megan Sophia Kildare," said the mother. And it seemed to be settled. "I'll call her Sophie."

Poma and Enash looked at one another and smiled through their tears. The scent of Gardenias overtook the river aromas. The fog reflected a purple glow. Time snapped once more and Poma and Enash found themselves back in the garden, their arms empty, except for each other. Poma sank deeper into his arms, crying softly.

He tried to soothe her. "Sh, now. It's alright."

Sophie was safe and loved. But it was quite a few days before Poma's depression lessened enough for her to want to go out. Enash and Starr stayed by her side. Finally she decided she was wasting time, and she got up and got dressed and announced it was time once more to visit Isaac.

The Fall

It was the end of March, and Poma had learned about the years and how they were numbered by the Christians. It was 1453, and many of the people of Constantinople had left the city. Folks lived in clusters around the churches and the neighborhoods were separated from one another, making the city's population appear as a group of villages.

Poma and Enash stood at the top of the hill near Isaac's house and stared in disbelief at the Sea of Marmora. The huge Turkish armada had made its way up the Dardanelles and was cruising on the blue waters.

"This is not good news," Enash said.

Poma took his hand. "Don't the Christians have good ships?" she asked.

"Oh, yes, far better than the Turks, but not nearly enough of them. The Sultan is a very smart man."

It was frightening. Only that morning there had been a small earthquake; the neighbors thought it a bad omen. What were the Turks planning?

Poma frowned. "It's pretty clear the city is surrounded. Won't the Pope send help?"

"The Emperor sent everywhere for help. I have heard the Pope will not send aid unless the Greek Church unites with the Roman Church. The realms of Eastern Europe are either too small or too greedy to want to help. The country of Hungary has problems of its own, and the Russians are too far away."

Poma's heart sank. "Well then, it doesn't look good for the Christians."

Soon they were sitting in Isaac's library, sipping tea. They discussed the siege that was likely to come. And then the three fell silent, each with their own thoughts.

Isaac put his cup down and studied Poma's face. "My dear, if anything happens to me, I want you to have all the scrolls. There are many recipes and years and years of research recorded. I don't want my life to have meant nothing."

Poma had many emotions bubble up at once. "Oh, certainly you have many long years ahead of you," she said.

"I represent many negative things to these Moslems." His smile at her was a sad and patient one. "I'm afraid my people are their ancient enemy. And they are a fierce people who love their religion more than life."

That did not seem to Poma to be anything new. "It seems to me if people live by what they believe, then their lives should be more important to them."

Isaac chuckled. "In a perfect world, eh, Enash?"

Enash smiled wryly. "Yes, sir, in a perfect world."

Isaac became serious once more. "You see, my dear, you are the only one I know who will understand my writings and perhaps do good and beautiful things because of them."

Poma longed to assure Isaac that he had, indeed, chosen exactly the right person. Because of their journey with Sophie, Poma now understood she could take his knowledge not only forward in time, but back into time as well. And she now had the wisdom to know just how much of that knowledge to share in any one dispensation of time. She smiled her secret smile, and was sure he caught a glimpse of it.

As each day brought the city closer to disaster, Enash, Poma and Starr all went out to help shore up any part of the walls that needed repair. The work was hard, but it gave them a sense they were helping in a cause that was bigger than they were.

Working at the walls when they could, they noticed that the Emperor had mixed the Greek, Venetian, and Genoese troops.

"This will keep the nationalistic quarrels in check," Enash explained.

Poma felt a nasty undercurrent of fear permeate the city, making it hard to keep an emotional balance. It had been a rainy spring, which did not help one's spirits. She looked up from her perch on the top of the wall, where she was stacking rocks. She frowned at the scene. Off in the distance a bright red and gold tent rose out of the ground like a bright mushroom. Shortly a great army appeared and set up camp in front of the big red tent.

"I think you'd better take a look at this," she called down to Enash.

He climbed up beside her. "Those are the colors of the Sultan," he said with a frown. "And those are the Janissary Guards. We'd better go and tell Father Rudolfo."

The siege began on April 11th. It was to last for six weeks. It was estimated the Turks had 80,000 men. The Emperor counted about 7,000 able-bodied men within the huge stretch of the city walls.

Father Rudolfo gathered the people of the Petrion Church together. "The Emperor has destroyed the bridges across the moats and closed the gates. We have enough grain and meat for awhile, but we must be prudent and use only enough to survive."

Then the cannons started up and the noise almost never ceased. Poma sat in her garden and tried to keep the happy times in her mind. She knew it was almost time for Enash to go into time again, and she feared for Starr and herself. She prayed now to the Christian God that they would survive this horrible war.

Word came that the Christians had won an important sea battle. Everyone was energized by the news. Poma and Starr climbed the small rise in back of the market place.

Starr stopped in her tracks. "What on earth is that?"

Poma looked where she pointed. It was an unbelievable sight. Teams of oxen were pulling a strange load over a newly built road on the other side of the waters of the Golden Horn.

It was difficult to see clearly, but after watching for awhile, Poma said, incredulous, "Boats. It's boats! I don't believe it. Boats going over the land."

Starr frowned. "Are you sure?"

They later heard that the Sultan had built a road and cradles on wheels for half his boats, and hauled them up an enormous hill, and across land from the Dardanelles to the Golden Horn, thereby regaining superiority over the Christian ships. The harbor was no longer secure. The city had lost control of the Golden Horn, and the Turks had accomplished the building of this road in only a few weeks, and the ships had been moved in only a few hours.

Poma and Starr hid themselves upstairs in their house in a closet during the nights when Enash went out to help repair the wall.

Finally, amid the agony and suffering, someone left a small gate open by mistake. The Turks poured into the city. The Christians fought gallantly, but victory eluded them because of the overwhelming Turkish forces.

Enash stood at the door of the Church. Upon hearing of the Turkish victory, he sent the fishermen to open the Petrion Gate and rejoined the people of the district to surrender. This saved them from the horrible fate that befell most of the other Christians in the city who lost their lives or were taken into slavery. Poma was proud of her husband, who was considered a hero for saving the small district from destruction. Unfortunately, in the confusion of the taking of the city, Enash disappeared. She and Starr looked everywhere for him. Rumor had it that he had been taken prisoner, but Poma knew better. They stood in their doorway and listened to the neighbors talking above the din of the looting and destruction. Poma was sad for herself, but happy he was safe. The Goddess would look after him.

Starr watched her face. "Was it his time to travel on?" she asked.

Poma was tired from the weeks of terror and the stress from the battle. She could only nod. Then she came alive. "Isaac!" she whispered. The two women feared the horses would draw too much attention, so they ran through the streets. Because of all the confusion, it took them quite a long time to reach Isaac's neighborhood. As they watched, the Turkish soldiers methodically killed and looted or destroyed everything. The stench of blood and death hung heavy in the smoky air. Curiously, the enemy soldiers left a flag in front of each building they went through. Poma thought of a herd of hungry pigs she had seen once, who ravaged part of a forest almost in the same manner. Only the pigs had left little piles of manure.

Poma was horrified to see a fire burning down the hill toward Isaac's house. They rushed into the house and found everything in disarray. The furniture was ripped apart and upside-down, Isaac's things had been turned to trash. The smells from his laboratory were now overpowering; bottles and jars were smashed, their contents mixing together on the floor in a bubbling lake. The owl and the cat were long gone. Isaac himself lay wounded near the brazier. He clutched his chest. Blood poured out of a large wound. Poma took him in her arms. Starr held his hand.

"Poma, you must save yourself. You must get to safety—" he said.

"Sh, just rest now." She tore off a corner of her petticoat and tried unsuccessfully to stop the bleeding.

"The scrolls—save the scrolls!"

The tears streamed down Poma's face. *How could they have attacked this old man? What a cursed thing to do.*

"Mother—get the scrolls from the library." Starr ran back down the hall.

"Isaac—the purple. What can you tell me about the purple?" She searched his face. His eyes seemed to lose focus. She leaned closer to him. "Isaac!"

"The secret—the secret is in the light," he whispered. His words were slurred.

"The light? What do you mean? Isaac? Isaac!"

The old man left her there, left her behind, left this world behind and took the secret with him. She was left with only a seemingly meaningless clue. She buried her face next to his and cried as he left her, and part of her life went with him.

Starr came running back into the room, her arms loaded with scrolls. She took one look at Isaac's face. "Come, hurry! The fire is almost here. Hurry! Poma, come on, we have to leave now."

Poma kissed the wrinkled brow and gently laid Isaac's head on the floor. She jumped up and gathered up all the scrolls she could find and they stuffed them all into two large baskets. They ran back through the city, hiding in places marked with the flags that indicated that dwelling or church had already been stripped of all its people and their possessions. They were thus kept safe as they made their way back to the safety of the Petrion district with their treasure of scrolls. They watched in horror as the Turks swept into the house next to the one they hid in along the way. They heard the screams of the women as the men were killed. As they listened, the mayhem of household goods being ripped and smashed seemed so senseless. Finally the women and crying children were led off, destined for slavery. They waited until it was safe, and then ran to the next house with a flag in front of it.

Poma was shaking and almost sick by the time they got home. But they were safe. Their neighbors were safe, and all their possessions were safe, including Estwynd and the other horses. She took a big breath and looked at the baskets of scrolls. She didn't realize the great amount of work she had ahead of her.

Esecheus

In the weeks and months after the city's fall, the Sultan's orders were carried out. The great church of the Holy Wisdom was turned into a mosque. It was now known as St. Sophia, and its blue dome rivaled the blue of the sea below it.

Poma and Starr visited there again and much to their amazement, most of the Christian mosaics had been preserved. Other churches had been completely destroyed. It seemed to Poma a miracle that the great art all across the caravan routes was recognized and kept as such.

The entire city gradually became Turkish at first glance. But the Byzantine influence crept out here and there in foundations and sometimes complete buildings, and the Christians who managed to survive tried to get along with their Turkish neighbors. It was really their only choice.

Poma and Starr gradually put their lives back together and Constantinople did the same. The summer brought an atmosphere of re-building and new life. A large Turkish family moved in next door in Carlo's old house. The lady of the house was a rug weaver, and Poma struck up a friendship with her. Soon Poma was doing the dyeing of yarns for several of her Turkish neighbors, and had money to buy fresh fruits and vegetables in the market place.

She made one of the upstairs bedrooms into a study, found an old desk that had survived the looting, and got her neighbors to help her get it home. Her study and its balcony faced the west, and her afternoons were spent at her desk, in the sun, reading Isaac's scrolls. After a few months she decided she needed to make a book of recipes, and try them out as she went.

Early morning generally meant a ride out into the countryside on Estwynd, hunting for dyestuff for her dye pot. Most of what Isaac had written was sound; some of it made no sense at all. Some of the ingredients held symbolic values. Others referred to the geographic locations where they originated. Poma's research took her into places and ideas she had never heard of before. She knew that all these bits of information were guideposts for her when she traveled back and forth in time. They would give her a better understanding of the alchemy of her art.

The months turned into years and Poma knew it would soon be time to travel on. So she took advantage of her steady Estwynd, the warm sun in the afternoons, and nice neighbors with whom she shared her art. The rugs she helped to create sported old patterns, and Poma recognized some very old symbols from her sojourn with the Saka people. Her Turkish neighbors became wealthy selling their rugs in the market to the merchants from the west.

Some of the scrolls bore historical records and stories of the old dye masters. One that intrigued her particularly told of a dyer's apprentice in the time of Nero. His name was Esecheus, and he was beheaded for being caught wearing the imperial purple. The dye master reported: *"When I came back to Rome in later years, I was told of Esecheus' abrupt end. I felt a great sorrow for the poor soul. He had worked hard to please me and the others he worked with. But my wife, Penelope, had cajoled him into thinking it was alright to wear the purple robe. That woman was poison from the first day I met her. When Esecheus was executed, she tried to take over the dyeworks, but the government would not allow her to dye the purple. The new emperor eventually had a friend take over the dyeworks. I felt a great sadness for Esecheus, but I was glad to be rid of the whole business. I took up farming in a northern province, and have not dyed a single piece of cloth from that day to this. And Penelope died from an experiment with arsenic and lead when she tried to make a cheaper red and avoid the madder merchants. She got what she deserved."*

Poma could not read his signature, but she saw by this bit of history some of the highs and lows people were taken to by their greed, even within her art.

Starr often came home from the theater very late, and Poma warmed her supper for her. "What an insufferable bore!" she said to Poma. They had spread out some bowls of soup and fresh bread on a low table on the garden porch.

Poma smiled. "Now who is insufferable?" she asked.

"Oh, it's that new director. He is so full of himself. He has changed up an entire scene just so his new actor friend can steal the whole first act. Wait until you see it! It's ruined the whole show."

Starr always came home filled with energy just as Poma was ready to go to bed. But she enjoyed hearing her mother's tales from the theater. It gave her life a certain balance. "Mother, I know you go into time shortly after I do, but I was wondering if you were going to really do that, or are you going to settle somewhere?"

"Oh, no, and gracious, I'm anxious to go this time. Can hardly wait to see what's next!" Starr said.

Such enthusiasm was inspiring. "I know I'll be going soon. I have my recipe book finished and packed in my basket. Mother, I will miss you."

"And I you, dear, sweet Poma. You are a fine lady. I'm glad Tigrax had some time with you. I know Enash will be waiting somewhere for you. We've had a good run together."

"A good run, mother, a good run." And she hugged the older woman and kissed her soft cheek.

Starr gave her a quizzical look. "And what has life taught you so far?" she asked.

Poma sat back and looked at the night sky. The warm air was thick with honeysuckle. Her mind wandered back to Hamora and the ugly lichens. She remembered the first time she saw the Egyptian tapestry. She thought of the green silk scarf she first saw that day so long ago at the market in Marakanda. The Saka people who became her family marched through her thoughts. She remembered Isaac's face as he lay dying on the cold floor of his laboratory. And always Enash, with the soft voice that held her life together. Her life was rich with color and enriched with people. "It's been quite a journey," she said softly. "I guess I've learned that we sometimes are led to achieve goals other than the ones we set for ourselves. We must learn the difference between our goals and the goals of Heaven." She brushed back a dark curl. "But I'm looking forward to the next place, too. I hope I've acquired some wisdom on the way. I'd like to find Sophie."

Her mother smiled at her, and they held hands and let the warm night envelope them.

The next morning Poma had her usual ride into the countryside. She wanted to check the cotton fields. Sure enough, madder was coming up in the fields as weeds. She would tell the neighbor children to come and collect it in the fall; to the cotton farmer it was only a weed. When she got home, Starr had already left for the theater.

Poma was eating her lunch on the balcony, watching the ships come and go on the Golden Horn. Suddenly a big, polished oriental caught her eye. She froze. She carefully put her bread down and jumped up to look closer. It couldn't be. A familiar, grizzled sailor was at the helm. Only now his hair was white. Ramatsu! *Was he there to find her? Had he come all this way just to hunt her down?* "Oh, my God," she whispered. *Where could she hide? What should she do?* She felt herself trembling all over. She turned and ran toward the stairway and tripped over a box of costumes in the hallway. She felt herself falling and the last thing she saw was one of the stone stairs coming right at her. As she hit her head, she could smell the Gardenias. The Goddess's face appeared as if in a purple dream. Her hand was held tightly. Time snapped. Her hand was dropped.

Yakimoto and his wife prospered with the sale of silk to Chinese merchants who came to Tottori and helped rebuild the harbor.

Ramatsu scoured the city and never found Poma. He never saw his son again. He later died in a storm at sea.

Himiko spent his life restoring the Buddhist art in the caves of Tun Huang.

Doctor stayed with him until he was a young man, and then went back to Chan Li's villa and married one of her daughters. He became a gardener famous for his vegetables, and never saw the sea again. He never forgot Poma and was saddened by her memory for the rest of his life.

Mohammed and Toru were, indeed, descended from Poma and her son, Targitaus. Toru taught his art to his sons, who carried on the wood carving tradition. Mohammed became a famous Islamic cleric and was known for his long and eloquent speeches.

Nik and Carlo eventually settled in Naples, where Carlo became a wealthy merchant. They had eleven children, three of whom lived. After Carlo's death, Nik became a nanny in the house of Medici, and taught the Medici children to spin as Poma had taught her.

Emar was stomped to death by a herd of wild camels.

Starr went back into time.

And no one ever knew what happened to Poma or her basket of treasures.

THE END